SHELTER FOR PENELOPE

BADGE OF HONOR, BOOK 15

SUSAN STOKER

Tucker "Moose" Jacobs paced back and forth impatiently across the hardwood floor in his bedroom. He should be sleeping. His alarm was going to go off in a few hours so he could get to Station 7 for his shift. But Penelope said she'd call.

He didn't know *when* she'd call, and he'd been staying up as late as he could every night to try to catch her call. The waiting and worrying was killing him. It had been a long six days since he'd last heard from her.

Not that being worried was anything new. From the second her brother, Sledge, a fellow firefighter, had told him that Penelope had quit her job at the station and taken off to, quote, "get her head together," Moose had worried.

A full week had gone by before he'd heard anything on her whereabouts, when she'd first left town. A week during which no one got much sleep for worrying

1

about their missing friend. Seven days during which Moose thought he would lose his ever-loving mind.

Then he'd gotten a call. From a man named Tex. Who'd told him that he knew exactly where Penelope was, and that she was fine. That he was helping her. Guiding her to places to stay where she and her crazy miniature donkey would be safe.

It should've made Moose feel better. Should've made the worry ease. But it didn't.

He still worried even after the first time Penelope herself had called. Even when she reassured him she was fine.

He still worried when she promised to call periodically to let him know where she was and how she was doing.

When it came to Penelope Turner, Moose had a feeling he'd never stop worrying.

He loved her. Completely and totally. When his feelings toward her had changed from friendship to something more, he wasn't exactly sure, but now that he knew he loved her, he couldn't just turn off the worry.

They were an odd-looking couple, that was for sure. At six foot three and very muscular, Moose didn't exactly blend into a crowd. He had dark brown hair and eyes, and usually some sort of five o'clock shadow. His facial hair grew quickly and shaving was a pain in the ass. With his size and the scruff, he looked intimidating, with a normal facial expression that

Penelope teased him for looking like "resting bitch face."

It wasn't that he was often mad or pissed; he just didn't like putting up with drama, and he supposed it showed on his face more than he was aware.

But what all of his friends knew was that, most of the time, he was actually very laid-back and mellow. He was a sucker for kids and animals, and he'd bend over backward to lend a helping hand whenever and wherever it was needed.

Penelope, in contrast to his rough and gruff, looked like a beautiful fairy. She was a foot shorter than he was, with blonde hair and blue eyes. It was no wonder the press had dubbed her the "American Princess" when she'd been held hostage over in Turkey. She looked ethereal and fragile and people were drawn to her.

But Penelope was anything but fragile. She was one of the strongest people Moose had ever met. Both physically and mentally. She'd been given the nickname "Tiger" by the SEAL team that had rescued her, and it fit her to a tee.

But somehow, over the years since she'd been rescued, she'd slowly but surely lost herself. She'd begun to question her reactions and actions at fires and other calls the firefighters had been sent on, and the confidence she used to wear like a cape had disappeared.

Moose wanted to help her find her confidence

again. Wanted her to laugh and joke with him and their other friends. Wanted to have the right and the privilege to call her his.

They'd been teased about how different they were—when they stood next to each other, he literally towered over her, and he was dark where she was light—but he knew deep down that they were perfect for each other.

Moose hadn't told Penelope that he loved her, simply because he wasn't sure how she'd react. He was pretty sure she had feelings toward him too, feelings she was denying. But until she dealt with what happened to her when she'd been taken captive by terrorists, the two of them didn't stand a chance.

So he hadn't insisted she come back to Texas.

He'd given her the space she thought she needed.

He hadn't pleaded with her to let him help. He'd simply been there for her.

Listened when she called to excitedly tell him about her adventures and travels, even though he could tell she was faking her enthusiasm most of the time.

And his heart bled when she cried and he wasn't there to hold her. When he couldn't fix what was hurting.

But during the last call, Penelope said she'd call him "soon." Then he hadn't heard from her since. He'd picked up the phone and almost called Tex a dozen times, demanding he tell Moose where Pen was so he could go get her. But in the end, he decided if he ever wanted Penelope to trust him, to love him the way he loved her, he needed to wait and let her call on her own time.

But the thought of her being hurt or falling into a pit of despair wouldn't leave his brain. She wasn't in a good place mentally. Something was eating her alive. He figured it had to be about the time she'd spent as a prisoner of war in Turkey, but she wasn't talking about it. Not to him. Not to anyone.

Moose was going absolutely crazy, and if she didn't call tonight, he was going to have to break his promise to himself to let her work through her emotions in her own way.

Lost in his head, envisioning all sorts of horrible things happening to the love of his life, he startled badly when the cell phone in his hand vibrated.

He closed his eyes in relief when he saw Penelope's name on the screen.

"Hello?"

"Hey, it's me," she said.

"Are you okay?" Moose asked.

He heard Penelope sigh. "Why is that always the first thing you ask?" she questioned in an irritated tone.

Exhausted and more worried than ever, Moose snapped back, "Because I'm worried about you. Because not having you here with me is driving me crazy. Because you're not here and I can't do a damn thing to help you because you've blocked me and all your friends out!"

Silence met his outburst.

Moose mentally swore.

"Sorry," he sighed. "It's been a long week, and I didn't mean to take it out on you."

"I didn't leave to stress you out," Penelope said softly.

"I know, sweetheart. And…I guess I ask you that question because I'm hoping one of these days you'll say that you're amazing, and that you're ready to come back to your life. And to me."

"I…I'm not sure what to say to that."

Moose wanted to kick himself. He'd pushed too hard, too fast. But the words had just tumbled out. "Forget I said it. Tell me where you are and what you and Smokey have been doing. How's the little rug rat doing?" Moose knew putting the attention on her donkey would lighten the mood.

"He's good. He's the most amazing travel companion, Moose. I was worried when we left because I wasn't sure how he'd do for long amounts of time in the car, but he just curls up into a ball and sleeps. He's only had a few accidents since we left—which is incredible for three months—and those were *my* fault because I left him alone too long."

"That's great, Pen. Where are you now?"

"California."

"That's a long way from Idaho, where you were when you last called me," Moose observed.

"Yeah, I know, and it's why it took so long for me to

get in touch. After I left Tex's friend Fish and his wife, I took my time driving south. I spent a few nights in Bryce Canyon in southern Utah. It was so amazing. Peaceful. I did a lot of thinking."

Moose took a deep, hopeful breath. "About?"

"Lots of things," she said vaguely.

Moose's stomach dropped. Just once he wanted Penelope to talk to him. To open up. To let him in. But it looked like she still wasn't ready. And that killed.

He didn't respond, knowing his hurt at her unwillingness to let him in would bleed through his words.

She obviously picked up on his disappointment anyway, because she went on quickly. "But now I'm in Riverton, California. It's beautiful here. I'm staying with one of the SEALs who helped rescue me."

For the first time in their many conversations, Moose felt a smidgeon of hope flare within him. "Yeah?"

"Yeah. His name is Matthew. His friends call him Wolf."

"I remember you talking about him."

"Right. Well, he and his wife Caroline don't have any kids, so it's easier for me to stay with them, with Smokey and all. Tomorrow, we're going to have a get-together on the beach with his team and their families."

Moose couldn't read her tone. "And are you excited about that?"

She was quiet so long, Moose was afraid he'd lost the connection.

Finally, she said in a low voice, "I don't know. I'm scared, Moose."

His heartrate sped up, and Moose prayed he'd say the right things. "What are you scared of, sweetheart?"

"Everything."

When she didn't elaborate, Moose wanted to reach through the phone and take her into his arms, but of course that was impossible. She was killing him. Slowly but surely killing him.

"I'm sure seeing the men who were with you in Turkey won't be easy."

"Yeah, it's weird. I know I'm a different person now than I was when I met them. Even though I'd just spent four months in captivity, I hadn't lost my spunk. I was snarky and high on the fact that I was finally getting rescued. I feel as if that happened to someone else, because I'm just not that way anymore. But...it's not just seeing them that I'm scared of."

"Then what is it? You know you can tell me anything, Pen. I'm not going to go and report back to your brother or the others. What you say stays between us."

"Is Cade driving you crazy?" she asked after a beat of silence.

Moose knew she was changing the subject, and he wanted to scream in frustration. She'd been so close to opening up, but had once again decided not to. "He's good. I tell him and the others when I talk to you and that you're fine, so they don't worry, and he knows better than to push me for details on what we talk about."

"Have you seen much of Blythe's baby?"

"A bit. She and Squirrel bring her by the station fairly often."

"Has she grown a lot? Is her hair coming in yet? What do Squirrel's sisters think about their new niece? And have they gotten together with Milena, Hope, Erin, and all *their* babies? I'm disappointed that I didn't get to spend more time with Erin and Lily, and Milena and Steven before I left. I was sorry to miss both Blythe's and Hope's babies being born, but I can just imagine the four kids having the time of their lives as they get older, especially since they're so close in age. I bet Steven and Carter are going to be super protective of Harper and Lily as they grow up. At least I hope they will."

Moose knew Penelope was sad she'd missed the births of their friends' babies. He'd hoped it would spur her to come home, but it hadn't. If anything, she'd almost seemed more determined to stay away after learning Blythe and Hope had given birth so soon after she'd taken off.

"I can send you pics," Moose told her. "All four already seem to be growing like weeds. Squirrel is super proud. It's almost annoying how much he talks about his daughter when he's on shift."

Penelope chuckled, as he'd wanted her to.

"Oh, and he and Blythe decided to go ahead and get married," Moose informed her.

"They did? No way!" Penelope exclaimed

"Yup."

"What else have I missed?" she asked quietly.

That was another thing Moose hated, how Penelope went from being happy to upset in a heartbeat. He wanted to tell her if she was home, that she'd be privy to everything going on in their friends' lives firsthand, but knew she didn't need to hear it. She knew that perfectly well already. But she was still staying away... to punish herself for something that wasn't her fault. Or because it was simply too painful to be around the people who knew her best.

"Taco proposed to Koren, and she said yes. They haven't chosen a date yet though."

He wasn't sure if he should tell her the next thing. But he'd promised he'd never lie to her, and not letting her know felt like a lie of omission.

"And...Sophie's pregnant. She and Chief just got back from visiting his mom on the reservation. They wanted to tell her first. I guess they had a blessing ceremony, and his mom was super excited. She's got about six more months to go."

When Penelope didn't say anything, Moose asked, "Pen? You still there?"

"I'm missing *everything*," she whispered.

"Then come home," Moose pleaded. He'd promised

he wouldn't, but the words just popped out. "Together, we can work through whatever has you so scared."

"I can't," Penelope told him.

"But you *are* coming home at some point, right?" Moose asked.

"I haven't decided."

Moose felt his heart break right in half at her words.

He'd had his suspicions that he'd lost the woman he loved, but until now, she'd never come right out and said that she might not come back to him. And it hurt.

She was shutting him out. Him and her brother and all the rest of her friends.

Feeling the tell-tale sign of tears forming behind his eyes, Moose stumbled backward until his legs came into contact with his bed and he sat down, hard. It was his turn to have nothing to say. The silence over the phone line was heavy and fraught with tension.

"Moose?"

"All I ever want is for you to be happy," Moose started, doing his damnedest to not let his voice crack. "When you were here and suffering, I did all I could to be there for you. I defended your need to keep Smokey, and I let him stay in my barn, and then my house when the barn was torched. After you left, I defended your need and right for some space to the guys. When you missed the birth of Blythe's daughter, I reassured her that you'd be back, that you were trying to get your head on straight after everything that had happened to you.

"And I'll have your back no matter what, Pen. I don't think it's a surprise that I love you."

Moose heard her take a deep breath, but he kept going. "I've loved you forever. I'd bend over backward to keep you safe. To do what you need to live your life the way you need to live it. But I need *you* to want that too. To want to stand by *my* side. To have *my* back. I get that you're struggling, I do, and I wish there was something I could do to help you. But I can't if you don't let me in.

"If you don't come back to San Antonio, I'm not sure I'll ever get over loving you. You're *it* for me. I feel that down to the marrow of my bones. I love the woman you are today, the woman you were yesterday, and the woman you're going to be in the future. I don't give a fuck if you have PTSD or if you can't ever be a firefighter again. You can stay home and raise miniature donkeys if that makes you happy. All I want is to be by your side while you do it.

"But if moving away from everyone who loves you exactly how you are, who supports you unconditionally, is what you need to be happy...so be it. Please thank the men who were able to get you out of hell for me, and tell them they have my undying gratitude. Don't forget to shoot Blythe a text to congratulate her on her marriage, and maybe Sophie too, for being pregnant. Stay safe...and know that I love you."

"Moose—"

"Thanks for calling," he interrupted her, not able to listen to her try to let him down gently.

He'd never come right out and told her he'd loved her before, but he couldn't keep the words in anymore. Not if she was deciding whether or not to come back to Texas. He wasn't about to play fair, not when it came to the woman he loved. He was almost forty; if Penelope didn't come home to him, he'd never get married. Never have a family. She was it for him. He knew that with no uncertainty.

"I'll talk to you later."

"Okay, Moose. Later."

Moose clicked off the phone and squeezed it so tightly in his fist he knew it was only a matter of seconds before it broke. He threw the phone onto his nightstand and bent over so his elbows were resting on his knees. He put his forehead in his hands and took a few deep breaths, willing himself to calm down.

He thought back over the last few months and lamented all the things he hadn't done for Penelope. When he'd first seen the signs of her struggle with PTSD and what had happened to her over in Turkey, he should've insisted she see a psychologist more regularly. Should've gotten her help back then rather than allowing her to just work it out on her own.

Moose wasn't an overly emotional man. He'd seen some pretty horrific things in his life. Car accidents that took the lives of entire families. Fires that wiped out all the houses in a single neighborhood. But nothing in his life hurt as much as hearing Penelope say that she wasn't sure she was ever coming back to San Antonio. Back to him.

Tears leaked out of his eyes and dripped onto his thighs, but Moose didn't move to wipe them away. He cried in frustration for not being able to help Penelope. For not being able to make her love him enough to turn to him when she was hurting. For losing the one thing he wanted more in this life than anything else. Her.

CHAPTER TWO

Penelope was in the worst mood. She hadn't exactly been Ms. Congeniality during the months she'd been on the road, but today was a new low, even for her.

She'd hurt the one person who had always been there for her. Who had always defended her and been able to make her smile even when she was at her lowest.

Sitting on the bed in Matthew "Wolf" Steel's basement and petting Smokey, she thought about her conversation with Moose the night before. When he'd flat-out asked when she was coming home, she'd panicked and said the first thing that came to her mind. That she wasn't sure she *was* coming back.

But the funny thing was, the second the words had left her lips, she knew she couldn't move away permanently. She loved San Antonio. Her brother was there. Her friends were there.

Moose was there.

The thought of going back was scary because she knew she'd have to face her demons. So far, she'd successfully managed to push to the back of her mind all the reasons she'd left, and the second she went back, she'd have to deal with them once more.

But the initial excitement of being on the road had been waning.

Hearing that Sophie was pregnant, and knowing there were *four* little babies she hadn't had the chance to get to know because she'd run like a fucking coward was almost too much at that moment.

But it was knowing she'd hurt Moose that made her want to pack her bags right that second and drive straight through the night to get back to him...and tell him that she loved him right back.

He *loved* her.

He'd come right out and said it.

She knew they had chemistry, and that over the last few years, her friendship with him had morphed into something more. She loved Moose more than she ever thought possible, but after what had happened in Turkey, she didn't think she had the courage to follow through on her feelings. Hell, she couldn't even deal with the deaths of fellow soldiers she hadn't even known that well.

If she got close to Moose and something happened to him, she knew it would permanently break her.

Moose had kinda snuck in under her radar. At first

he was just another firefighter at the station. But as she'd gotten to know him, she'd liked him more and more. He was the opposite of the kind of men she'd been attracted to previously. She loved that he was so much taller than she was. She hadn't really wanted to fall in love with another firefighter, the hours were wonky and it'd be easier if she was with someone with a normal nine-to-five job.

But Moose was different from any other man she'd met. He was big and buff, yet if they went to a scene where there were injured children, he'd make a beeline for them and have them giggling and laughing in the midst of whatever tragedy might be going on.

There were so *many* things about him that drew her...and it was more than his good looks and his love of kids. It was his dedication to his job. His loyalty. The way he gave his all in his friendships. It was also some deep quality inside him; something that made her feel safe in a world that she'd found out firsthand wasn't safe at all.

The last thing she wanted to do was drag him down to the hell she'd experienced...and was still having a hard time climbing out of.

The bottom line was that she was a coward. In every sense of the word—and Penelope hated that.

What had happened to her? She used to be so kickass. She didn't take shit from anyone, not even the terrorists who'd imprisoned her. But now she was so weak, she couldn't even do her job. She'd fucking *run* when shit became too much.

Moose was better off without her. He'd find someone else. Someone better. Stronger.

The thought of him kissing some other woman sent a jolt of pain through Penelope. The idea of him joking with some faceless female, of giving *her* his love, made her want to puke.

God, she was a mess. She didn't have the strength to claim Moose as her own, but she didn't want him with anyone else either.

Penelope closed her eyes and flopped back on the bed. Smokey, thinking she was playing a game, nudged her with his muzzle and tried to lift her hand back to his head.

"Shhhh, Smokey. Just let me lie here for a second." But she dutifully began to stroke his head, and he rested it on her belly, the weight heavy and comforting against her.

"I didn't mean to hurt him," she whispered to her donkey. Smokey was a good listener. Didn't judge and never tried to talk over her or tell her that everything would be all right when she knew it wouldn't be. Couldn't be.

Penelope thought about the last few months. She'd been floundering so badly. Still was. All the men and women Tex had sent her to had been extremely welcoming. Some had tried to talk to her about their own experiences with PTSD, and what they'd done to manage it, but at the beginning of her trip, Penelope hadn't been ready. It was preferable and easier to run away from her problems, rather than trying to solve them.

She'd first stayed with a man in Pueblo, Colorado, who'd had a horrendous childhood and had joined the Army to get away from it all. And while he—and his brothers and their families—had been extremely welcoming and funny, she didn't really see how any of their situations were in any way similar to hers, so she'd shut down any talk of Turkey and her captivity.

Then Tex had sent her to Colorado Springs, and she'd stayed in the basement guest room of a large house in Black Forest, where a former Navy SEAL— now some sort of private security guy—lived with his wife. Again, when they'd tried to talk about their experiences, she'd firmly steered the conversation in another direction.

It wasn't that she didn't appreciate their willingness to help; she just had a hard time *letting* people help.

But as time went on, and Tex sent her to more and more friends who were either retired from the military or who'd been through horrific situations of their own, as she listened to their stories, Penelope realized she'd left Texas to sort out her *own* shit. And she wasn't even trying, despite Tex's best efforts.

She was running from issues that she really *did* want to fix.

So when she'd shown up in Idaho on the doorstep

of Fish, a medically retired Delta Force soldier, Penelope was in a slightly better headspace. Determined to at least *try* to get to the bottom of what was bothering her and find a way to fix it. And upon seeing Fish's prosthetic arm, while also noting how comfortable he seemed with both his handicap *and* his life, she did her best to talk to him.

Surprisingly, it wasn't Fish who'd gotten through to her the most during her time in Idaho—it was his wife, Bryn.

As a high-functioning autistic, everything in Bryn's world was black and white. There was hardly any gray. So when Penelope had admitted what had happened at the last fire she'd attended, how she'd had a major trust issue and ran from the scene, and how she felt *equally* guilty for surviving in Turkey when so many other good soldiers hadn't, Bryn had looked at her and asked, "So you'd rather be dead?"

It was so blunt—and something no one had ever *dared* say to her before; her friends were too busy stepping on her emotional eggshells.

All Penelope could do was shake her head in denial.

Bryn had continued, "Then figure out a way to deal with the stuff going on in your head and live."

Of course, she made it sound simple, and Penelope knew it was anything but...though, it made her really think about what she was currently doing. Why was she going from house to house, pretending she was on some grand adventure, instead of knuckling down and getting her head screwed on straight once and for all?

She *didn't* want to die...and she hated being away from her friends and her life back in Texas.

A light knock sounded on the door at the top of the stairs, interrupting Penelope's musings, and she was actually glad for the reprieve from her own thoughts. "I'm up!" she called out.

Within seconds, Caroline, Wolf's wife, was peering around the door. "Good morning," she said brightly.

"Morning," Penelope said as she sat up.

"Did you sleep okay?"

"Great," Penelope lied. She hadn't slept well at all, but not because the bed wasn't comfortable, or Caroline and Wolf's hospitality was lacking in any way.

Caroline's head tilted and she studied Penelope for a long moment before saying, "Why do I get the feeling you're saying what you think I want to hear, rather than the truth?"

Penelope couldn't help but smile at the astute woman. "Because you're smart?"

Caroline looked uncertain for a moment and bit her lip. Then she asked, "Can I sit for a second?"

Penelope nodded. She knew Caroline was only a few years older than her, but in many ways, she seemed so much more worldly and wise. At this point—especially after her heart-wrenching conversation with Moose last night—she'd take just about any advice she could get.

She had to admit it—she wasn't doing all that great at figuring out her life on her own. She knew she should go back to the Army doctor she'd seen a few times at home, but she'd put it off for so long, it felt weird to simply call him up out of the blue and make an appointment. Which was stupid…but it was how she felt.

Caroline had come down and sat on the bed beside her, and she was studying her when Penelope emerged from her own musings.

Blushing, Penelope said, "Sorry, I do that a lot… start thinking about something and the next thing I know, minutes have gone by and everyone's staring at me, wondering what the hell I'm thinking about so hard."

Caroline shrugged. "I get it. I do. I'm assuming you know my story, Penelope? What happened to me after I met Matthew for the first time and how we got together?"

"Yeah. I knew some of it, and Tex filled me in on a few details before he sent me down here."

"Tex. God, I love that man," Caroline breathed. "Seriously, he's so amazing at what he does, but more importantly, he *cares*."

Nodding, Penelope said, "When he sent me the tracker your guys arranged for me to have, after my rescue, I wore it all the time at first. But as time went on, it felt weak to rely on it as much as I did. So I took it off and put it aside. At the last minute, however, when I was leaving San Antonio, I grabbed it. And when he called me the first night I was gone, and asked where I was going and what I was doing, I was pretty shocked. I didn't really think he would actually be monitoring it. I admitted that I had no plans, and I just needed some space to get my head together. He gave me the first of several names and addresses of former military buddies, and he's been directing my impromptu trip ever since."

"That sounds like Tex...and just so this doesn't get weird, I have to admit that I read every interview about you I could get my hands on. Not that you did that many. But I was curious and wanted to know every-thing I could about the American Princess."

Penelope winced.

"And even though our situations weren't exactly the same, I just wanted to let you know that what happened to you was terrible. It sucked, and no one will ever truly understand what you went through and how it felt to be in a situation where you had no control over anything. But...I've been there. Again, not exactly, but I know what it feels like to be scared out of your mind and think you might not live to see another day. I know how it feels to come home and have everyone ask over and over if you're okay. To have people stare at you as if they're wondering when you're going to freak out. It's hard to smile on the outside and feel like you're slowly crumbling on the inside."

Penelope just stared at the other woman. To look at

her, you'd never guess she was anything but a military spouse with no concerns in the world other than the normal everyday things. But Penelope knew Caroline had been kidnapped. That she'd been drugged, beaten, and almost killed. And how it had happened a *second* time when she got caught up in another friend's drama and was kidnapped along with her.

Penelope wondered if the second time she'd been taken had been scarier than the first, knowing how things could turn out for the worse.

Regardless, the words meant a lot more coming from someone like her. Someone who'd also been taken against her will.

But hadn't Beth, her brother's girlfriend, tried to tell her the same thing?

And Erin? And Corrie?

She'd blown off her friends...even though they'd *all* been kidnapped, and had to fight for their lives, as well.

Why was it different coming from Caroline?

Penelope had no idea.

But the thing was...no one had died during their time in captivity, as people had in *hers*.

Penelope couldn't stop second-guessing every single decision she'd made, wondering if, had she done something different, her friends would still be alive today. Or that poor Australian soldier.

And if she'd run faster, given more clues to her whereabouts, and helped them find her sooner, maybe some of the first men who'd saved her wouldn't have died, maybe their helicopter wouldn't have been shot out of the sky.

Survivor's guilt. The psychologist had said her feelings had a name, but reducing that huge black ball of emotions inside her would take more than giving them a cliché title and diagnosis.

And why was she also now doubting her fellow firefighters? Why hadn't she been able to go into that burning condo to save Taco and Koren?

She understood the guilt, but in all the time she'd been gone, she hadn't come any closer to finding the answer or solution to her recent trust issues.

Penelope knew she should say something to Caroline. Smile and nod. Agree and thank her for her words of wisdom, but she couldn't get anything past the lump in her throat.

Caroline seemed to know. She leaned over and put her hand on Penelope's knee. "It's okay not to want to talk about it with me. You don't know me. But you *have* to talk to someone. I know you've probably already heard that, but it's one hundred percent true. And before you ask, yes, I talked about my own issues with Matthew. It was hard on both of us; him, because he hated to see me in pain and knew exactly what I'd gone through, and me, because I was, and still am, ashamed of how terrified I was at the time. Everyone told me how brave I was. How amazingly well I held up. But inside, I was screaming in terror the entire time, and hearing that others thought I was brave made me feel even more like a fraud."

"Yes," Penelope whispered. Inside, she was wondering who she could talk to as Caroline had. Moose loved her, but would he tell her what she needed to hear, or what he thought she *wanted* to hear? Her friends would be sympathetic, but Penelope wasn't sure talking to them would all of a sudden make her trust her fellow firefighters again.

She wanted to talk to *someone* about what happened over in Turkey. Specifically, how and why she'd been captured. But she couldn't.

As hard as she tried, Penelope just couldn't remember.

The missing memories of those few moments had weighed heavier and heavier on her since her rescue, until she was sure that she'd blocked them out because she'd done something horribly wrong.

She hadn't talked about it with *anyone*, and now didn't seem like the right time or place either.

The hand on her leg squeezed in a show of sympathy, and as if Caroline could read her mind, she said, "Talk to someone, Penelope. Someone you trust. Someone you know won't just agree with whatever you're saying to try to get you to feel better. Someone who will let you scream and cry and rail against the world for the unfairness of it all. It helps. It doesn't make the terror completely disappear, but it makes it easier to get through each day. And each day that you get through makes what you experienced fade a tiny little bit. You'll never forget. That event will always be with you. But time, and knowing you're still here and you have people and animals around who love you no matter what, makes the power the memories have over you fade."

While Caroline had been talking, Smokey had scooted over even closer to Penelope and buried his head in her lap. He'd thrown one of his front legs over her own and was practically purring as she rhythmically petted his head.

She thought again of her friends, and the desire to talk to Moose above all others was almost overwhelming. She knew beyond a doubt that he'd listen without judgement. That he'd let her do all the things Caroline mentioned. He was her rock. Had been since she'd gotten home from hell on earth. He didn't treat her like a fragile piece of glass. But he also didn't put her on a pedestal and treat her like she was Wonder Woman. He laughed with her, scowled at her when she messed up, and had gone out of his way to make her feel safe and loved, even when she didn't really deserve it.

He *loved* her.

She had a really hard time believing she was worthy of his love though. She was completely fucked in the head. How the hell could he love her? It made no sense.

She also hadn't missed the emotion in his voice over the phone line. It was that emotion that had her tossing and turning the night before. The fact that she had the power to hurt him as much as she clearly had.

She hated that, had to make it right. Because she loved him right back. She hadn't said it, but knew deep down it was true, even if she didn't believe she deserved his love.

Tucker Jacobs was the one man she could see herself with for the rest of her life. She'd never get bored with him. And he'd proven over and over that he would be there for her no matter what.

Penelope realized that Caroline was staring at her with a small smile on her face. "Sorry...you gave me a lot to think about."

"I did. And I know that I didn't really let you talk much. I apologize. I just started babbling away about my own experiences, not really even giving you a choice to do anything but listen."

"No, I appreciate it. I mean, honestly, if you'd asked me if I wanted to talk, I probably would've told you no, like I have to everyone else."

The women smiled at each other in understanding.

"If you aren't ready for today, you can stay here," Caroline told her as she stood.

"No, I need some fresh air, and I'm looking forward to seeing all the guys again."

"Okay. But if seeing them brings back any memories you can't deal with, just let me know and I'll make up an excuse to get us out of there."

Penelope took a deep breath to keep her tears at

bay. Caroline reminded her of her friends back home. They would've said the same thing. "You're a good person, Caroline," Penelope replied.

Looking surprised, Caroline smiled down at her. "I've just been where you are. Some days are harder than others, and the smallest thing can trigger a lot of memories you'd rather forget. With that being said, I know all the women are looking forward to meeting you. They've heard a lot about you from their men. And wait until you meet all the kids! If you can't keep them straight, don't worry. I swear sometimes even *I* forget their names, and I've known them their entire lives." She winked to let Penelope know she was joking.

Chuckling, Penelope nodded. "Deal. Names aren't my strong suit." She slowly disentangled herself from Smokey, then lifted him down from the bed so he didn't jump and hurt himself. "I need to get Smokey outside so he can do his business, then get changed."

Caroline led the way to the stairs. "No problem. We've got about an hour and a half before we need to head out. I'll get breakfast ready while you're changing."

"Thanks. I'll come help after letting Smokey out."

"Sounds good."

As Penelope headed up the stairs behind Caroline, Smokey almost tripped her as he barreled up from behind, knocking into her legs. Laughing, Penelope decided to put all her deep thoughts behind her for now. She had a reunion with some very amazing men, and women, and she wanted to enjoy that more than she wanted to brood on her own situation.

Hours later, Penelope's cheeks hurt from smiling so much. She couldn't remember the last time she'd relaxed enough to let herself simply enjoy spending time with other people. Seeing Wolf, Abe, Cookie, Mozart, Dude, and Benny again hadn't been easy, but they'd kept things lighthearted and hadn't said anything about Turkey. Hearing them use the nickname they'd christened her with while saving her life had taken a bit of getting used to, but it was comforting at the same time.

"So, Tiger, you ready to run for the hills yet?" Abe asked.

She and the six-man SEAL team were sitting together away from the other women and children, and Penelope had thought that might be awkward, but instead she felt as if she'd known and hung out with them for years. She had nothing to hide from these men. She didn't feel the need to bullshit them about how she hadn't been scared or traumatized by what she'd been through. They knew.

"Ready to run because of how amazing and awesome your wives and children are?" she scoffed. "Hardly."

"But you *are* ready to run," Dude said with the same uncanny insight as Abe.

She looked over at the dark-haired man and met his intense gaze. "Not in the way you think."

"Explain," Dude requested.

Penelope couldn't help but smile. That was exactly what she figured he'd say. "I'm actually ready to *stop* running. I needed this time away. To think. To be alone. I thought I was going to take the time away from Texas to work through my shit, but instead, most of the time I refused to even acknowledge I *had* any shit to work through."

"It's okay to hurt," Cookie said quietly.

Penelope turned to stare at the huge man. All the men towered over her diminutive five-foot-two frame. Even when they were all sitting in low beach chairs, they seemed larger than life. But they'd never given her shit about her height.

She felt the same way around her friends and fellow firefighters back home. *Everyone* was taller than she was, but she never felt as if her size was a handicap, simply because they didn't treat her differently from anyone else. They expected her to carry her own weight and be able to haul hoses and climb ladders like any other firefighter. They didn't think she was weak or somehow lesser because she was short and female.

Not like the terrorists had.

Back in Turkey, when she was held captive, she'd felt like a little kid. Fragile. Small. She'd covered those feelings with bravado. And she *had* been pissed off they were holding her hostage, of course. But she'd also been terrified.

When she realized it had been several moments since anyone had said anything, and she'd been lost in her own head again, she blushed. "I'm sorry, what?"

"I said, it's okay to feel a little lost. I'm not sure if anyone's ever said that to you before," Cookie said. "After Fiona got back to the States, after being held hostage for months, everyone told her how strong and brave she was. But no one ever told her it was okay to be scared. Or to hurt. Or to be mad about what had happened to her. So I'm telling you right now that, no matter how much time goes by, it's okay to hurt and to be any or all of those things."

His words meant so much to her, Penelope wasn't sure how to express it. Swallowing hard, not wanting to cry in front of the men, she simply said, "Thank you."

"None of us know what's goin' through your head, but one thing we *do* know is that half of it is probably bullshit," Mozart said succinctly. "And we know that because after our women went through their ordeals, and they opened up to each of us, half of what was going through *their* heads was bullshit."

Penelope couldn't help but smile at that.

"The worst is the what-if feeling," Benny told her. "What if you did this instead of that? What if you fought back? What if you didn't? What if you were killed instead of your friends? What if you'd said something differently? All the what-ifs in the world won't change what you went through. Won't change the outcome. You can't go back. You can only go forward."

"You have the what-ifs?" Penelope asked.

"All the fucking time," Benny said solemnly. "My situation wasn't near what you went through, but I hate that Jess had to kill someone because of me. *Hate* it. She seems okay with what happened, but I still go through that day in my head all the damn time. And when I do, Jessyka always seems to know, and she helps me pull my head out of my ass.

"What's done is done. The best thing we can do is be happy. Being pissed off or holding on to our anger doesn't change anything. Being happy and living the best life we can is the best 'fuck you' to those who've hurt you. Jess and I have our kids and each other. And it helps to focus on the here and now instead of dwelling on the past. I know that's easier said than done, but it truly does help."

Penelope nodded and looked to Abe and Wolf. "You guys gonna put in your two cents?"

Abe chuckled. "There's the snark we know and love. The only advice I have for you, Tiger, is that words have power. It doesn't matter if they're said in anger or frustration. They can cut just as deep if they're said carelessly or without thought than if they're intentional. So when you go back to your man, and you get overwhelmed and scared, remember that."

Penelope thought back to Moose's tone the night before, and she nodded slowly. She hadn't meant to imply that she wouldn't *ever* be coming back to San Antonio, but that was how Moose had taken it, and she hadn't bothered to immediately correct his assumption.

"You impressed the hell out of us, Tiger. I don't think you really understand that. We were ready to deal with whatever state you were in when we found you. But when Dude saw you for the first time, you said something to the effect of 'about damn time,'" Wolf said.

Everyone chuckled, and Penelope winced.

"Not only that, but you did exactly what had to be done without question. You trusted us to get you out of there, and to this day, I remember how proud I was to fight by your side. I'm not saying these things to heap more emotion on your already overloaded brain, I'm just callin' it like I see it. A person's true self comes out in situations like the one you went through. I'm guessing you're feeling a lot of guilt about surviving when others didn't. I bet you're second-guessing every single moment you spent in the hands of those assholes. But no matter what you think or what the press says about you, we all know the truth."

When he didn't continue, Penelope got up the courage to ask, "And what's that?"

"That you're one hell of a woman. I wish I had the words that would take away the pain of what you went through, Tiger," Wolf continued. "What you're *still* going through as a result of your time as a POW, but I don't. And that sucks. No one can take it away. It's as much a part of you as your blonde hair and short stature."

"Gee, thanks for pointing *that* out," Penelope griped with a small smile, trying to ignore the little voice inside her saying Wolf was just placating her. That he didn't really think she was brave. That he was blowing smoke up her ass just so she didn't start crying like the baby she really was. But something he said struck a nerve.

"I trusted you to get me out of there," she agreed, "so why am I suddenly finding it so hard to trust people around me now?"

Wolf hesitated, and Penelope could see that he was really thinking about his words before he said them. "I can't really answer that without knowing all the facts. But I'm guessing it's because at the time, things were moving extremely quickly. You didn't have a chance to think about trusting us or not. You just acted. But now your head has had the time to reflect on what happened over there, and it's messing with you."

"Understatement of the year," Penelope muttered.

"You'll figure it out," Wolf said confidently. "Something else you should know is that if you need us, we're here," Wolf went on, his gaze intense and comforting at the same time. "You need a safe place to land, you got it. Right here with us. We'll have your back and front and stand between you and the world if that's what you need."

Penelope's eyes filled with tears and she looked down at her hands to try to hide them.

"But the thing is, I don't think you'll need it," Wolf said in a confident tone.

She glanced back at him briefly.

"I think you've already got a tribe of people who would move heaven and earth to make sure you're safe. That you get what you need. Don't you?" Wolf asked.

Penelope swallowed hard and thought about everyone she'd left behind without so much as a good-bye. The women who'd shown time and time again that she was an important part of their group. Hope, Milena, Erin, Hayden, Laine, Corrie, Mickie, and Mackenzie. They were hilarious and fun, and even though they'd all been through their own traumas, they never hesitated to offer a shoulder to cry on or take her out for a relaxing girls' night.

And the girlfriends, fiancées, and wives of her fellow firefighters were the same. Beth had been through hell, and despite her quirks and coping mechanisms, she still managed to be a rock for anyone who needed her. Adeline and her dog Coco had been godsends in helping Penelope with Smokey after he'd almost died a second time in the arson fire that had been set in Moose's barn. Sophie, who dealt with a stutter, and Quinn with her large birthmark made her proud to know them every damn day. They were so good at ignoring people who discriminated against them because of their disabilities. Blythe was a pillar of strength, despite previously being homeless, and Koren, who Penelope didn't know too well, was still one of nicest people she'd ever met.

But even with knowing all that, and acknowledging that they were good friends and had been through their own shit, Penelope still wasn't sure they'd understand what *she* was going through. How could they when she didn't understand it herself?

"They'll understand," Wolf told her, as if he knew exactly what she was thinking. "That's the thing about friends, they let you get away with stupid shit because they love you."

"Thanks, guys."

"You're welcome," they all said in unison, as if they'd planned it.

Penelope chuckled.

"Come on. Looks like Smokey needs a break from our little ones," Benny said. He stood and held out his hand to Penelope. She grabbed it and let him help her out of the beach chair. The others also stood.

"We'll be there in just a second," Dude said as he held Penelope back with a hand on her arm.

She was curious as to what he had to say out of earshot of his teammates. When they were alone, Dude turned to her.

"Sometimes, the best thing you can do is give everything over to your man."

Penelope frowned. "What do you mean?"

Dude sighed. "I'm just going to come out and say this and not beat around the bush."

"Good. I prefer that."

"I'm what's known in certain circles as a dominant. I like to be in charge, and I need that. I'm not talking in everyday life, although I'm sure Cheyenne would probably disagree with me." He let out a small snort of laughter at himself, then continued. "But in intimate situations between me and Cheyenne, I need to be in charge, and she lets me. It's freeing for her. She can let go and not have to worry about anything other than feeling. She doesn't think about what happened when she was kidnapped and almost blown to pieces. She can just be herself and enjoy how I'm making her body feel. She knows I'll do whatever it takes to make things good for her. She doesn't have to worry about saying or doing the wrong thing, or where to put her hands or *anything*, because she knows I'll tell her exactly what I want her to do."

"So you're telling me I should be submissive in bed and it'll fix my problems?"

Dude blew out a breath. "No. But *maybe*. Look, there's no doubt you're a kick-ass soldier and fire-fighter. You didn't freak out in Turkey, you took over the care of Abe's leg without having to be told. You frequently have to take control at accident or fire scenes. Decisions you make could be life or death. They *have been* life or death. All I'm saying is maybe, with someone you trust implicitly, you can give up some of that iron control you've let yourself believe you have to have at all times. Let your man take the lead. Let him help you, help make decisions with you, even make some decisions *for* you. I think it could be empowering and freeing for you."

Penelope wanted to roll her eyes at the man. Tell him she didn't have a submissive bone in her entire body.

But when she thought about giving control over to Moose...something inside her clicked.

And she knew Dude wasn't talking solely about sex.

Penelope didn't used to be so high strung. Before she'd been a POW, she'd been pretty relaxed. Didn't have to be in control all the time. It was easy to let others at the station lead, but she'd also had no problem stepping in and making life-or-death decisions when the situation called for it.

But somewhere between her coming back from Turkey and right before she'd quit her job, things had changed. She no longer wanted anyone making any decisions that might affect her adversely. She had to be in control of *everything*.

Because she didn't trust anyone? Because she didn't trust herself? Penelope had no idea, but the idea of letting Moose take control, make decisions for her, didn't freak her out for some reason. Maybe because, like Dude had said, she trusted him. Implicitly. He wouldn't ever do anything that would hurt her if he could help it.

She'd left Texas because the constant pressure of trying to control everything around her and the guilt over her fellow soldiers' deaths was getting worse. She still felt guilty as hell and she still didn't trust anyone, including herself. But after thinking about what Bryn and Caroline had said, and what the guys tonight had told her, Penelope was starting to understand that no amount of control would help with her trust issues.

"I see you're thinking about it," Dude commented.

Penelope nodded. "But that doesn't mean I'm gonna go to a sex club with you and Cheyenne," she joked.

Dude's lips quirked upward. "Noted." Then he reached out and put his arms around her and pulled her in close. Penelope didn't fight the embrace, didn't stiffen like she usually did when others tried to show her affection. For once, it felt okay to relax and lean into someone.

"That's it, Tiger. Let someone else take on your burdens for a while. Not forever, just for a moment or two. Let your mind relax for a single second. Cut yourself some slack."

Nodding against him, Penelope felt lighter than she had in months.

But seconds after she felt herself relax, she quickly stiffened again.

She shouldn't be here with *this* man. It wasn't *his* arms she wanted around her.

It was Moose's.

The second her muscles tightened, Dude let her go, stepping back and giving her space. He eyed her for a long moment, then nodded as if whatever he'd seen was acceptable to him. "Come on, let's go rescue your poor donkey from the ragamuffins. He's gonna sleep well tonight, that's for sure."

Feeling relieved, but still a little unsettled at all the advice she'd gotten, Penelope let Dude lead her back to the chaos and excitement of the beach party.

That night, lying in bed and listening to Smokey snore at her feet, Penelope thought about her day, and her time in Idaho, and the weeks before that…and came to the realization that the itchy feeling she'd felt inside her for weeks was a yearning to go back to Texas.

She wanted to go back. She wanted to make things right with Moose. Wanted to see all the new babies who'd been born while she'd been on the run from something she now knew she couldn't outrun. Wanted to see her brother and Beth finally tie the knot. Wanted to participate in the next law enforcement/firefighter softball game. Wanted to give Smokey a stable place to feel safe.

The more she thought about it, the more she missed home.

She felt better about this decision than any she'd

made since hitting the road. Running away hadn't been the solution to her problems. She'd deluded herself into thinking she'd left to solve them, but that wasn't what happened. Instead, she'd avoided them entirely until recently.

It wasn't that she didn't *want* to talk about everything she'd been through, it was that she wasn't talking with the right person.

She missed Moose. Missed hanging out at his house and simply watching television together. Missed riding in the fire truck with him. Missed seeing him joking and laughing with their friends at the station. She'd held back from talking about her experiences in Turkey with him—hell, with anyone—because she didn't want to look weak in anyone's eyes.

But she had the sudden certainty that Moose would *never* think of her that way. He loved her. If it was *him* who'd been through what she had, she'd have no problem letting him talk about his feelings. About what had happened. She'd never see him as weak. No way.

So why was she holding back on him?

She was done with that. Tomorrow, she'd head back to Texas and hopefully fix whatever she'd broken between them. If Moose had given up on her, she didn't know what she'd do, but she hoped and prayed that it wasn't too late.

Penelope also didn't know what she was going to do about her job. Wasn't sure she wanted to be a firefighter anymore, wasn't sure she could handle the pressure of being responsible for other people's lives, but she'd think about that later. She didn't even know if the chief would let her come back after she'd up and quit the way she had.

First things first. Get back to Texas. Make things right with Moose. Then worry about what she was going to do with the rest of her life.

Penelope leaned over and picked up her phone from the nightstand. She wasn't ready to *talk* to Moose yet, even though she missed him terribly. The next time they spoke, she wanted to be face-to-face with him. But she *could* text to let him know what was going on.

Pen: I'm leaving in the morning to head back to Texas.

Pen: I always meant to come back. I didn't mean for you to think I wasn't.

Pen: I've messed up in a lot of ways. I've let a lot of people down. But the last person I ever wanted to disappoint was you. *I'm sorry.*

She knew Moose was on shift, and the fact that he didn't respond right away to her texts was actually a relief. He'd just say she hadn't disappointed him and she hadn't let anyone down...and she knew she had. But she was going to fix it. If she could.

. . .

Pen: I'll see you soon and we can hopefully talk.

Pen: Be safe. Tell Cade and the others I'm coming home. I still don't know about going back to work at the station though. We can talk about it.

Pen: I'll keep you updated on my progress but I'm planning on driving as far as I can every day before stopping. And yes, I'll be safe. See you soon. (If you still want to see me, that is.)

Then she clicked off her phone so she wouldn't be woken up by any incoming texts or emails, and rolled over, curling herself around Smokey, who was snoring in the bed next to her.

What she'd just done scared the hell out of her, opening herself up like that, even if just in a text, but the bottom line was that she trusted Moose. He wouldn't let her down; he hadn't yet. *She'd* been the one to run. To block him out. He'd been more than patient with her, and it was time she stopped running and faced her demons.

Maybe with Moose by her side, she could beat them. She sure as hell hoped so.

CHAPTER THREE

Moose couldn't sit still.

He'd been on a call for a grass fire when Penelope's texts had come through and he hadn't seen them until hours later, when he'd returned to the station. He wanted to immediately call her. Wanted to hear her voice. But it was okay. She was coming home. He could wait to talk to her when he saw her again.

As she'd requested, he told her brother and the others at the station that she would probably be home in a couple of days. Everyone was excited and couldn't wait to see her.

Moose didn't know what her plans were. Was she going to move back into her apartment? Would she come straight to his place to drop off Smokey? He didn't know, but he was more than ready for her, and more than ready to do whatever he could to convince her to stay with him.

Penelope was the bravest woman he knew, even if she didn't feel that way. He didn't know how she felt about him, but the fact that she was coming home, and had told *him* and not her brother, had to mean she felt *something*, didn't it?

Moose was done tiptoeing around his feelings. He'd known she'd been struggling mentally, and hadn't wanted to add anymore stress to her already full plate. But fuck that. He loved her. He wasn't going to throw in the towel yet.

He didn't know if Penelope loved him back, or *could* love him, but he'd do everything in his power to show her how good they could be together. That no matter what she thought about herself or what issues they had to fight, he'd always love her.

Moose knew it wouldn't be easy, but he'd be damned if he was going to let her push him away this time. These last few months without her had sucked. It was a small glimpse into what his life would be like if she left permanently, and he had no intention of going through that again. He wanted Pen by his side, from here on out, and he'd do whatever it took to make that happen.

While Penelope had been gone, he'd had his barn rebuilt, complete with fire alarms and security cameras. He had a feeling, however, that it might be impossible to convince both woman and donkey that a barn was where Smokey should be sleeping. He knew Smokey had been sleeping in Penelope's bed while they'd been on the road, and separating the two would probably be impossible. Luckily, he had a king-size bed, and he didn't give a damn about sharing with the four-legged beast. Not if it meant having Penelope in bed with them.

Looking at his watch for the hundredth time, Moose knew Penelope should probably be arriving at any moment. If she truly did drive as long as possible each day, it should've only taken her two days to drive from the California coast back to Texas. He knew he could call Tex and find out exactly where she was, but he didn't want to abuse her trust that way.

So he paced. It was silly. She might go straight to her apartment. Or to see her brother. Or to see Blythe's or Hope's new babies. There were a million places she could go once she got back to town. But he hoped and prayed she'd come to him.

As if his thoughts alone had conjured her, Moose heard a car pulling down his driveway. He hurried over to the window and looked out.

Sure enough, Penelope's PT Cruiser was pulling up in front of his house.

Taking a deep breath, Moose hurried out his door and stood on his porch and waited.

It had been months since he'd seen Penelope, and his eyes drank in the sight of her in the waning daylight as she climbed out of the driver's seat. It looked like she'd lost a little weight while she'd been gone, and maybe some muscle tone, but regardless, she looked good. Her blonde hair was up in a ponytail, wisps of hair escaping its confines and blowing across her face. She had no makeup on, but still looked more beautiful than anyone he'd ever seen before. She was wearing her normal jeans and T-shirt and had her favorite pair of sneakers on her feet.

Penelope's gaze met his, and Moose sighed in relief at what he saw there.

She still had demons, that was easy to see, but she seemed more settled than when he'd last seen her. Less frantic. Less haunted. Her impromptu trip had ripped his heart out of his chest, but he couldn't deny it seemed to have done her good.

He wanted to run to her. To take her in his arms and order her never to leave him again, but his feet felt as if they were glued to the boards beneath them. Maybe she regretted coming back. Maybe she'd just stopped by his house to tell him she needed more time and space.

That she couldn't ever love him...

Before either of them could say anything, Smokey had exited the car and seen him. He made a noise somewhere between a bray and a yell and came barreling toward Moose as fast as his little legs could carry him.

Moose heard Penelope laugh before he knelt to catch Smokey as he ran full tilt into him. Moose fell back on his butt and laughed as the miniature donkey did his best to let him know exactly how much he'd been missed. Smokey brayed and rubbed his head all over Moose's chest in excitement. It was all he could do to stay upright under the exuberant donkey's affection.

"It looks like he missed you," Penelope said softly.

As thrilled as he was that Smokey hadn't forgotten about him, Moose was more eager to greet the animal's mistress than continue to get slobbered on by the beast. Extricating himself from the donkey's overly enthusiastic greeting, Moose climbed off the floor and stared down at Penelope.

She was standing on the ground at the bottom of the three stairs that led up to the porch, which made her seem even smaller than she was. Moose knew they were an odd sight together. His six-three height to her five-two made him look even more like a giant. His muscular biceps were three times as big as hers. He was as big all over as she was small. Most of the time when he was around Penelope, he felt even more ungainly and hulking than usual, though she never made fun of his size and brawn. And normally around someone as small as she was, he'd be scared of hurting her. Not Penelope. Her personality and strength made her seem bigger than she was.

But at that moment, for the first time, Moose was scared to death to touch her. He'd loved her forever, but not knowing how she felt about him made him cautious. He didn't want to say or do the wrong thing that might make her put him in the friend zone once and for all. He felt stupid, like a gangly teenager all over again. And he stood frozen at the top of the stairs. He didn't know what to say or what to do.

But Penelope, being Penelope, didn't give him much time to fret. In a blink, she came at him almost as fast as her donkey had. One second he was standing on his porch staring down at her, and the next, she was in his arms.

Sighing with a relief so profound it literally took him to his knees, Moose wrapped his arms around her waist and buried his face into her stomach. She clung to him just as desperately. No words passed between them for the longest time. They just held on to each other as if their lives depended on it.

Moose felt her hands in his hair, and he knew he'd never known anything better in his life. He could hardly believe she was there. It was almost as good a feeling as it had been the first time he'd hugged her after she'd returned from Turkey, after her captivity.

Finally, he tilted his head back and looked up at her. "Welcome back, sweetheart."

"Thanks. It's good to be back."

He slowly stood, not breaking eye contact. He had a thousand things he wanted to say but couldn't get even one out of his mouth.

But again, he needn't have worried. Penelope took the reins. "You should know, I'm not sorry I left. I needed the time away to think. But I realized while I was traveling around, and watching others with their families and friends, that I'd done you and *our* friends a disservice. I need you guys. Even though I'm scared that I'm never going to find my way back to the person I used to be."

"But that's the thing, Pen, you don't have to. We love the person you are today."

"I don't even know who that is."

"Then we'll help show you."

Penelope nodded and bit her lip. Moose swallowed hard, wanting more than anything to take her lips with his. To tie her to him so tightly she'd never even consider taking off again, but he knew he had to tread lightly. His Pen was fragile right now, even if she didn't look it on the outside.

"What if I don't like her?" she asked. "She's a coward, Moose. I couldn't go into that burning house because I knew I'd let you all down. I couldn't be responsible for saving Taco and Koren because deep down, I knew I'd fail. Not only that, but how in the hell can I trust you and the others when I can't even trust myself? Something happened over there, and try as I might, I can't remember. I'm afraid I did something horrible...something that got people killed. I'm scared to try to remember, but I'm scared *not* to."

"Listen to me, Pen," Moose said firmly, putting one hand on her shoulder and the other under her chin, forcing her to look at him. Surprisingly, she let him. Didn't try to pull away. The vulnerability in her eyes hit him hard. He'd never seen her show so many emotions before.

"You are *not* a coward. Not in the least."

She looked away from him then, and Moose hated that.

"I'm done hiding my feelings for you. I did that for too long. I love you, Penelope. I love the way you don't take any shit from anyone. I love how you didn't shy away from taking on Smokey as a pet. I love that you're strong...but the thing is, you don't always *have* to be that way.

"Life is hard. Downright terrifying sometimes, and you don't have to fight your demons by yourself anymore. Nothing you say or do will make me love you any less. You can talk to me about anything. Or your brother. Or Beth, Sophie, or any of the other women. Hell, you've got those Delta Force men and even those SEALs out in California who would bend over backward to help you talk through the military shit you don't think I can understand.

"The person you are today is *amazing*, and I think if you give her a shot, you'll find that she's a badass motherfucker who can take on anything and make it through to the other side."

She smiled a bit at that. "I'm screwed up, Moose. I'm afraid I'm going to screw up you and everyone else I come into contact with as well."

"You won't."

Penelope stared at him for a long moment. "You really mean that," she said after a while.

"I do."

"I was responsible for at least six deaths out there in Turkey."

Moose immediately shook his head. "No, you weren't."

"You don't know what happened," she protested.

"And I don't have to know the details. I know without a shred of doubt that you did the best you could out there. If there was any way to save others, without getting yourself killed in the process, you would've done it. Is this what's been eating you alive all this time?"

Penelope shrugged. "Partly. That, and I feel like I can't trust anyone. Myself included."

Moose felt determination well up inside him. Everything made sense now. Her reluctance to take the lead at accident and fire scenes. The way she'd run away at Koren's condo when that shit went down. Guilt and lack of trust were insidious things. They could eat away at the strongest person.

He recognized what a huge step she'd just taken in telling him what was bothering her. He wished she'd told him months ago, but he couldn't change the past anymore than she could.

Now that he knew, Moose wasn't going to let fear and doubt break his Penelope. "We're going to beat this," he told her. "What you went through in Turkey would've broken a weaker person." At her look of skepticism, Moose shook his head. "It would've. And the fact that it took as long as it did to knock you down a peg proves it. I'm going to do whatever I can to help. I can't do it all *for* you, but I can be right by your side as you fight."

"Why?"

Moose didn't understand her question. "Because I love you."

Penelope shook her head. "You shouldn't. I'm a mess! I have no idea why you're still here when I've treated you like shit, used you, and been a horrible friend."

"I don't love you because you're perfect, Penelope. I love you because even with your flaws, you're still the most beautiful person inside and out I've ever met." When she looked skeptical, he went on. "If you were the horrible person you think you are, you wouldn't care what happened to Henry White and Thomas Black. Or Robert Wilson. Or the Australian soldier. You'd be thankful *you* didn't die and that would be that. You would've capitalized on the whole American Princess thing and signed book and movie deals and gone on every news and talk show that asked. But you didn't. You hid away and went back to your forty-thousand-a-year job as a firefighter, quietly saving lives behind the scenes and not asking for a damn thing in return."

Tears filled her eyes, and as much as Moose hated seeing them, he was glad. Penelope very rarely let down her guard in front of him, or anyone, really.

He pulled her against his chest, and closed his eyes

in relief when he felt her arms go around him and hug him back. How long they stood like that, on his porch in the setting sun, holding each other as if it was the very first time, Moose had no idea. But it wasn't until Smokey nudged his leg with his snout that he realized Penelope was probably tired and hungry after driving all day.

It didn't escape his notice that she hadn't returned his declaration of love, but that was all right. For now, he loved her enough for the both of them.

He pulled back and said, "Let's get you inside and settled. I'll call for Chinese if you want."

Penelope looked up at him, and Moose couldn't read the look in her eyes, but she nodded. "Sounds perfect."

He didn't want to do anything to make her tense up, but he had to know. "Are you staying here tonight?"

She nodded again. "If that's okay?"

"Of course it is," Moose confirmed quickly. "You can stay as long as you want. Forever if it works for you." It was too soon, but he didn't regret his words when he saw the look of relief cross her face.

"We'll start with tonight. How's that?" she said with a hint of her old snark.

"Sounds good."

Penelope looked in the direction of his barn and blinked in surprise. "You had it rebuilt?"

"Yeah. Hoped when you came home that it would help convince you and Smokey to stay. But I'm guessing the little guy isn't going to want to sleep outside in a nice, comfy bed of hay after getting used to being on a mattress, huh?"

Penelope smiled, and Moose melted inside at seeing the genuine happiness on her face.

"I'm guessing you're probably right."

"Then we'll just have to find other donkeys, horses, or whatever other animals you think need rescuing to fill up the barn, then," Moose told her.

"Seriously?" she asked with wide eyes.

Moose shrugged a little self-consciously. "It's been too quiet around here without the two of you."

"You're too good to me."

"Not possible," Moose told her. "Come on. Let's get you guys inside so I can feed you."

Moose had to let Sledge know his sister was home safe and sound, but that could wait until Penelope was settled. He knew the next few months weren't going to be easy. But he was as determined as ever to help Penelope love the new woman she was and deal with her past. Only then could they look toward the future… hopefully together.

CHAPTER FOUR

Penelope took a deep breath and let it out slowly. She'd been back in San Antonio a week and had yet to get together with the guys. It was past time.

Cade and Beth had come over to see her at Moose's house, and she'd been overjoyed to see them. After an hour, when Beth had apologized and said she wasn't having a good day as far as her agoraphobia went, and needed to get home, Penelope studied her brother carefully and didn't see even one ounce of impatience or irritation on his face. All she saw was concern and love for his woman.

It was a little eye opening. Beth took no shit from anyone. She was a beast behind the keyboard. She could do just about anything if it had to do with electronics. But she had her demons too. And Cade obviously loved her anyway. It gave Penelope hope that maybe she wasn't too far gone that she couldn't have an amazing life in the near future.

She couldn't help but look over at Moose after her epiphany, and she'd seen him watching her with an inscrutable look on his face, before he'd smiled gently.

Penelope was really nervous about seeing the other guys from the station today. She hadn't heard from them since her return, and that stressed her out. She hated not knowing what was going on in their heads, so she was sucking it up and going in today to get this first meeting out of the way.

She had no idea what to expect. She wouldn't blame them if they were upset with her; if one of them had done what she had, she'd want answers, and wouldn't be afraid to let him know she was mad that he hadn't kept in touch.

She dreaded it, but she couldn't fix anything broken until she faced them.

Not wanting to think about doing this same thing with the women of their group, she tamped down that worry to deal with another day.

"If you need more time, I'll take you home," Moose said quietly as they sat in his truck in the parking lot at Station 7.

Penelope was trying to get up the courage to get out of the vehicle and go inside, but was finding it difficult. She hated this new indecision of hers, but couldn't seem to make her muscles work. "Tell me honestly," she said after a minute. "Are they really pissed at me?"

Moose looked shocked at her questions. "No," he said immediately. "Is that what you think?"

"I'm not sure *what* to think. I left so abruptly. I quit and didn't even bother to say good-bye to anyone. They haven't called or texted me since I've been back."

"Look at me," Moose ordered.

Sighing, Penelope turned her head and met his brown gaze.

"They aren't pissed. At all. They were worried as fuck. Worried about *you*. Worried that you'd never come back. That they wouldn't get the chance to tell you how much they all care about you. They were giving you time and space to sort through shit in your head."

His words made her sigh in semi-relief, but the stress didn't really ease. "But I was a coward. I'm sure I've lost their trust, which is ironic, considering the trust issues I've got."

"Pen, you aren't a coward and never were one. But I know I'm never going to convince you of anything. The best thing you can do is suck it up and go inside and see for yourself what the guys think."

Penelope looked up at Moose in surprise. In the past, he'd been nothing but gentle and supportive. She liked that he wasn't beating around the bush and was encouraging her to go see their friends.

When she looked into his eyes, she still saw the love and support she always did.

Taking a deep breath, she nodded. The fact of the

matter was, she *was* being a coward by sitting in the truck, stewing about things. She was never this way in the past. And as much as she knew she couldn't go back to being the person she was before she'd been taken captive in Turkey, she didn't want to be this meek, scared person either. So she had to get her shit together.

Without a word, she opened the door and got out. By the time she was at the front of Moose's truck, he was there too. He took her hand in his...the first time she could ever remember him doing so.

With no time to feel awkward about holding his hand—probably because she was still freaking out about seeing the guys—Penelope held her breath as he pushed open the door to the station.

They walked into the large main room, and it took a second before anyone saw them. But the second Squirrel noticed they were there, he bolted up from the couch and made a beeline for Penelope.

"About damn time," he mumbled, before pushing Moose out of the way and sweeping her into a hug.

The second his arms wrapped around her, Penelope relaxed completely.

"Good to see you, Pen," Squirrel said emotionally.

"Congrats on your baby girl," she mumbled into his shoulder.

"Thanks," he said, then pulled back a fraction to look into her eyes. "You good?"

"No. But I'm doing my best to get there," Penelope said honestly.

"I hope you're planning on going to see Blythe soon. She asks about you just about every day. And," he winked, "we could use a babysitter for a night or so. You know how hard it is to get some quality bedroom time when there's a baby in the house?"

Penelope burst into laughter. Leave it to Squirrel to break the tension by talking about his sex life...or lack thereof. "Heard you finally made an honest woman out of Blythe."

"I did. Wish you could've been here, but you comin' home just gives us an excuse to have another party."

"Stop hogging her!" Driftwood complained. "Let the rest of us in there."

Squirrel dutifully let go of her, but said, "Just remember that since I asked first, I get first dibs on the babysitting."

"Great to see you, Pen," Driftwood said as he rolled his eyes at Squirrel's comment, then hugged her.

Even though she'd never been touchy-feely with her coworkers and friends, having them not hesitate to hug her felt good. It had been a long time since she'd been touched, and even though she hadn't really missed it over the last few months, right now, it hit home how much these men meant to her. "You too," she told Driftwood.

He let go of her, and Penelope turned to Chief. He was standing watching them with his arms over his chest, looking every inch like she imagined his ancestors did back in the day. She hesitated.

"What are you waiting for? Get over here," he said gruffly, finally holding out his arms.

Penelope walked into his embrace.

"'Bout time you got home, girl," he said gruffly.

She tilted her head back to look him in the eye. "I heard you and Soph are going to have a baby. Congratulations."

Chief nodded. "She's scared she's gonna pass her stuttering down to our kid."

"So what if she does?" Penelope asked with a huff. "Your kid'll have Harper, Lily, Steven, and Carter to stand up for him or her in school, and there are two dozen honorary aunts and uncles to make sure he or she has a healthy self-esteem and can deal with anyone stupid enough to bully them."

Chief's lips quirked up in a smile. "Missed you, Pen. Things haven't been the same around here without you. Go see Soph, would ya?"

"I will."

Then Penelope was passed over to Crash. After a big hug, he asked, "How's Smokey doing? I swear Coco has been depressed ever since you left. That dog's been moping around and staring at the door longingly. I knew I'd never be able to take Adeline's place in that dog's affection, but I never thought I'd come in third place behind a donkey."

Everyone laughed at Crash's mock indignation.

Penelope turned to give her brother a hug, words unnecessary since she'd actually visited with him and Beth not too long ago.

She then turned to the last person in their group. Taco.

She felt utterly at a loss as to what to say or do, but Taco took the decision out of her hands when he engulfed her in a bear hug.

Tears welled in Penelope's eyes. She felt as if she'd let Taco down in the worst way a fellow firefighter could, and yet it seemed as if he wasn't holding it against her. "I'm sorry," she whispered against his neck. "I'm so sorry."

"It's over and done and we're all okay," Taco told her.

Penelope pulled back and forced herself to meet his gaze. "If I could change *anything* in my past, it wouldn't be not getting taken hostage. It wouldn't be for my fellow soldiers to have survived. It would be that I didn't run like a coward and leave you and Koren in that house." The words came from her soul, and she knew they were the absolute truth—which made her feel even worse, since Taco and Koren were alive and well, when her soldier friends weren't.

Taco took her face in his hands, and Penelope felt a hand settle on her lower back. Without looking, she knew it was Moose. Just having him there comforted her.

"It's okay, Pen. I understand."

"You do? I wish you would explain it to me then," she said with a watery chuckle.

"You're gonna find yourself again, I know it," Taco said. "After what Jennifer did, I didn't ever want to date again. I just knew I was going to end up an old, bitter man with hair growing out his ears and nose with no one to tell him to snip that shit."

Penelope chuckled again and felt her tears ease. This is what she needed. Her fellow firefighters to pull her out of her doldrums. Taco's acceptance, and his forgiveness of what she'd done—essentially leaving him and Koren in her burning condo—felt good, but she wasn't sure she could ever forgive *herself* for that ultimate act of cowardice.

"The question we all want to know is...are you coming back, Pen?" Crash asked.

The room was so quiet, she could hear the old clock on the wall ticking each second as it passed. "I...I don't know. I just... I don't know."

Not able to bear any possible looks of disappointment or censure on her friends' faces, she looked down at the floor, uneasy.

Before anyone could respond, the tones went off in the quiet room, scaring the shit out of her. Penelope jumped, and she heard Moose say quietly, "Easy, Pen."

The other six men quickly said their goodbyes and hurried to the garage to put on their bunker gear and jump into the trucks.

When it was just her and Moose once more, she

turned to him. "I'm not sure if that went well or not. I mean, they were happy to hug me and all, but it still felt a little weird."

"It did. Give them some time," Moose advised. "And yourself. You just got back. I know for a fact that the chief didn't accept your resignation."

"He didn't?" Penelope replied, shocked.

"Nope. You've officially been on a leave of absence."

Penelope stared up at Moose, a feeling of hope in her belly for the first time. She'd thought she'd burned that particular bridge. She wasn't ready to come back yet, wasn't sure she'd ever be ready, but knowing that maybe she *could* if she decided to was a huge weight taken off her shoulders. The fact of the matter was that if she didn't go back to being a firefighter, she had no idea what she'd do. She wasn't really qualified to do anything else, and working in some hourly minimum-wage job didn't appeal in the least.

"You want to wait here until they get back, or head out?" Moose asked.

Penelope thought about it. On the one hand, she wanted to get the hell out of the station so she didn't have to deal with any questions about her returning or why she'd left. But on the other hand, these were her friends. They'd shown it unconditionally by their acceptance and welcoming of her. She felt comfortable here, even if she was *un*comfortable thinking about why she didn't feel right about returning to work. She had a lot of great memories in this fire station, and she wanted to stay.

"Here."

Moose smiled at her. "Want to help me make something for lunch for when they get back?"

"Absolutely."

Working with Moose in the kitchen also brought back a ton of good memories. Thinking about what Wolf had said when she'd been in California about her "tribe" really struck home. This was where she felt most comfortable. But at the same time, it was also where she felt the most *uncomfortable*, as if she somehow didn't really belong there anymore. Like she was a fraud.

But she'd cross that bridge later. Not today and not now. For now, she was going to do her best to relax and make some lunch for her friends.

Three hours later, Penelope felt better than she had in months. The guys came back right as she and Moose were finishing up the vegetable soup and sandwiches they'd put together for lunch. They'd all laughed and joked just as they used to. It felt good.

She told the group stories about where she'd been over the last few months and the people she'd met. She recounted funny stories about Smokey, and how he'd gained attention and friends everywhere they'd gone.

In turn, the guys got her caught up on what had been going on in their lives. About half their group was married now, while the other half was engaged. It dawned on Penelope that she and Moose were the only two of their group who were still single.

But...it didn't feel that way. Moose was sitting next to her on one of the couches. His thigh was touching hers, and every now and then, he'd put his hand on her leg or his arm behind her on the back of the couch, his fingers playing with her hair.

It shouldn't have come as a surprise when her brother asked the question she had a feeling he'd been dying to ask since she'd returned a week ago.

"So...you and Moose have finally admitted you like each other and are dating now?"

"Yes."

"No."

She and Moose answered at the same time.

Penelope blushed when Moose raised an eyebrow at her. "It's complicated," she finally said lamely.

"Have you even been back to your apartment since you've returned?" Sledge asked.

"Yes," Penelope said defensively.

"For more than just to grab clothes and stuff?" her brother clarified.

"Moose has a barn, and it's easier for Smokey," Penelope said defensively. As soon as the words left her mouth, she knew she was once again being a coward, and she'd promised herself she was going to do her best to stop lying about things.

Moose didn't contradict her...not in words. He stayed silent and let her take the lead on this, which she appreciated, but she figured the hand resting on her thigh in a way she'd never let one of the *other* guys touch her spoke volumes.

Steeling her spine, she took a deep breath. "Fine, if you must know, I've been staying over at Moose's house. And not because of Smokey. He sleeps with me anyway, so he doesn't need a barn. I've been sharing Moose's bed and we're making loud, kinky sex all night long. Happy now?"

She heard more than saw Moose suck in a surprised breath, but she kept her gaze on Cade, glaring at him. She was lying, mostly. While she and Moose had been sharing a bed, Smokey was always between them, and all they'd done was sleep.

The other guys all burst out laughing, congratulating Moose, but Penelope stared at her brother, trying to gauge his reaction. Wasn't there some code that said men didn't hook up with their friends' sisters? Was Cade upset that she and Moose might get together? She hadn't ever let herself think about that before because she'd been fighting her feelings for Moose so hard. But now that she was back, and Moose had told her exactly how he felt about her, she was more sensitive to what the people around her thought.

Cade smiled at her and shook his head in exasperation. "I don't ever want to get a blow-by-blow of what my little sister is doing in the bedroom, but for the record, I would be the happiest man alive—well, maybe not as happy as Moose—if you two got together. I trust

Moose with my life, but more importantly, I trust him with *yours*. All I've ever wanted is for you to be happy, Pen. And I have to say, it's been a very long time—since before you went over to Turkey for that humanitarian mission—that I've seen you happy. When you were missing, the only thing I wanted was for you to come home. I didn't care what shape you were in, as long as you were alive."

The room got quiet as everyone sobered at Sledge's words.

"I was over the moon when you survived what those assholes tried to do to you. I wanted to move you into my house and never let you out of my sight, but of course you wouldn't have let me do that if I'd tried. The next best thing was having you working with me here at the station. I could see you every day and know that you were all right, physically if not mentally. But over the last year, even though you've been here, you haven't really *been here*, if that makes sense. We all knew you were struggling, and it killed us that you wouldn't let us help.

"I don't know what happened while you were gone these last few months with Smokey, but the woman I see sitting in front of me today is just a little more like the sister I used to play War with in our backyard. And I have a feeling the man sitting next to you is a big part of that. Not downplaying the shit you still have to figure out in your head, because it's obvious you're still working on that, but it's also clear that Moose will move heaven and earth to make your path easier...if you let him. So I don't care if you're having loud, kinky sex with Moose—as long as it helps bring back the little sister I know is hiding in there somewhere."

"You need to back off," Moose said in a warning tone.

Penelope looked up at him in surprise. Her brother's words *were* hard to hear, but she was actually glad he'd said them. She didn't realize until right that minute exactly how much everyone had been tiptoeing around her. Scared to say the slightest thing that might upset her or make her even think about her time as a POW...as if she could ever forget.

"The last thing your sister needs is pressure to be the person she used to be," Moose said. "That woman's gone, and the Penelope who's taken her place is someone I like a hell of a lot. And I didn't have shit to do with who Penelope is right now. She's done that all on her own. She doesn't need a man to cure her of her PTSD. For one, she isn't ever *going* to be cured. That's a simple fact of post-traumatic stress disorder. And two, she's doing a hell of a job pulling herself out of the mental hell she's been through. She'll learn to deal with her memories, and if she wants me by her side, that's where I'll be."

"Moose, it's okay," Penelope said quietly, putting her hand over his. She could see that he was way more upset about this conversation than she was...and somehow that comforted her.

"It's not," Moose said, still staring at Sledge. "I love her, man. As you said, I'll do whatever it takes to help her figure her shit out, but I won't sit here and let you guys make her feel uncomfortable about her choices."

Penelope was floored that he'd come right out and said that he loved her in front of all the guys. She wanted to say it right back. Tell her brother that she loved Moose too and whatever they decided to do with their relationship was on them, but she couldn't get the words out. Wasn't ready to tie him to her in a way that she knew he'd never let her back away from if things got too bad inside her head.

She wouldn't do that to him. Wouldn't make him feel like he couldn't leave if she was going to be a fucking mental case for the rest of her life.

"No one's trying to make anyone uncomfortable," Chief said quietly. "We love Pen too."

Moose actually growled at that, and Penelope kinda wanted to laugh.

"Not like that, man, jeez," Taco complained.

"All I'm saying is that if I had to pick a man for you to be with, Moose would be that man," her brother explained. "I respect him, but even if I didn't, I'd still be supportive of any relationship the two of you might have, for the simple fact that I see more of my little sister in your eyes today than I have since you've been back from Turkey. Maybe it's because of your trip, but I have a feeling it's also a result of the man at your side."

Penelope couldn't respond. Didn't know what to

say. She thought any kind of relationship with Moose would be awkward since they worked together, and that the guys might not like to see them together at the station. But looking at them, all she saw was concern and acceptance.

Words stuck in the back of her throat. She wanted to ask them how in the world they could stand to be around her after she'd failed them so spectacularly at the fire at Koren's condo. How they could be supportive of her and Moose when they couldn't trust her anymore. Her head spun with recriminations and questions, but she couldn't get the words to come out of her mouth to ask. She knew in the past, she would've made some smart-ass comment and everyone would laugh and the tension would ease... but that wasn't her anymore. Somewhere between her rescue and now, she'd lost that part of herself.

"Hey, there's another softball game coming up," Crash said, breaking the tension. "Now that you're back, Pen, the teams can be even. What d'ya say?"

Swallowing the lump in her throat, Penelope nodded. "I'd like that. Although I'm probably not in the best shape."

Crash snorted. "As if that makes a difference. You're the best distraction though. The guys'll go out of their way not to rock the boat when it comes to you, and that'll give us a leg up."

Penelope couldn't help but laugh. Leave it to her friends to think the fact that she was emotionally fragile right now would be a positive thing when it came to winning a softball game. Everyone cheated anyway, so it wasn't as if the game was life or death.

The more time she spent around her friends, the more she remembered how awesome they were and how they made her forget her worries.

"You want me to not shower for a week and come to the game wearing the same clothes I've been sleeping in? That might make me look even more pathetic," she deadpanned.

For a second, no one said anything—then her brother laughed, and the rest of the group joined in.

"Would you?" Taco asked. "Because that would be awesome."

Penelope picked up a pen from the table and threw it at Taco. "No. I was kidding."

"Maybe you can wear a knee brace or something, make 'em think you're hurt. That would put all the attention on you so we can outmaneuver them," Squirrel suggested.

While the rest of the guys continued to offer up crazy ideas on how to outsmart the police officers and use Penelope's return as a distraction, she turned to look at Moose. He was staring at her with a look she couldn't interpret.

"You okay?" Moose asked.

Penelope nodded. "Surprisingly, yes."

"They aren't overstepping?"

She rolled her eyes. "No. It actually feels good to joke about my situation for once."

"I don't think I've ever seen or heard you talk about the effect your captivity's had on you like this before."

"Like how?"

"So nonchalantly."

Penelope thought about that, and realized he was right. And for just a second she felt like her old self. But as soon as the feeling swept over her, it was replaced by a memory of her joking and laughing with White, Black, and Wilson as they played soccer in the humanitarian camp during their down time. How happy they'd all been before things had gone to shit and they'd been captured.

"Shit," Moose murmured before pulling her up and off the couch. "We're going to head out," he announced to the room.

Penelope knew she should say something. Tell Moose she was all right. Joke with the guys and get back to the mellow mood she'd been in, but all she could think about in that moment was how she would never see her Army friends again. How she'd somehow let them down.

She didn't remember what had happened immediately after they'd been captured, or the capture itself. She'd felt uneasy about the section of camp they'd been ordered to patrol and had complained to the major about it, but he'd reprimanded her in front of the entire squad and sent them off anyway. She'd obviously been correct in her fears, but the next thing she remembered was being in a tent, getting beaten by a group of men before being left alone. She'd never seen White, Black, or Wilson again, and had later learned they'd been beheaded and set on fire for the terrorists' propaganda videos.

Feeling sick, Penelope didn't realize she'd let out a quiet moan until Moose put his arm around her waist and pulled her into his side. "Easy, Pen, I'll have you home in a jiffy."

Forcing herself to concentrate on something other than her dead friends, Penelope focused on how she fit against Moose perfectly. She'd always hated her short stature, but being tucked against his much larger frame made her feel safe. It was a feeling she desperately needed right now.

She heard him saying goodbye to the others and telling Sledge that he'd text him later, but she didn't have the mental energy to lift her head and say her own goodbyes.

At that moment, she hated herself. Hated what she'd become. She'd thought she was doing better, that she could come back to San Antonio and not be quite so mental anymore. She'd admitted to having guilt and trust issues, and had hoped that alone was enough to have her well on her way to feeling stronger, to letting go of those feelings. But that wasn't the case.

She let Moose lead her to his truck and get her settled on the passenger side. When he'd started the vehicle and headed back toward his house, she whispered, "They haunt me, Moose."

"Who, sweetheart?"

"White. And Black. And even Wilson."

"Tell me about them."

Blinking, Penelope looked over at Moose. He glanced at her before returning his attention to the road. "I know they were in your unit, but I haven't heard you say much about them. They must've been amazing men to have earned your loyalty like they did."

"They were. They were hilarious. But, if I'm being honest, they could annoy me sometimes too. Kinda like brothers. But they didn't deserve what happened to them," she said softly.

"Just as you didn't deserve what happened to you," Moose insisted. "Now, tell me about them."

And she did. For the rest of the drive home, she recounted how White and Black had nothing in common, but somehow they'd clicked. Thomas Black was from Maine and had red hair and freckles. Henry White was from Mississippi and had the darkest skin she'd ever seen. They were the complete opposites of their names, which struck everyone as funny, and they had become close friends.

Black was a klutz, hopeless at any kind of sport, but he was the guy everyone wanted on their team when they were playing trivia. White was Black's protector of sorts, standing up for him when the other guys in the unit tried to pick on him. No one wanted to cross

White; he could be one mean motherfucker. But to her and Black, he was silly, funny, and loyal.

Before she knew it, they were pulling up to Moose's house and she'd been talking nonstop for the entire trip. It had been nice to remember the men as they'd been before the shit had hit the fan. After her rescue, she'd made the mistake of looking up the videos the terrorists had made of their deaths, and for a while, as Moose drove and she told funny stories about the men, she'd forgotten the looks of terror that had been on their faces before they'd been beheaded. She'd forgotten how fast their bodies had gone up in flames as the terrorists read their manifesto with the pyres in the background.

"What about Robert Wilson?" Moose asked, as if he could read her mind and knew how close to the edge she was. He'd come around her side of the truck and helped her out as he asked the question.

Almost desperately, Penelope talked about how Wilson had been a ball hog whenever they played soccer, although he'd mostly kept to himself outside of their missions. He seemed like a good man, but she didn't know a lot about him.

The next thing she knew, Moose had led her into his bedroom. She had no idea what time it was, but he turned on the bathtub faucet and, after the water got hot, plugged the drain and poured in an obscene amount of bubble bath.

"I'm going to go let Smokey out. Get in the tub, and

when I get back, be ready to tell me more stories about your friends." He grinned. "There will be enough bubbles in the tub to preserve your modesty." Then he lifted her chin, and the intensity in his gaze mesmerized Penelope. "Don't think about anything but the good times. I mean it, Pen."

"Okay."

Then Moose ever so slowly leaned toward her.

For a second, she thought he was going to kiss her, and she wanted that. More than she'd ever wanted anything in her life. She could lose herself in Moose. Not have to think about anything. Not about her dead friends. Not about how she'd let down her fellow firefighters.

Not about how lately, she wished more and more that she'd died over there in Turkey.

But instead of pressing his lips to hers and taking her the way she'd recently begun fantasizing about, Moose kissed her forehead. He left his lips on her skin for a very long time, until Penelope swayed on her feet. Then he pulled back. "I'll bring up a glass of wine. Relax, Pen. I'll be right back."

One second he was there, keeping the bad memories at bay, and the next he was gone, leaving Penelope alone with her morose thoughts.

"Get it together, Pen," she mumbled before stripping off all her clothes and leaving them in a heap on the tile floor and climbing into the tub.

CHAPTER FIVE

Moose lay awake for hours after helping Penelope to bed. For the first time, he usurped Smokey's place beside his mistress and pulled Penelope into his arms, leaving the donkey to curl up at their feet instead of between them.

Penelope hadn't complained, had simply melted into him and fallen to sleep almost instantly. Moose was glad. He knew she hadn't been sleeping well, and he'd done everything he could to relax her tonight. Wine, hot bubble bath, and keeping her talking about the good times she remembered about her friends.

She'd talked about White the most. Apparently, she and him had spent quite a few nights talking about their lives back home. Penelope said White had talked a lot about his mama. How she was a struggling single mother who made the best cornbread he'd ever tasted in his life, and she was the reason he was in the Army

Reserves. He'd been on the verge of getting fully immersed into the gang life in Mississippi, and his mama had sat him down one day and talked to him for hours. Told him what would happen to him if he continued on the path he was on. Told him it would probably end up killing him, which in turn, would kill her too.

White had told Penelope that his mama meant the world to him, and he admired her so much. He was lucky she cared enough to get in his face and tell him he had to straighten up or he'd die. To her, it was that simple.

An idea niggled at the back of Moose's mind. He wasn't sure what Penelope would think, or even if it was a good idea at all, but once it came to him, it wouldn't let go. Before mentioning it to Penelope, he'd have to think about it some more.

Sighing, he tightened his hold on the woman in his arms. Penelope snuggled deeper into him, and he couldn't help but close his eyes and pretend things were different. That Penelope loved him back. That they were *together*-together. That she'd somehow found her way back from the hell she was living in now. It killed him that he couldn't do more for her. That he couldn't take away her pain. But he knew that wasn't how things worked. Penelope had to fight her own battles. All he could do was remain by her side as she did it.

With every day that passed, Moose was more and

more impressed by her. What would've broken a weaker person had only temporarily knocked her off her life path. He had no doubt whatsoever that she'd find her way back and be stronger as a result.

The only thing he wasn't sure about was if she'd leave him behind when she did.

It was a real concern. He might be a kind of trigger in her memory, of things she'd rather forget. But he hoped that since she'd come home to him after all those months on the road, that meant he had a chance. She was here now, in his house, in his bed, in his arms, that had to mean something…didn't it?

Moose hated the insecurity he felt about their relationship. He wanted what was best for her, but if that meant letting her go or seeing her in the arms of someone else, he wasn't sure he could take it.

Moose was tired. Needed to get some sleep as he was supposed to go into the station tomorrow. He'd taken some days off to be with Pen, to help her get settled, but it was time for him to get back to his normal schedule. Maybe that would help Penelope get back to her own semblance of normal as well. He simply wasn't sure.

Just as he was dozing off, the woman in his arms whimpered. The sound was enough to make Moose jerk awake, as if he'd been sleeping for hours and was completely refreshed.

She whimpered again and shook her head back and forth.

"Penelope, wake up. It's Moose...you're fine."

As if she didn't hear him, Penelope continued to whip her head to and fro, and she brought her arms up in front of her, as if trying to ward someone off. "No, stop. Please!"

Hating the terror in her voice, Moose tried to wake her once more. "Penelope... Wake up! You're having a bad dream."

But she was too far into the nightmare. His words seemed to frighten her more, not comfort her.

"Get away from them! Stop! We're surrendering! Stop hitting them!"

Having a feeling she was dreaming about the friends she'd talked so much about earlier that night, Moose felt guilty. He'd encouraged her to tell him about them, and it had obviously triggered some sort of memory.

She was on her back and her feet were flailing, almost hitting poor Smokey, who hadn't fully awakened yet. Moose grabbed hold of one of Penelope's arms and held it tightly in his hand, trying to figure out how to wake her.

But apparently grabbing hold of her was the wrong thing to do, because her eyes popped open and she stared sightlessly at him and opened her mouth and let out the most terrifying, heartbreaking wail he'd ever heard in his life. It startled him so badly, he immediately let go of her arm.

She turned away and curled into a ball on his bed

and covered her head with her arms and hands as best she could, as if to protect herself from him.

Smokey had woken up by that time, and he walked up the bed to Penelope and lay down next to her, nudging her with his head, softly braying and rubbing against her. Amazingly, that seemed to work, unlike anything Moose had tried. Penelope grabbed hold of the donkey, buried her head in his fur, and held on to him tightly.

Flummoxed, Moose could only watch as the four-legged animal did his best to soothe his mistress. It was obvious that Penelope and Smokey had been through this routine before. He didn't like knowing she had nightmares, and had been suffering through them alone.

No. He *loathed* that. Equally loathed that he couldn't do anything when she was hurting, and Smokey obviously could. Feeling jealous of a damn donkey was ridiculous, but Moose was sick that he hadn't been able to help her.

Taking a deep breath and forcing himself to turn away, Moose headed out of the bedroom. He'd sleep on the couch to give her some space.

He hated leaving her. It felt as if he was being split in two. But without a sound, he closed the bedroom door and walked down the stairs.

* * *

The next morning, Moose was at the counter pouring himself a cup of coffee when Penelope wandered down the stairs. She was wearing one of his T-shirts, which was huge on her. Her hair was in disarray and she had the most adorable sleepy look on her face. Smokey was at her heels, but he immediately veered off toward the back door.

Impressed all over again at how the damn donkey was housetrained, Moose wandered over and let him out as Penelope sat at the small table near the kitchen.

"Coffee?" Moose asked softly as he came back toward her.

"Please."

He poured her a cup, black, just how she liked it, and put it in front of her. She lifted the mug up to her face and inhaled deeply, her eyes closed. Moose could do little more than stare at her. She seemed…good this morning. He was afraid she'd be tired after her nightmare, but he doubted she even remembered it, if the way she was acting was any indication.

"Sleep okay?" he asked.

"Like the dead," she reassured him. "I don't know what it is about your mattress, but I swear I sleep better here than I have anywhere in the last few months."

Her answer made him feel both better and worse about what had happened. He grabbed his own mug and slipped into the chair next to her. "I have a confession," he told her.

She arched a brow at him as she sipped her coffee.

"You had a nightmare last night." He'd debated not telling her, but if it was him, he'd want to know. He wouldn't want her keeping something like that from him.

Her mug hit the table with a loud thud as she put it down. "I did?"

Moose nodded.

"Was it bad?"

He nodded again.

"That's so weird because I don't remember it at all."

"I tried to wake you up, but you freaked. Thought I was trying to hurt you."

Her face paled. "You wouldn't hurt me."

Moose gave her a small smile. "Of course not. But when you were in the middle of the nightmare, you didn't know it was me."

"I'm sorry."

Moose shook his head. "This isn't your fault, sweetheart. But that being said, I really think you need to talk to someone about what you went through."

Penelope sat up straighter in her chair, and he could see her jaw clench. "No, I'm doing okay."

"You are. You're doing amazing. But you have to admit that things aren't exactly good."

He thought she might immediately argue with him, but she simply pressed her lips together. Moose pushed a little more. "You said yourself that you don't remember what happened when you were taken captive. What exactly happened to White, Black, and

Wilson. I think it might do you some good to see if, under hypnosis, you can remember. I think it could help you heal. At least you'll know once and for all."

Penelope shook her head and gripped her mug with both hands so tightly, Moose saw her knuckles turn white. He reached over and took one of her hands in his and let her hold on to him, rather than the hard ceramic. "You were fighting someone and yelling out the word 'no.' Telling whoever it was to 'leave them alone.' What are you afraid of, when it comes to finding out what really happened that day?"

She was quiet so long, Moose thought she wasn't going to answer. But finally she said softly, "That I did something to get them killed."

Moose leaned over and put his hand behind Penelope's neck and turned her so she had no choice but to look at him. "You didn't."

"You don't know that."

"I do."

She shook her head slightly. "You don't."

"Pen, I've worked with you for years. I've seen you hold your own in the worst possible situations. Not only that, but when there's been any kind of altercation between the rest of us and a civilian, you've tried to dissipate the tension or physically protect someone. Remember that one time we were called to a domestic, and the cops thought the situation was under control and you were treating the woman? The boyfriend got all riled up again and managed to grab a knife and come after his girlfriend? You stood *between* them until the officers could control the guy."

Penelope stared at him with wide eyes. The need to believe him was easy to read in her gaze.

"And the time there was that big fight downtown. It was complete chaos, and some asshole ran up behind Taco and was ready to bash him in the head with a tire iron. You wrestled it away from him, even took a hit or two yourself before me and Crash could subdue him.

"Pen, I don't know what happened in that refugee camp, but whatever it was, I am one hundred percent sure that *nothing* you did or said got your friends killed. They were executed by terrorists with fucked-up ideologies who wanted to try to blackmail other countries into doing their bidding. You were all in the wrong place at the wrong time. That's it."

"I remember being angry. So fucking *angry*," Penelope told him. "What if I said something that changed their plans from holding all of us to killing them?"

"I'm thinking they knew exactly what they were going to do with y'all before they even got their hands on you. If anything, I'm betting the fact that you were a woman, a beautiful one at that, saved your life. If you'd been a man, they probably would've killed you quickly, right along with the others."

At that, her eyes closed tightly. "I don't know, Moose."

He leaned forward and rested his forehead on hers. "I tried to wake you up last night. I did everything I could think of…and the only thing I managed was to scare you more. It took Smokey to get you out of your head and to get you back to sleep. I hated seeing you look at me with such terror in your eyes."

"I'm sorry."

Moose shook his head. "I'm not telling you this to add more guilt to your plate. I'm telling you because I'll do *anything* to prevent that from happening again. Even if means pushing you to do something you might not want to do."

"Like see a hypnotist?" she asked.

Moose nodded.

"Will you come with me?"

"Of course. I wouldn't let you go *without* me."

He felt Penelope take a deep breath, and then she pulled back. He dropped his hand from her nape reluctantly.

"*Let* me?"

Moose was thrilled to hear a bit of the old Penelope in her words. He gave her a small grin. "Yeah, Pen. *Let* you. Now, what do you want for breakfast? I'm heading into the station soon for a twelve-hour shift, and I want to make sure I feed my girl before I go."

"Twelve hours, not twenty-four?" she asked.

Moose nodded as he pushed back from the table, stood, and headed over to the back door. "Yeah. I asked the chief if I could do shorter shifts so I could be home with you more often." That wasn't the only reason, but he wasn't sure he should tell her that right now. She had enough on her plate without having to worry about his issues.

"Afraid I'm going to run again?" she asked with a tilt of her head. Her question wasn't snarky, it was actually fairly unemotional.

Moose let Smokey back inside and turned to face Penelope. "Are you?" he challenged instead of answering her question.

After a beat, she shook her head. "No. I'm done running."

"Good. Now…breakfast?"

"An omelet?"

"Cheese, peppers, and mushrooms?"

"Is there any other way to make an omelet?" she asked with a smile.

Moose's mind was going a million miles an hour with plans he needed to make regarding the next suggestion he had for Penelope. He was going to help her heal, no matter what it took. He'd watched from the sidelines for far too long. He should've stepped up way before now, but almost losing her, knowing she'd been *this* close to never coming back to San Antonio, had shaken him out of his complacency. Penelope might fight him every step of the way, but he didn't think so.

She wanted to get past what happened to her as much as *he* wanted her to. She just needed a little nudge. Or a big one. But since he'd already talked her into one scary thing for the day, he could wait to tell her about his other plans.

After they'd eaten breakfast and he'd changed into his work clothes, Moose asked, "What are your plans for today?"

Penelope took a deep breath and said, "I think I'll call Blythe and see if I can go over and meet little Harper."

Moose was thrilled. She'd take one look at their friend's beautiful baby girl and fall head over heels in love. Selfishly, he thought it would be that much harder for her to leave again, after she spent time with all the new babies who had recently been born. "Sounds like a perfect plan. I'll call when I get off shift and am on my way home. It'll be late, after dinner. You'll be all right?"

She chuckled. "I might be messed up in the head, Moose, but I think I can manage to feed myself. I did it for the last few months while I was on the road."

He stalked toward her and watched as her eyes widened, but she didn't back away from him. Even that little bit of defiance thrilled him to no end. He liked how she stood up to him. Liked that even with his size, he didn't scare her...at least when she wasn't in the middle of a fucking nightmare. "You gonna have my dinner waiting for me when I get home, woman?"

She narrowed her eyes and put her hands on her hips. "If you think I'm gonna play the happy little housewife while I'm here, you're crazy. Since when have I ever..." Her voice trailed off as she glared up at him.

Moose knew he was grinning like a fool, but he couldn't help it. His Penelope was still in there. As ornery and prickly as ever. And he was as happy as could be that she'd shown her face once more.

"You're fucking with me, aren't you?" she asked.

"Yup. But if there are leftovers from whatever you make for dinner, I'd be happy to eat them," he told her. "Make yourself at home. Take a nap. Bake cookies and mess up my kitchen as much as you want. Read a book, surf the web all day, binge-watch television. I don't give a shit what you do, as long as you're happy doing it."

"Is it weird that I'm staying here? I should probably go back to my apartment," she said uneasily.

"No!" Moose said more forcefully than he wanted. He gentled his tone. "Sorry, no, stay. I like having you here. You know how I feel about you. I want you in my space. It'll make me feel better knowing you're here. Visit with Blythe, make arrangements for a girls' night out with the others… Just don't leave."

"Okay."

"Okay," he confirmed, then leaned down and touched his lips to hers.

It was the first time he'd kissed her since he'd said he loved her. He wanted nothing more than to deepen the kiss. Learn her taste. But now wasn't the time. She hadn't indicated she wanted anything from him other than a place to stay. For now, it was enough.

"I'll text you later. If you need anything, and I mean *anything*, just let me know."

"I will. Thanks, Moose. For everything."

"You're welcome."

"Moose?"

"Yeah, sweetheart?"

"I'm not scared of you. No matter what I say or do while I'm asleep, I'm not afraid of you. When I woke up this morning, and you weren't there, I have to admit it scared me a little. It's stupid, because I knew you were probably just down here making breakfast, but...please don't leave me again."

She ripped his heart out without even trying.

"I won't," he vowed. It might kill him to have her fight and flail against him, but last night was the last time he'd leave her alone in his bed.

CHAPTER SIX

A few hours later, Penelope knocked on the door to Squirrel and Blythe's house. She heard a muffled voice yell out for her to come in, that the door was unlocked. She slowly pushed it open—and was taken aback by the stench inside the house.

She followed the sound of a baby's cries up the stairs. She stopped in her tracks just outside baby Harper's room and stared in disbelief.

There was baby poop literally all over the wall behind the changing table and all over both the table itself and the baby lying on it. Harper was wailing uncontrollably, her little face bright red, and her fists were waving in the air.

Blythe turned to the door when Penelope arrived— and immediately burst into tears.

Penelope had no idea what was wrong, but it was obvious Blythe had reached the end of her rope.

Breathing through her mouth instead of her nose, Penelope strode forward and gently pushed her friend out of the way. "I got this. Go get changed, take a breather."

"Do...do you know anything about babies?" Blythe asked, even as she did as Penelope asked, stepping away from the changing table.

"I know enough. Now go."

As a testament to how off kilter she was, Blythe simply nodded and headed for the door.

Harper hadn't stopped screaming, but Penelope took a deep breath, grabbed a bunch of baby wipes and got to work.

Twenty minutes later, the room was cleaned up and smelled a bit better. Blythe hadn't returned, so Penelope picked up the freshly washed baby and held her against her chest, bouncing her up and down gently. Harper had stopped screaming but still wasn't exactly happy, so Penelope left the room to find her mom.

She stopped in the doorway of the master bedroom...and her heart almost broke for her friend. Blythe was sitting on the bed with her knees drawn up and her arms around her legs. Her eyes were red and she had clear tear tracks down her face.

Penelope cautiously approached the bed. "You okay?" she asked.

Blythe looked up at her and pressed her lips together and shook her head.

"What's wrong? What can I do? Should I call Squirrel?"

Taking a deep breath, Blythe wiped her face. "No. He'll be home tonight. I don't want to bother him."

When she didn't reach for her baby, who was still a bit fussy, Penelope *really* started to worry. She sat on the bed next to Blythe and reached out a hand. "Talk to me, Blythe. I know I've been gone, and I missed all the hoopla regarding this little one's birth, but you can still talk to me. I hope I'm still your friend."

With that, tears reformed in Blythe's eyes and she started crying again.

Alarmed now, Penelope felt helpless. She was great in situations where someone was bleeding to death. Or if the room was on fire. But crying babies and friends were something outside her comfort zone. Just as she was beginning to panic, Blythe took a deep breath and got herself under control.

"I'm so glad you're back," she said with only a small hitch in her voice. "I'm so scared."

"Of what?" Penelope asked.

"Of *her*," Blythe said, gesturing toward the now sleeping baby in Penelope's arms.

Shocked, Penelope looked down at Harper, then back up at Blythe. Trying to lighten the situation, she asked, "Why? Is she a vampire? Will she wake up and want to suck all the blood from my body? Maybe she's a shapeshifter? Is that what freaked you out?"

Blythe's lips quirked upward then she got serious

again. "I don't know *anything* about babies. Not too long ago, I couldn't even take care of myself, and now I'm completely responsible for keeping a baby alive and well. I was on the freaking *streets*, Penelope. I couldn't even figure out how to keep a roof over my head. I'm the worst mother in the world, and I couldn't live with myself if I did anything to hurt her. I haven't showered in two days, and that poop incident you walked in on wasn't even the first! I'm sure she's gonna get some sort of bacterial disease because I can't manage to change a diaper properly. Squirrel will never forgive me if I kill his baby giiiiiirl!"

The last was said on a wail, and Penelope finally understood what was going on. Blythe had postpartum depression, and more than a healthy dose of new-mom jitters. She wished Squirrel was there, but he wasn't. So it was up to her to calm Blythe and figure out the next steps.

"Harper's fine," she said softly. "She's fat and happy. And babies poop. Take a deep breath, Blythe."

Her friend did as she was told.

"Good. Now another."

Blythe did, and some of the panic disappeared from her face, but now she just looked sad. "I'm losing my mind, Penelope. One second I'm overjoyed at the fact I'm a mom, and the next I look at her and just know everything is gonna be taken from me. That Child Protective Services is going to bust into my house and take her away because I'm a mess."

"Have you talked to Squirrel about how you're feeling?" Penelope asked.

Blythe shook her head. "He's been so happy. So thrilled that he's a father that I haven't had the heart to tell him that I'm struggling."

"You have to talk to him," Penelope said firmly. "How do you think he's going to feel when he *does* find out what a hard time you've been having? He's gonna be devastated, and he'll probably blame himself for missing the signs. You love him, and he loves you. Your hormones are all out of whack, making you feel everything a hundred times more intensely. You're not a bad mom if you need a break from your baby. And, Blythe, you aren't alone anymore. You aren't homeless on the streets. You have so many friends who would be happy to help you when things get overwhelming. Squirrel's mom, his sisters, Sophie, Adeline, Quinn, even Tadd and Louise."

"I didn't want to bother them," Blythe said. "I'm afraid they'll think I'm being stupid. Or weak."

Penelope reached out a hand and put it on Blythe's arm. "How about we call them together? I can explain about the postpartum so you don't have to. They aren't going to hesitate to help you, Blythe."

"I'm just so tired," she whispered.

"Then lie down and take a nap."

"I can't leave you alone with her," Blythe protested.

"Why not? We'll be fine. Harper's asleep and content enough for now."

"She's going to be hungry soon," Blythe said. "She seems to always be hungry, and I'm not sure I'm producing enough milk for her." Tears filled her eyes.

"We'll figure this out," Penelope said quickly, not wanting her friend to start crying again. "Just for a little while, close your eyes and get some sleep. I'll be here the whole time and nothing's going to happen to Harper or you."

"Are you sure?"

Penelope figured she was asking more about whether she was sure it was okay for her to take a nap, and not if she was sure nothing would happen to her baby. "I'm sure," she told her confidently.

"Okay. Just for a little while though. I need to do laundry. And deep-clean Harper's changing table and make something for dinner."

"Shhhhh. Stretch out and relax, Blythe," Penelope ordered.

Within a minute or two of lying flat on the bed, Blythe was breathing deeply, and Penelope relaxed. She got up and tiptoed out of the room, closing the door behind her. She looked down at Harper and couldn't help but smile. It wasn't hard to see both parents in her face.

Closing her eyes, Penelope was suddenly very thankful she'd decided to visit Blythe today. She'd expected a light and fluffy visit, where she'd talk about some of the places she'd been over the last few months, and Blythe would recount stories of Harper's first month of life. But instead, it seemed as if she'd arrived just in time to prevent Blythe from having a full-blown mental breakdown.

Taking a deep breath, Penelope knew she had a lot of work to do while Blythe was napping. Unless she absolutely needed to, she wasn't going to wake her up.

Heading to the living room, Penelope carefully put Harper into the bassinet sitting in the middle of the floor. The space was messy and needed to be tidied. There were dishes in the sink, and it was more than obvious Blythe hadn't had the time or energy to keep things clean.

She'd get to the kitchen, but first things first. Penelope pulled out her phone and called Beth. She needed to rally the troops, but before that, she wanted to find Squirrel's mother's phone number. She'd met her once before, and she knew without a doubt that the older woman was the perfect person to put in charge of this operation.

Three hours later, Riley Young was sitting on the couch in her son's living room, her granddaughter snuggled in her arms, and watching as Penelope and two of Riley's daughters, Natalie and Charlotte, finished folding the last round of laundry they'd just taken out of the dryer.

Blythe wandered into the room, looking much better than she had when Penelope had arrived. Her eyes widened at seeing her sisters-in-law and her mother-in-law in her living room.

"Um...hi."

Penelope immediately went over to Blythe and put her arm around her. She pulled her farther into the room. "Riley, Natalie, and Charlotte are going to babysit Harper tonight. After you feed her, and pump some milk so she's got some for later, you and me are going out."

"Oh, I can't! I need to—"

"You need to get out of the house," Penelope said firmly. "I talked to Adeline and Sophie, and they're meeting us at The Sloppy Cow. Milena, Erin, and Mackenzie are meeting us there too. You need some adult interaction. We're going to have dinner and some girl time. That's it. We'll have you home by eight so you can feed Harper again, and so you're home before Squirrel gets off shift."

Blythe looked at Penelope for a long moment, then turned to her mother-in-law. "Are you okay with staying for a while?"

Riley stood up and handed baby Harper off to Charlotte. The baby cooed and wiggled her arms and legs happily as her aunt held her. Squirrel's mom walked over to Blythe and put her hands on her shoulders.

"Of course I am. I'm thrilled to get to spend *any* time with my granddaughter. But more than that, I'm happy I can give you a break. Blythe, you aren't alone. Anytime you need help, or a break, all you have to do is call me. I'm not that far away and will be happy to come over.

"I don't talk about this much, but...after I had Sawyer, I was almost hospitalized because I had such a severe case of postpartum depression. It got so bad, I was afraid of physically harming him. One night, I sat in the corner of Sawyer's room and watched him cry for two hours straight. I knew I should get up and hold him, or feed him, or make sure he had a clean diaper... but the only thing I could do was fantasize about putting a pillow over his face to get him to stop crying. That was when I knew I needed help. I finally got up the nerve to tell my doctor, and she immediately put me on medication. It changed my life. It was like night and day.

"You aren't the first new mom to feel overwhelmed, depressed, and scared. Babies are hard. Everyone thinks new moms are all canaries and rainbows after having a child, and that it's all smiles and giggles, but we both know it's not."

Riley put her hand on Blythe's cheek and caressed her with a thumb. "You aren't alone, sweet girl. You aren't homeless, hiding in the corner of an abandoned building anymore. You've got family who loves you very much. And friends who would do anything for you." Her eyes flicked over to Penelope then back to Blythe. "Feed Harper, take a shower, and go out and have some fun. Penelope and I also worked on a schedule, where your friends and I will rotate in and out of here, helping with the housework and to simply give you a break from being on your own with Harper when Sawyer's working. Nothing intrusive, but just enough during the days when Sawyer's on shift so that you don't feel so alone. Okay?"

Blythe nodded, and Penelope watched in satisfaction as Squirrel's mom engulfed Blythe in a bear hug. Several moments later, Riley gestured to her daughter to bring the baby closer, and Blythe took her from her sister-in-law. "Thanks, Charlotte."

"Anytime, Blythe. And I mean that."

Nodding, Blythe turned and headed back up the stairs with Harper to feed her.

Squirrel's mom then walked over to Penelope and looked her in the eye. The other woman wasn't a lot taller than Penelope, but like most people, still had to look down at her. "Thank you."

Penelope shrugged. "It wasn't anything anyone else wouldn't have done."

"Maybe not, but I didn't see anyone else doing it. *You* did. I knew she was struggling, but I didn't want to overstep. Didn't want her to think I was being a pushy mother-in-law," Riley sighed. "But I should've anyway. I should've recognized the signs."

"Did you *really* want to smother Sawyer?" Natalie asked her mom.

Riley turned to her youngest daughter. "Yeah, baby. I'm certainly not proud of it, but I was overwhelmed, scared, and frustrated."

Charlotte shrugged. "I've wanted to smother him at times too, so I totally understand."

Everyone laughed.

Riley turned back to Penelope and studied her with narrowed eyes.

Penelope braced for whatever she was going to say next.

"I don't know you very well, but after what you did for my family today, I'm in your debt."

Penelope shook her head and opened her mouth to say that she didn't owe her anything, but Riley continued before she had a chance.

"I know a little bit of your story. I'd have to live in a cave and be completely clueless not to, and I can see you've still got some ghosts haunting you. Seems to me that, like Blythe, you've got an amazing tribe of friends who would move heaven and earth to give you a hand...if you'd only reach out and grab it."

Penelope stared at Riley with wide eyes as the other woman continued to study her. It was interesting that she'd used the word "tribe," just as Wolf had.

Suddenly, Penelope felt guilty. She'd gotten so good at pushing people away and ignoring their offers of help that it had become second nature. She'd done exactly what Blythe had. Pushed ahead on her own, doing her best to cope and not allowing anyone to help her.

She thought back to this morning, and how Moose had suggested seeing a hypnotist. She'd agreed, but now she wasn't so sure. She just wanted all the shit in her head to go away. She'd been living with the guilt and the uncertainty for so long, it had become a part of her.

But what if talking about it with her friends could help dispel it from her brain? What if they really could help her climb her way out of the pit she'd dug for herself? She was still afraid of remembering what exactly had happened in the chaos of being captured, but one thing she knew without a doubt was that her friends wouldn't turn their backs on her. In fact, they'd probably close ranks around her even tighter. Just as they were doing for Blythe.

"I can see you're thinking about what I said, so I'll leave it at that," Riley said with satisfaction. "And just so you know, you can add my daughters and me to your list of people in your tribe. I'll never forget what you've done here for my son and daughter-in-law. You might think it's not a big deal, but it's huge. I've been where Blythe is, and it's scary as hell and there's never any guarantee that things will turn out all right in the end. But now that we're aware of what's going on, we'll make sure Blythe gets the help she needs. Thank you."

"No thanks are necessary. I love Blythe and Squirrel, and just as I have your son's back in a fire, I'll have it here at his home too."

Penelope didn't even think about her words before she said them. She didn't use the past tense when talking about having Squirrel's back at a fire scene. And it felt right. She wasn't ready to put on her uniform and leap back into the thick of things, but maybe, just maybe, she'd someday be back on the trucks and doing what she used to love again.

Blythe reappeared at the top of the stairs with Harper in her arms and her hair still damp from the shower she'd obviously taken. She looked a hundred times more relaxed than she had when Penelope had arrived, and the slight smile on her face was worth any uneasiness Penelope might've felt at going behind her back to call her mother-in-law and arranging a night out without asking first.

"You ready to go?" Penelope asked.

"Yeah. I just need to go over a few things with Riley."

Penelope listened for ten minutes as "a few things" turned into a dissertation of Harper's bowel movements and how she liked to be held and which of her blankets and toys were her favorites. But Riley didn't look even one bit annoyed or put out that Blythe was going on and on.

Finally, Penelope couldn't stand it. "Enough, Blythe. If you stand here and talk any longer, Harper's gonna be headed off to kindergarten and we'll be old ladies. Time to go."

Charlotte and Natalie laughed, and Squirrel's mom did her best to choke down the chuckle that threatened to burst forth.

"Fine. You have my number, right?" she asked Riley.

"You can call or text if you have any questions or need anything. We won't be that far away, and I can be home in ten minutes or less."

"I've got it, child. Go on. Have some fun. Relax. We've got this."

"Thank you," Blythe said softly. "There isn't a day that's gone by since I've had Harper that I haven't missed my mom and wished she could meet my daughter...but you being here goes a long way toward making that ache less."

It was Riley's turn to tear up. "Thank you," she whispered. "I can't take your mom's place, but I have no doubt she's looking down on you both and is as proud as can be."

When Penelope felt her own throat closing up, she said, "Okay, we're going. I can't stand anymore of this touchy-feely crap. Come on, Blythe. Time to get our butts in gear."

"Keep your shirt on, I'm comin'," Blythe said. She quickly hugged Riley, kissed Harper's forehead, and grabbed her purse from the kitchen counter.

"Call if you need me!" Blythe called out.

"We will!" Charlotte yelled back.

The second the door closed behind them, Blythe hesitated.

Penelope hooked her arm with hers and pulled her away from the door. "They'll be fine," she reassured her friend.

"Promise?"

"Promise," Penelope said without any doubt in her voice. "Let's go. I'm sure the others are waiting for us."

After they'd climbed into Penelope's PT Cruiser and were on their way to The Sloppy Cow, Blythe said, "Thanks, Pen. I'm sorry for being so psychotic."

"That's what friends are for," Penelope replied.

"I owe ya one."

"And I might just take you up on that someday," Penelope told her, feeling less stressed about the possibility than she might've even a few hours ago. Being there for Blythe and not wanting anything in return made her realize that was exactly how her friends probably felt about helping *her*. It was a sobering thought—and one that confirmed she'd had her head up her ass for a very long time, and it was about time to get it out and start living her life again. ISIS had done their best to break her, and for a long time, they'd succeeded. But no more.

Penelope might not be ready to go back to work, but she was more determined than ever to do whatever she could to fix the shit going on in her head so she could get back to the job she loved.

For the first time in a long time, Penelope looked forward to the next day. It wouldn't be easy, but with friends like Blythe and the other women they were heading to meet—not to mention, Moose, her brother, and the rest of the gang at Station 7—she had the hope that she just might make it out to the other side.

CHAPTER SEVEN

Forty minutes later, seven women sat at a back table in The Sloppy Cow, laughing hysterically at Mackenzie's retelling of a story about how her man, Daxton, and Weston King, a fellow Texas Ranger, had literally found themselves covered in cow shit as they desperately tried to wrangle a couple of wayward cows that had escaped their pasture and led their pursuers on a wild and crazy trip.

"So Daxton had gotten in front of the last cow they needed to catch and Wes was sneaking up behind her. Their plan was for Wes to lasso the cow from behind and lead it back the half mile to the waiting trailer. Well, he got the rope over its head, but that *literally* scared the shit out of the poor animal and it took off running! Wes refused to let go of the rope and was dragged behind it. Dax tried to help by adding his body weight to the rope to get the poor cow to stop, but *that* didn't work. So here was this cow, sprinting away in terror, pooping as she ran, and Dax and Wes doing everything in their power to stop her, all while being dragged through the extremely fresh poo the cow was spewing from its body!"

"Oh my God, stop—please stop!" Milena begged.

"I think my episiotomy stitches are gonna bust open," Blythe added between guffaws.

"Did they ever stop the cow?" Penelope asked, feeling a bit sorry for the Texas Rangers because she'd been in a situation a lot like the one Mackenzie was describing. Luckily, they'd been able to corral the loose cows quickly.

"Yeah, but not because of anything *they* did. They eventually had to let go of the rope because they were being dragged over all these rocks and stuff. Anyway, Daxton and Wes stood up, and they were covered in cow shit and their uniforms were all torn. They were trying to figure out what to do next; they couldn't just leave this poor cow wandering around. It was getting dark and if someone hit it on the back roads, it would certainly kill both the cow and anyone unlucky enough to be in the car.

"Dispatch was finally able to get ahold of the owner, and he came driving up in his *Mercedes*, got out, did some sort of weird whistle thing, and the cow simply turned around and trotted right up to him. Without even a word of thanks to Daxton or Wes, he headed for the trailer with the cow following docilely behind him as if she hadn't literally dragged two men through her shit."

The laugher at the table rang out again, and Penelope held her stomach as she laughed so hard she almost couldn't breathe.

"Holy shit, you are too much," Blythe said when she'd gotten control of herself again.

Penelope smiled. It had been forever since she'd let herself stop thinking about all the crap in her head and just let go.

"I love hanging out with you guys," Milena said. "It's such a nice break. I mean, it's never easy having a baby, but throw a toddler in the mix who isn't sure he *wants* a baby brother, and it's a whole new level of difficult."

"How's JT doing with everything?" Adeline asked.

"Honestly? Good. He's got his moments, but I can't blame him. He went from being the only child and having TJ spoil him rotten, to having this additional little baby being brought into his space, and now he has to share his mom and dad. It's not easy," Milena said.

"How are *you* doing, Erin?" Mackenzie asked. "You talked about it a bit before...your struggle with your weight and your body image and having a baby?"

Penelope leaned forward with one hand on her chin and watched her friend. They all knew being pregnant had been hard for Erin, and not only because it was her first. She'd come a long way since she'd weighed over four hundred pounds and had weight loss surgery, and they all knew she'd struggled with gaining any weight at all after working so hard to take it off.

"I'm okay," she said. "I can't say it's been easy, but refusing to weigh myself and to even look in the mirror after showering has helped. I'm never going to love my body, but Conor says that's okay; he'll love it enough for both of us."

Everyone chuckled and nodded. They got it.

Looking around, Penelope realized once more that she wasn't the only one in their group with internal issues they were dealing with. Which was stupid, because she'd been there when they'd all gone through their own kinds of hell. It was very selfish of her to think she was the only one who was going through a tough time. It seemed that being normal and perfectly adjusted wasn't exactly common in their group.

For the first time in a long time, she accepted what so many had been trying to tell her—that maybe she wasn't as alone as she'd always felt. No, none of the women around her had been kidnapped and held by ISIS, but they'd all gone through their share of shit.

"Knowing what you know now—that things would turn out for the best and you'd be either married or engaged to men who love you more than life itself—would you still choose to go through what you all went through to get to this point?" Penelope asked.

When everyone's heads swiveled to stare at her, she blushed, but forced herself to explain. "I just... Mack, if you knew you'd be buried alive and literally *die* from it, would you do it again, knowing you'd end up with Dax? Erin, would you suffer through everything you did with your weight loss journey, then being kidnapped by that psycho who wanted to hunt you like a wild animal for fun, and almost dying by those fire ant bites, if it meant being with Conor? And, Blythe, would you be homeless all over again and go through what you did to be where you are today, married with a baby and postpartum depression?"

Everyone stared at her as if she'd just sprouted another head.

"I mean, it just seems unfair that you've all had to suffer as much as you have to get your happily ever after. And even then, there's no guarantee it'll last. That all the pain will be worth it."

"I'm s-speaking for m-myself here, but I'm guessing that everyone feels the s-same way," Sophie said. "It's absolutely worth it. No, the journey hasn't been easy. It plain ol' s-sucked s-sometimes. I hate m-my s-stutter. I had a hellacious childhood as a result. I almost died twice, once because of that s-skinwalker and that damn carbon monoxide leak, and once in that fire downtown, but in the end, when I fall asleep next to Roman and feel his heartbeat against m-my own, I know in m-my heart that it was *all* worth it."

"What happened to you was terrible," Adeline said softly, her hand gripping Penelope's tightly. "But as the saying goes, 'what doesn't kill you, makes you stronger.'"

"But what if it doesn't?" Penelope asked. "What if it makes you weaker?"

Blythe laughed then. Didn't even try to hide it.

Penelope's feelings were a bit hurt, and she frowned at the other woman.

"Sorry," Blythe said, not sounding sorry at all. "But it's absolutely hilarious that you think you're weak."

Penelope pressed her lips together hard. She wasn't going to go into all the ways she *was* weak. Not in front of her friends.

"Seriously, Pen, no one is saying that what happened to you didn't suck. It did. And we don't even know the level of suckage it probably *really* was... because you won't tell anyone. But that's beside the point," Mackenzie said earnestly. "You can't compare your suckage to anyone else's because it's not a competition. Would you sit there and tell me what you went through was worse than being buried alive? Or that Erin being hunted was worse than Sophie being stuck in a burning building? Or Quinn being almost burned alive by a psychopath, or what Beth went through at the hands of that serial killer out in California?"

"You know I wouldn't," Penelope protested.

"Exactly. It's not what happens to you that shapes your life—it's how you deal with it. If I couldn't have gotten over being the target of a serial killer, then he would've won. And I really, *really* didn't want him to win."

Everyone was silent as Mackenzie's words soaked in.

Penelope blinked, then closed her eyes and hung her head. Mack was right. She was exactly right. It wasn't a competition. Not in the least.

But even knowing that, Penelope couldn't shake the guilt she felt over her friends. Had White and Black died blaming her for what happened? Had they hated her? And why did she survive when they didn't? It wasn't fair.

"I'm not saying you shouldn't feel bad about what happened to you," Mackenzie said gently. "It fucks with your head. I still have nightmares sometimes. I think I'm back in that coffin and can't get out. I know Daxton is right there. He's pounding on the lid but he can't get to me, and I know I'm going to die. They're scary as hell, but after I wake up, I tell Daxton all about my dream, he holds me, and I know that whatever happened in the past, I've beat it. I'm here, and I'm going to be okay."

"I wonder if that's what my friends thought right before they got their heads chopped off," Penelope said without thinking. "That everything would be okay, and then...*boom*...their heads were rolling around on the ground, with all the terrorists laughing."

"When I thought I was going to die, I was thinking about Daxton and how I hoped he didn't blame himself," Mackenzie said into the silence that followed Penelope's harsh statement.

"I was thinking about Coco, and how it would be hard for him to adjust to not having me around, but that Dean would take care of him," Adeline said.

"I was mad," Erin added. "I had just had this great realization that my body was exactly the way it was so I could escape the asshole hunting me, then I was taken down by fucking *ants*."

"All I could think about was JT, and I hoped he'd somehow remember how much I loved him, and how I would do anything to keep him safe. I was glad it was me and not him," Milena said.

"I knew Chief would do everything in his power to get to m-me, and I hoped, like M-Mackenzie, that he wouldn't blame himself for m-my death," Sophie said.

Penelope sighed and looked at Blythe. She was the only one who hadn't chimed in.

She shrugged. "I was more worried about Squirrel than I was about myself. I was upset that he might die because of me."

Penelope closed her eyes again and swallowed hard. She wanted to believe that White and Black hadn't blamed her in their last moments. That they might've forgiven her for anything she might've said or done. "Moose suggested I get hypnotized so I could try to remember what happened when we were taken hostage."

She felt Adeline's fingers tighten on her own, and she opened her eyes.

"I think that's a great idea," she said.

"Me too," Mackenzie said.

"Me three," Erin threw in.

The others all agreed.

"But what if I remember something I did to get them killed?" she asked.

"What if you remember that you did everything you were trained to do and were captured anyway?" Milena countered.

"Besides, you can't possibly beat yourself up anymore than you already are," Erin said.

"If you want us to be there, we will," Sophie added.

Their support meant the world to Penelope, but there was no way she wanted anyone there to witness what could be her ultimate shame. No one but Moose, anyway. She trusted him more than she trusted herself at this point. "Moose'll go with me."

The girls all nodded.

Penelope did her best to get herself together. "This was supposed to be about Blythe and supporting her as she deals with her overactive hormones." She grinned weakly.

"You know what?" Blythe said. "This is exactly what I needed."

"What, to rehash all the shit that's happened in our lives?" Penelope asked a little shakily.

Blythe smiled. "Actually, yeah. It reminds me how lucky I am to have friends like all of you, and to be married to the man of my dreams and that we had a freaking *baby* together. Squirrel told me once that he dreamed of holding our child, and now that dream has come true. I'm not saying things will be easier from here on out, I'm not an idiot, but knowing that I have all of you to lean on goes a long way toward making me feel not quite so alone. That, and knowing Sawyer's mom felt the same way after having *him*."

"She did?" Erin asked.

"Yeah. She said one day she came close to smothering him with a pillow."

"I've felt like that many nights when he snored so damn loud at the station that I couldn't get to sleep," Penelope muttered.

And with that, the tension around the table was broken. Everyone laughed again, and the next hour went by without anymore mentions of postpartum or Penelope's PTSD. By the time she was driving Blythe home, she knew the night had been exactly what they'd *both* needed.

It was way past dinner, and Penelope felt a pang of guilt that she hadn't made anything for Moose, but he was an adult, just like she'd said *she* was earlier, and he'd been fending for himself a long time now. She'd sent him a text to let him know where she was, so he wouldn't worry, but she couldn't help looking forward to going back to his house and seeing him again.

"You gonna be all right?" Blythe asked when Penelope pulled into her driveway.

"I think that's my line," Penelope said with a self-deprecating chuckle.

"Thanks to you, I'm gonna be fine," Blythe told her. "I have a feeling Grandma is going to be making an appearance more frequently, as are my sisters-in-law. Harper is going to be the most spoiled baby ever, which I'm totally okay with. Thank you, Pen. I know we haven't exactly been the closest, but I'll never forget what you did for me tonight. And even though I know you won't ask, if you ever need anything, I'll be there for you."

"I know you will," Penelope told her. And she did. Asking for help wasn't her forte, but after seeing how close Blythe had been to the edge tonight, and Penelope being pissed she hadn't reached out for help, she realized how stupid it was for *her* not to ask for help when it was needed. "And I appreciate it."

"You gonna do the hypnosis thing?"

Penelope nodded. "I think I have to. It's obvious my brain isn't going to let it go."

"You're gonna get through this. You wanna know how I know?"

"How?"

"Because you're the American Princess," Blythe said with a straight face, before breaking into a huge smile.

"Fuck you," Penelope said, and mock punched her friend in the arm.

Before she could say anything else, Blythe leaned across the car and awkwardly wrapped her arms around Penelope as best she could in the small space. "Love you, Pen. Give Smokey a pet for me and tell Moose to get his butt to the house to see Harper sometime soon. She needs to see her honorary uncles more."

"Will do," Penelope reassured her, and sat in the car watching as Blythe climbed out and walked up to her door. She stayed there until the door opened, and both Blythe and Squirrel's mom waved to her before shutting it. Only then did she back out of the driveway and head home.

Home.

To Moose.

She didn't want to talk about everything that had happened. She had a lot to think about. But she *did* want to feel Moose's arms around her, holding her tight to him. It's where she felt the safest. Where she felt nothing could get to her, not even her own thoughts and fears. He was like her own personal force field. It wasn't fair to use him as a crutch, but somehow she didn't think he'd mind.

Driving faster than she should, and hoping if she got pulled over, it would be by one of her tribe's men, Penelope realized the best part of her day would be seeing Moose and listening to him talk about his workday and the calls he'd been on. When such mundane things had become the highlight of her life, she didn't know, but she also didn't care. With every day that passed, Moose was becoming more and more important to her, and the reason she strove to overcome the demons in her head.

Without him, she had no doubt she would've already succumbed to the voices in her head telling her she was worthless, and the world would be a better place without her in it to fuck up other people's lives.

Moose sighed in relief when Penelope finally walked through the door. He knew she was hanging out with some of the other women, since she'd texted. He'd also heard from Squirrel, who'd talked to his mom, that Penelope had intervened with Blythe, who was suffering from postpartum depression to such a degree that Squirrel had been ready to take a leave of absence right then and there to make sure his wife was all right. His mother talked him down, telling him that Penelope had taken care of it, and that a schedule had been set up to rotate helpers in and out of the house until Blythe was over the worst of her depression.

But the only thing Moose could think about was seeing Penelope. Making sure she was all right after the long day she'd had. She was supposed to go over to Blythe's, meet baby Harper, and have a nice relaxing chat with her friend. But of course when Pen realized Blythe needed help, she hadn't hesitated to give her that assistance.

It was such a Penelope thing to do. And it killed Moose that she couldn't see how badly he and all the rest of her friends would do the same for her. He knew she had some nasty demons in her head, and he was as determined to help rid her of those as she'd been to help Blythe.

The second Penelope crossed the threshold of the door, Moose was there. He took her in his arms and held her to him for a long moment. Instead of holding herself stiff in his embrace, as she sometimes did, depending on her mood, Penelope melted into him.

"Hey," he murmured.

"Hey," she replied.

"You okay?"

Looking up at him, Penelope shook her head. "No."

Alarmed, Moose started to step away to further assess her, but Penelope clutched him harder, not letting him go. "I just need you to hold me," she said, resting her cheek against his chest.

Feeling his love for her well up inside him, Moose swallowed hard and tightened his hold. He couldn't remember a time that Penelope had asked for anything. Sure, she relied on him at the station to have her back, just as he relied on her, but this was different. Penelope was the most self-sufficient woman he'd ever met in his life. She could hold her own against any of her male counterparts and even surpass them sometimes.

But this, her needing him to hold her, was something she'd never asked for. And it felt good. Damn good.

They stood there for several minutes before she said, without looking up, "Were you serious about going with me to the psychologist to undergo hypnosis?"

"Yes," Moose said simply.

"How soon do you think I can get an appointment?"

"I'm not sure, but if the VA won't approve it or doesn't move fast enough, we'll go around them and find someone on our own."

"Okay," Penelope said. "Moose?"

"Yeah, sweetheart?"

"Thank you."

"You don't have to thank me for anything."

"Maybe. Maybe not. I'm aware that I haven't been that forthcoming as to what's going on with me, but I've gotten to the point where I can't sleep much, and I obviously can't do my job. I'm all about telling Blythe that she needs to ask for help, but I'm a hypocrite because I haven't either. I'm not ready to let Cade know how fucked up I am, but I also can't fight this alone anymore. It's not fair to drag you into this with me, to let you see how screwed up my head is…but I'm weak."

"Listen to me," Moose said, taking Penelope's face in his hands and tilting her head up so she had to look at him. "You aren't weak. You're the strongest person I know. Hell, even Superman had his kryptonite. I'm honored that you've asked me for help. You won't regret it."

"I already do," she whispered.

"Don't," he ordered. "I have no doubts whatsoever

that when your memories come back, they're going to set you free of this guilt you've been carrying."

"How can you be so sure?"

"Because I *know* you, Pen. I love you."

She closed her eyes then. "You shouldn't."

"Can't help it," Moose said lightly. "You wormed your way into my heart when I wasn't looking. At first I just admired you and your work ethic. Then you had to go and be funny, kick-ass, and caring. The more I worked with you, the more I fell in love with the woman you are inside. You could no more give up on or leave behind a teammate than you could ignore a cry for help. I see you, Penelope. And I love what I see."

She opened her mouth to reply, but he put a finger over her lips. "I'm not pressuring you, Pen. You have enough on your plate. Let's get through the next few weeks. Once you're feeling more like you, I'll let you say whatever you want, but the last thing I want is for you to mistake gratitude for my help for something else. Okay?"

"That's not fair to you."

Moose chuckled. "You of all people should know life isn't fair."

"True. But you have to know, Moose, I wouldn't be here if I didn't care about you."

"I know, sweetheart. And that means the world to me. You hungry?"

She shook her head. "No, we had snacks at the bar. And I had a few drinks to fill me up."

"Okay. You want to watch TV or are you tired?"

"I'm tired, but I'm not sure I can fall asleep yet. Too many things going through my head. Will you lie with me in bed and tell me about your shift?"

"Nothing would please me more. Go on upstairs and get ready. I'll be up after I let Smokey out and lock up."

"Oh...was Smokey good while I was gone?" she asked.

Surprised she'd forgotten about her beloved donkey, but happy that the first thing she'd thought about was being with him, Moose said, "Of course. He did go upstairs and grab some T-shirts out of the dirty clothes hamper to add to his nest down here, but that's it."

Penelope smiled. "I don't think he'll ever grow out of that. He loves having something that smells like me to sleep with."

"Smart animal. So do I," Moose couldn't resist saying.

Snorting and rolling her eyes, Penelope pulled away from him. "On that note, I'm headed up."

"I'll be there soon."

She nodded and padded away from him and, after stopping to pet Smokey, disappeared up the stairs.

Moose was tired from the long shift he'd had that day, but the thought of talking about the calls he'd been on with Penelope made him sigh in contentment. She was everything he'd ever wanted in a partner, both at work and out of it. She was smart and compassionate. She might be down right now, but she wasn't out. And he'd do anything to help bring her back to the confident woman she'd always been.

With that in mind, he made a mental note to make the phone call that would set in motion another step in her healing process. He had no idea how she would react, but first things first. Hypnosis and dealing with the issues *that* brought up. Moose didn't care how much it cost or whether or not the VA would cover it; now that she was on board, he'd make sure the appointment happened sooner rather than later.

He wanted his Penelope back, and proving to her that she hadn't done anything to get her teammates killed was the first step.

CHAPTER EIGHT

"Maybe we should wait a little longer to do this," Penelope said as she bit her lip. They'd pulled up outside the small, nondescript brown office building in Killeen, Texas, outside Fort Hood, with thirty minutes to spare before her appointment with one of the most recommended psychologists in Texas, who specialized in treating veterans with hypnosis.

Moose had pulled as many strings as possible, including getting in touch with one of the Delta Force operatives who had ultimately rescued Penelope, after the helicopter she'd been on with her SEAL rescuers had crashed. After Moose explained what was going on, and why he was calling him, the Delta had done some research and gotten back to him with the name of the doctor they were now there to see.

Maybe because it was Penelope, and because of the reputation she had, the VA had immediately scheduled the appointment, and probably pulled some of their own strings to get it arranged within a week and a half of the request.

Moose hoped he hadn't overstepped *too* much by agreeing to a meeting with the Delta Force team after her appointment.

He had faith in his Penelope that nothing she found out today would put her into a downward mental spiral. On the contrary, he had a feeling what she found out would put her on the path to recovery all that much faster.

"We can go back to San Antonio if you want," Moose told her, lying through his teeth, "but I don't think you really want to."

Penelope let out a long sigh and shook her head. "I don't. But I'm scared to freaking death, Moose."

"Don't be."

"How can you be so calm?" she asked.

"Because I know that whatever happened in that refugee camp isn't nearly as bad as you're thinking. I've seen you under pressure, sweetheart, and I have no doubt that you handled things as best you could."

"Yeah, just like I did when Koren's condo was burning down with her and Taco inside, right?"

Moose knew it would take her a lot more time to come to terms with *that*, so he didn't rise to the bait. "Come on, let's get this over with."

He opened his door and hoped like hell Penelope wouldn't leap over to the driver's side and decide to take off. But by the time he got around to her side of the truck, she had the door open and one leg already out. He took hold of her hand and didn't let go after she had both feet on the ground. He could feel how tense she was, and Moose wished he could do this for her. That he could shield her from this pain. But that was impossible. The best he could do was stand at her side as she tackled her problems.

The check-in process was fairly painless, and right on time they were led to a very comfortable room and told that Doctor Melton would be with them shortly. Penelope sat on the very edge of a comfortable armchair and fidgeted nervously.

Too restless to sit, Moose stood by the window in the room and kept his eye on Penelope. She had a wild look in her eyes, much like the one he'd seen right before she'd balked at going into Koren's burning condo. He hated seeing her like this. Moose wanted to sit next to her, to take her hand in his and reassure her that everything would be all right, but all he could do was look on helplessly.

The door opened and Penelope jerked in her chair.

"Sorry for startling you," said the woman who entered. "I'm Ivy. Ivy Melton." She held out her hand to Penelope.

The two women shook hands and Moose took the opportunity to study the psychologist. She was a little taller than Penelope but not by much. She looked to be around the same age too, which surprised him, as he'd thought for some reason that she'd be much older than her early thirties, especially considering her reputation.

She'd been working with soldiers and veterans for almost four years, and in that time had gained quite the reputation for being down to earth and caring. But one of the main reasons why she'd come so highly recommended was because of her use of hypnosis to get to the root of a person's PTSD.

Moose had a feeling that was exactly what Penelope needed. She was beating herself up about something she couldn't even remember. He didn't care if the "old" Penelope never made a reappearance, but she couldn't go on like she had been. Every now and then, he'd see a spark of the woman she'd once been, and while he knew she likely couldn't ever go back completely, he wanted to see her confidence return more than he'd ever wanted anything in his life.

"I'm really nervous about this," Penelope blurted.

The doctor chuckled. "I'd be worried about you if you weren't," she said without a trace of guile. "But before we get started, I'd just like to get to know you a bit, if that's okay?"

Penelope glanced over at Moose, then back at the doctor.

Seeing where her gaze went, the doctor asked, "Would you prefer some privacy for your session?"

"No!" Penelope practically shouted in panic.

Moose stood up straight and his hands fisted in an effort to stay where he was. To not rush to Pen's side.

She had to do this on her own. Well, not entirely on her own. He wanted to be there to listen, to support her. But if she really wanted him to leave, he would. Even though it would kill.

"Okay, he can stay. And you are?" Ivy asked, as she turned to Moose and held out her hand.

Moose shook her hand and said, "I'm Tucker Jacobs. Pen's my girlfriend."

The words had just come out. And for a second, he was worried Penelope would protest. Would tell the doctor that he was just kidding and was just a friend, but when he met her gaze, she simply gave him a smile.

"Right. Okay, Tucker, you can stay, but I need you to sit in that chair over there and simply listen, all right? There might be a time when I have questions for you, but for now, I want to talk to Penelope."

Moose's respect for the doctor went up a few notches. He nodded. "I understand."

"Good." Ivy turned back to Penelope then sat in a large, overstuffed armchair across from her patient. "Why don't you start by giving me a quick rundown as to why you're here to see me today, and what you hope to get out of the session."

Moose listened as Penelope haltingly told her story. He watched the doctor and was pleased to see that all her attention was focused on Penelope. She didn't frown, didn't give Pen any platitudes or false sympathy. She simply listened.

After fifteen minutes, Penelope wound down.

"So the whole world knows me as the American Princess, but they don't know the real story. How every time I hear that moniker I die a little inside. I'm no hero. I'm scared to death that one of these days someone is going to come forward and call me out. Tell the world that the American Princess is a coward. A fraud."

"What does your heart tell you happened that day?" Dr. Melton asked.

"I…I don't know."

"Close your eyes."

"Are we…are we starting?" Penelope asked.

Ivy grinned. "No, I just want you to stop thinking so hard, and closing your eyes is a good way to block out everything but your thoughts."

"I'm not sure I want to be alone with my thoughts," Penelope muttered before doing as the doctor asked and closing her eyes.

Ivy chuckled, but went on. "Without thinking about your answer, tell me what kind of soldier you were."

"Tough, but fair," Penelope said without hesitation.

Moose hadn't ever been prouder of her than he was right this minute. And he didn't know Penelope in the role of soldier, but he could picture her just as she'd said. She was probably tough as nails, but when push came to shove, not a hardass.

"Think back to the morning your patrol started. What are you feeling?"

"Pissed."

"Why?"

"The major was new to the unit, and he wanted to prove himself or something. He ordered us to patrol a section of the refugee camp that we knew had been very volatile. I questioned his order, and he called me out in front of the entire unit. Said that if I was too scared to follow orders, he'd put me on KP since that was more suited to someone like me."

Moose ground his teeth together. What a misogynic asshole.

"And what did he mean by that?" the doctor asked.

"That because I was a woman, I should be in the kitchen," Penelope said.

"And how did that make you feel?"

"Like I said, pissed," Penelope said.

"And what about your friends, what did they think?"

"White and Black were upset on my behalf. They thought the same as I did about the major's plan."

"Did they speak up? Defend you? Say anything?"

Penelope shook her head.

"Why not?"

"Because. That's not how things work in the military. You follow orders. And if you don't, things don't go well."

"Were you pissed at your friends for not standing up for you?"

"No. I understood. And I wouldn't've been happy if they'd gotten in trouble because of me."

"Open your eyes," Ivy said.

Penelope did, and Moose could see the confusion clouding them from across the room. "Was that it?"

The doctor smiled gently. "No. But I think we're ready to see if I can put you under."

Penelope took a deep breath and nodded.

"Do you want to sit, or lie down on the couch over there? Which would you be more comfortable in?" Ivy asked, gesturing to the chair, then a couch against the wall.

"I'm good here," Penelope said. Then she bit her lip and glanced over at Moose again.

Proving she was as good at reading people as her reputation indicated, Dr. Melton asked, "Would you like Tucker to come closer?"

"Is it allowed?"

The doctor chuckled. "There are no hard and fast rules about this, Penelope. Basically whatever puts you at ease and makes you the most comfortable is what works best."

"Moose makes me comfortable," Penelope blurted.

"Moose?" Ivy asked.

"That's me," Moose said. "It's a nickname. I'm as big as a moose, you see."

The good doctor's gaze went from his head all the way to his toes before moving back up his body. He didn't get the feeling she was examining him like a piece of meat though; she was just observant. "I see.

Well then, Moose, please come over here next to Penelope's chair."

Moose did as requested and automatically reached out for Penelope's hand as he got close. She clung to him as if he was the only thing keeping her from leaping out of the chair and getting the hell out of the room.

Ivy didn't miss anything when it came to her client, and she nodded. Her gaze was intense and serious when she met his. "Here's how this is going to work. I think it'll be good for Penelope to keep hold of your hand while she's under. But you are not to speak under any circumstances. Understand?"

Moose nodded.

"I'm serious. You could do irreparable harm if you bring her out of her hypnosis before she's ready. And simply hearing your voice could do that."

"I won't say a word. I swear."

"Now, Penelope, here's what's going to happen, you're going to close your eyes when I tell you to and concentrate on nothing but the sound of my voice. I want you to relax as much as possible. Sometimes this works and sometimes it doesn't. I don't want you to worry about anything other than breathing deeply and my words. You'll be safe at all times, nothing can hurt you while you're here and while Moose is holding your hand, all right?"

Penelope nodded, and Moose was surprised to see that she already seemed calmer. He got down on his knees next to the chair and rested his and Penelope's clenched hands on the arm of the chair.

"Good. Go ahead and rest your head on the back of the chair, just like that. Now close your eyes and take a deep breath. Perfect. And another. Now I want you to count backward from twenty to one, breathing in through your nose and out through your mouth."

Moose only half listened as Dr. Melton wove her magic around Penelope. She relaxed more and more until he thought she might have fallen asleep. But he knew she wasn't when Ivy instructed her to squeeze his hand and she did without hesitation.

"Okay, Penelope, you're doing amazing. The important thing to remember is that you're safe. I want you to think back to your time in Turkey. You were deployed to the refugee camp to keep the peace and to make sure violence didn't break out amongst the people who had gone there for shelter, food, and water, right?"

Penelope nodded slowly.

"Picture yourself sitting right where you are now, in a nice comfy chair, watching a huge big-screen television in front of you. You can see yourself on the screen. As well as your friends, White, Black, and Wilson. In your hand is a remote control, look at it now."

Moose saw Penelope's head dip down, but she didn't open her eyes.

"See the big red button on the remote?" The doctor waited until Penelope nodded. "Good, that's the pause button. Whenever things on the screen get too intense, you can push the red button to take a break. Everything will stop and you can remember that you're safe and that you're only watching a movie. Everything that's happening on the screen happened in the past and can't hurt you today. It's okay to be scared, but always remember that what you're seeing is part of the movie. It's not happening in real time. Also, can you feel Moose's hand in your own?"

Penelope's fingers twitched around his, and Moose was fascinated. Even though he'd pushed for Pen to come today, to get hypnotized to see if she could remember the details from the day she'd been captured, he hadn't really been sure it would work. But he was definitely a believer now.

"Good. When you get scared, just remember that Moose is here. He's holding your hand and won't let anything bad happen to you. It's just a movie, okay?"

"Okay," Penelope whispered.

"All right, go ahead and push the green button on the remote in your hand to start up the video of your time in Turkey in the camp."

The index finger on Penelope's free hand pushed down on the arm of the chair.

"What do you see?"

"I'm sitting on the floor of a tent with White and Black, and we're playing cards."

"Are you having a good time?" Ivy asks.

Penelope nods her head.

"Good. Now go ahead and turn up the volume. I'm not there, so I can't see the movie. Talk me through it as if we're on the phone together. Tell me what everyone is saying and what's going on. Step by step, Penelope. Don't leave anything out."

Moose was fascinated by the way Penelope immediately began recounting the scene playing out before her very eyes.

"Go fish."

"Damn, Sarg, I swear you're cheating somehow, but hell if I can figure out how."

"Face it, White, I'm just a better Go Fish player than you are."

"I'm never gonna live this down back home. Beaten by a girl, what's the world coming to?"

"Hey! I can kick your ass any day of the week, and you know it."

White smiled at her. "That's true."

"How'd you get so good at hand-to-hand, Sarg?" Black asked, his face bright red from the heat of the desert. His freckles were even more apparent when he was flushed, like he was now.

"My brother."

"That's right, Cameron? Cain? What's his name again?"

Penelope kicked her foot out and nailed White in the thigh. "Cade."

White laughed, his teeth bright against his black-as-midnight face.

"Right, Cade. He's the reason you became a firefighter, right?"

"Yup. He's awesome. A pain in the butt, as most brothers are, but I don't know what I'd do without him."

"You're lucky," Black said. "I'm an only child, and I could'a used a big brother to beat up the bullies when I was growing up."

"You got picked on a lot?" Penelope asked him.

"Look at me," Black said, gesturing to himself. "Bright red hair, freckles everywhere and skin so pale, if I was outside for more than twenty minutes at a time, I turned beet red. Yeah, I got picked on."

"Assholes," White muttered. "If anyone dares to look at you cross-eyed, Black, you just let me or Sarg know and we'll kick their asses for you." He turned to Penelope. "Fight like a girl, right, Sarg? You kicked that first-sergeant's ass and showed him exactly *how girls fight."*

"That's right. And then you started following me around like a puppy, begging me to show you all my moves so you *could fight like a girl too."*

All three laughed.

"Good times, Sarg. Good times," White mused.

When Penelope paused in her reminiscence, Dr. Melton said, "So you, White, and Black were close, right?"

"Yeah. They reminded me a lot of the guys at the station. I had their backs and they had mine. I never worried about what would happen when I was patrolling with them."

"Good. Okay, Penelope, I want you to hit the fast-forward button on your remote until you get to the time right before you headed out on patrol that last day. Then stop it and once again tell us what you're seeing. And remember, you're watching things happen, but you aren't there. You can't be hurt."

Moose hated the way Penelope whimpered slightly in her throat, but her finger pressed down on the arm of the chair as if she really was using a remote control.

"Good. Now walk me through what you're seeing."

"This isn't a good idea," White muttered

"I know, but there's nothing we can do about it. We just have to keep our heads down and do our job," Penelope told him.

"Maybe we can go and talk to the major, now that he's not in front of the formation," Black suggested.

"It won't do any good. I hurt his ego, there's no way he'll let us patrol anywhere else now. Sorry, guys, I should've kept my mouth shut."

"Fuck that," White said. "The day you keep your mouth shut is the day I quit the Army and go back to Mississippi and start up a bakery."

139

Penelope laughed. "What do you mean? I'm the spitting image of the stereotypical fifties housewife," she teased.

Black rolled his eyes, then looked around to see if anyone was listening. He leaned into Penelope and White. "If anything happens out there...are we allowed to fire our weapons?"

"Of course we are," Penelope reassured him.

"It's just that...I'm not sure we can overpower a huge mob if it comes to that."

Penelope put her hand on Black's shoulder and looked him in the eye. "All you have to do is fight like a girl, Black. We'll be back here tonight, and I'll even let you win at Go Fish if you want."

As she hoped, the younger man grinned back at her. "Deal."

"Hey, guys, we ready to head out?"

Penelope looked over at Wilson and nodded. She didn't know the other soldier all that well, but he'd always been respectful of her, hadn't ever pulled any bullshit when it came to her gender.

"Let's get this over with, yeah?" she asked her small crew. They all strapped the heavy Kevlar helmets onto their heads. They were bulky, and it had taken her a long time to get used to wearing it when she'd first started patrolling the camp. But even if she sweated like a pig when she wore it, there was no way she was leaving it behind.

The four soldiers slung their rifles across their backs, checked the map of the camp one more time, then set out.

. . .

"Moose?" Penelope cried out suddenly, squeezing his hand so tightly her fingernails drew blood. He opened his mouth to reassure her that he was there, but the doctor's hand slicing through the air stopped him at the last second. She frowned and put her index finger to her lips.

Moose nodded and pressed his lips together. He hated not being able to comfort Penelope, especially when she sounded so scared, but he'd promised to stay quiet, and the last thing he wanted was to do something that would set her back.

"He's right here next to you, Penelope," Dr. Melton said in an easy, calm voice. "You're holding his hand. That's right...he's right there."

"I'm scared!" Penelope said. "I don't want to watch anymore!"

"What are you scared of?" Ivy asked.

"I...know what's coming, and I don't want to see it. I'm not safe!"

"You *are* safe," the doctor reassured her. "Remember, you're watching a movie. You're not there, you're here, and Moose is right here with you, holding your hand."

"Why can't I see him?" she asked, squeezing his hand harder.

"Because he's not at the movies with you. He needs you to tell him what's happening."

"I don't want to," Penelope said, her head shaking back and forth on the cushion it was resting against.

"Why?"

"Because. I want him to keep loving me."

"And if you tell him what you're seeing, he won't love you anymore?"

"No. Maybe…I just…he's the best thing to ever happen to me, and I don't want to let him down."

"How will you let him down?"

"If he knows that I'm scared. That I'm *always* scared. He said he loved me but he might stop if he knows."

Moose closed his eyes and pressed his lips together even tighter. He wanted to tell Penelope that she couldn't let him down. That he'd always have her back, that she didn't need to be scared, but all he could do was sit there and hold her hand and listen.

"What if he finds out what happens in your movie and loves you anyway?"

There was silence for a moment as Penelope pondered the doctor's question. Then she asked in a tone that was so unlike his Penelope, Moose would've had a hard time knowing it was her if he wasn't sitting right next to her.

"You think he could?"

"Yes, Penelope. I do. Now, it's time to hit play again. Moose is holding your hand, you're safe and just watching the movie. Nothing can hurt you. Go ahead and start it back up and tell me what you're seeing, what's going on."

Penelope whimpered again but her fingers pressed

on the imaginary play button, and she started relaying what she was seeing in her head.

"Stay alert, guys, I don't like this at all."

"You and me both, Sarg," Black said nervously.

"Wilson, you and White take point, me and Black will have your backs."

"You got it, Sarg," White said confidently.

They walked amongst the western end of the camp, which was eerily devoid of people. Normally, there should have been refugees everywhere. Sitting around outside their tents trying to get some fresh, if not much cooler air. Cooking over small fires. Chatting in groups. But today, a sense of menace rested over the camp. A sense of anticipation, of...something.

The four soldiers suddenly heard a ruckus ahead of them.

"Easy, everyone," Penelope said softly.

They cautiously approached the area where they'd heard the yells and scuffle. The second they stepped out from behind a row of tents, Penelope knew they were in trouble.

A group of around fifty men were harassing several older gentlemen. They were slapping them, pushing them to the ground. Penelope couldn't understand what they were saying, but she didn't need to. The air of hostility was almost smothering.

As soldiers, they were there to prevent this sort of thing from escalating out of control, but Penelope knew with only four of them, they were outnumbered. There was nothing they could do right this minute. They needed to report back to headquarters and get some reinforcements.

"Back up slowly," she said softly to the men around her.

But it was too late. They'd been spotted.

Within seconds, the young men had given up their game of harassing the old refugees, and had turned on them.

"Hold your ground," Penelope said.

As soon as the words left her mouth, Wilson turned and bolted away, back the way they'd come. Penelope gaped, shocked to her core that he'd abandoned them.

His retreat seemed to snap the group of men out of whatever indecision held them frozen, and immediately ten or more men gave chase.

"Back to back," Penelope ordered, pointing her rifle at the riled crowd. She felt White and Black move against her, their own weapons at the ready. They were in a small triangle now, facing off against overwhelming odds.

"You need to disperse," Penelope said loudly, hoping against hope that someone in the crowd understood English.

Someone seemed to, as he called out to the rest of the group, but instead of breaking up, the men laughed and inched closer.

"I'm serious. As inhabitants of this refugee camp, you are required to follow the United Nations' rules. You are to disperse immediately."

One of the men yelled something back at her, and everyone around them cheered.

Penelope flipped off the safety on her rifle, sweat dripping *down her back. Her head felt as if it weighed a hundred pounds, and she swayed just slightly on her feet.*

"Easy, Sarg," White murmured.

His words were enough to bolster her.

"Step back!" Penelope ordered.

Instead of doing as she asked, the men pressed in even closer.

Things were beyond dicey now. They were not in a good position, and she knew both White and Black were also aware of it. They were in a standoff with a mob of pissed-off men. It would take next to nothing to set them off. They should start shooting...but Penelope also knew that would create an international incident. Even though the three of them could probably take down most of the men, mass casualties would change the nature of the Army's presence in Turkey and any goodwill they'd managed to forge would be lost in a heartbeat.

No one said anything for several minutes, they just stared at each other, waiting for someone to make a move.

A commotion off to their right made most of the mob turn to look. Penelope didn't move her body at all, but her eyes shifted to the right—and she gasped at what she saw.

"No!"

"Easy, Penelope. Hit the pause button," the doctor said calmly.

Penelope was panting as hard as if she'd just run the obstacle course at the Fire Training Academy. Moose looked down and saw a trail of blood slide down the back of his hand from her fingernails digging into his skin. He didn't even feel the pain. All he could feel was Penelope's anguish—and at that moment, he would endure anything, *do* anything, to make it stop.

"You're doing great, Penelope," Ivy said. "Remember, this is only a movie of what happened. You aren't there anymore."

She whimpered.

"So Wilson ran, correct? Left you and your soldiers there to face the mob of angry men?" the doctor asked.

Penelope nodded. "I can't believe he just left!"

"Do you think he was a coward?"

Remarkably, Penelope shook her head. "No, he was just scared. I was too. We all were."

"Go on, play the rest."

"I don't want to!"

"I know, but you need to. You need to remember it all so you can move on. True bravery is being scared out of your mind, but doing what needs to be done anyway."

The doctor's words seemed to encourage Penelope. She took a deep breath and nodded. "Moose won't leave me?"

"No, he won't leave you. He's holding your hand tightly."

"Okay."

. . .

146

Looking to her right, Penelope gasped. Wilson was being dragged by his feet closer and closer to where she stood with White and Black.

"Fuck," White muttered.

"Stop!" Penelope ordered.

A few men had the audacity to laugh at her words. Instead of letting Wilson go, the men closest to him began kicking him, yelling something as they did so. Whatever they yelled got the rest of the men riled up, and everyone began to chant and cheer.

"Leave me alone!" Wilson screamed. "Take her! She's a woman, you can have your fun with her! Just let me go!"

Penelope gawked at Wilson in horror, his betrayal cutting deep. Had he really just said that? She'd trusted him to have her back, to do whatever it took to make sure they all got home safely. To hear him beg the mob to let him go and take her instead was shocking.

"Whatever happens, do not give up," White said, loud enough to be heard over the screaming of the mob. "The major will find out what happened and send in troops to rescue us."

Penelope couldn't say anything. Her mouth was suddenly drier than the desert sand all around them.

"Put down your weapons," a man ordered. He walked out of the group of men as if he were a messiah.

"How about you give us back our friend and let us be on our way?" Black countered.

The man grinned, then he said something Penelope didn't understand and made some sort of gesture.

Suddenly, at least a dozen men pulled out weapons and pointed them at their heads.

Penelope didn't know where all the guns had come from, as weapons were forbidden in the camp and searches were conducted regularly, but at this point, it didn't matter. All that mattered was that one of the men walked over to where Wilson was lying unconscious in the dirt. His helmet was gone, as was his rifle and his Kevlar vest. He was wearing only a brown T-shirt, pants, and his boots.

The man who'd spoken in English repeated his order. "Put down your weapons."

"Pen?" White asked, the uncertainty and anger easy to hear in his voice.

Penelope didn't want to. She wanted to fight. The situation had gone from trying to break up a mob to them being in mortal danger. The soldier inside her didn't want to give up. But the dozen or so weapons pointed at her head definitely changed the situation.

"I'm doing it," Black said, even as he and White were already removing the slings over their heads and slowly kneeling to put their rifles down on the hot sand in front of them.

"Sarg, do it," White hissed.

Feeling as if she was moving through quicksand, Penelope slowly followed suit.

Grinning wider, the man gestured to a few of his friends nearby, and they ran forward and snatched up the three rifles and disappeared into the crowd. Then he walked closer, ignoring the five men who grabbed hold of

148

Wilson and dragged him around a set of tents and out of view.

"You shouldn't have come here," he said, before smiling a smile so evil, Penelope knew she'd see it again in her nightmares.

Then he nodded his head and yelled something to the crowd.

The next thing Penelope knew, she was fighting for her life.

Fists came at her from all directions, and she did her best to keep White and Black at her back, but it was no use. She was pulled away from her friends, and what seemed like thousands of hands began to pummel her. Her helmet was ripped off her head, taking strands of her blonde hair with it, as the fists continued to beat her.

She fought back as hard as she could, feeling satisfaction anytime someone yelped in pain when she got in a lucky blow.

But it wasn't enough. There were too many of them.

Frantically looking around for White and Black, she saw them fighting for their own lives, and not having any better luck than she was. She saw a man pick up a rock and lift it over his head, and she screamed out in warning. "White!"

"Fight like a girl!" he yelled back. "Fight like a fuckin' girl, Sarg!"

It was the last thing she heard him say before the rock came down on his head and the larger-than-life man fell like a stone to the desert floor.

She saw Black seconds before he was dragged away. He

was still kicking and flailing, but he had blood flowing down the side of his face fast enough to stain his T-shirt bright red.

He glanced at her with terror in his eyes, but neither had time to say anything before the leader of the mob, the one who'd spoken to them in English and apparently given the order to attack, came toward her.

She was on the ground, being held fast by a dozen men who spat on her even as she continued to struggle. Her ribs hurt; she figured some were definitely broken or cracked. She felt a trickle of blood drip from her temple down the side of her head, and one of her ankles was definitely sprained. Penelope glared up at the man with hatred in her heart.

Fight like a girl.

She could do that. She'd hang on for White. And Black. And even Wilson. The Army would come for them.

They had to, the alternative was unthinkable.

"We have no use for your friends. But you, we can use. Pretty blonde American. Your government will listen to us when they see you pleading with them to cooperate.

"Fuck you," Penelope slurred, her lips so swollen she could barely talk. "I'll never do what you want. My government doesn't negotiate with terrorists."

"You'd better hope they do—because if not, you'll end up with your head on a pike, just like your friends."

And with that, Penelope lost it. She snarled deep in her throat and thrashed, doing everything she could to break free of the many hands holding her down. She'd kill the asshole threatening her and her friends with her bare hands.

But she didn't get a chance. The harder she struggled, the

more men came to beat on her. They kicked and punched her so hard, she eventually lost consciousness. The last thing she remembered seeing was White's helmet lying forlornly on the ground. His last name was upside down, and it was hard to see through the blowing sand and blood in her eyes, but Penelope vowed right then and there to fight like a girl. For White.

As long as she was alive, there was hope she'd be rescued.

A young boy, probably no more than fourteen years old, walked over to where Penelope was lying on the sand, broken and bleeding, and grinned down at her. "American whore," he spat, before pulling back his leg and kicking her in the head.

The world went completely black.

"Okay, Penelope, that's enough. Push the stop button."

Moose held his breath and stared at the love of his life in absolute agony. On the plus side, she hadn't done one thing to be ashamed of. Not one. Just as he'd known she hadn't. All her fears and worries that had been eating her alive for so long had been for nothing.

But he now understood more about what was eating at her. She'd been part of a team, and that team had let her down. Wilson had bolted, and then the bastard had tried to make the mob turn on *her* instead of him. Her backup was taken away, forcing her to fight a battle she couldn't hope to win on her own.

He got it now. Understood why, when things had

gotten so intense at Koren's condo, she hadn't been able to walk into the burning building.

Walking into smoke and fire went against everything a person had learned about danger their entire life. Firefighters relied on their equipment and the men at their backs every second they went into the flames. Subconsciously, she was probably remembering how Wilson had shattered her trust when he'd run...when he'd begged the men to take her instead. When she'd been left alone without backup when she'd needed them the most.

Moose didn't have time to contemplate how best to help his woman when he realized the doctor was having a hard time reconnecting with Penelope.

While she'd been reciting everything she'd seen in her mind, her eyes had been shut, but now they were open, and she was staring straight ahead with no emotion on her face.

"The movie's over now, Penelope. You're safe."

Nothing. Not a twitch of an eyebrow. Not a flinch. Even her hand was lax in his. Moose didn't like this at all, but he'd promised not to talk.

Dr. Melton looked over at him for a second, and he could see the concern in her eyes.

Fuck. He had to *do* something.

As the psychologist did her best to reassure Penelope that she was safe and sound in Texas and not in Turkey, not in the hands of the terrorists, Moose slowly turned his hand over, ignoring the way the small wounds in his skin burned at the contact with the fabric of the chair. He leaned close and brushed his mouth over the back of Penelope's hand, letting her feel the bite of his five o'clock shadow on her skin. Then he nuzzled her fingers, doing what he could think to let her know he was still there, waiting for her to come back to him.

"Feel that, Penelope?" the doctor said, obviously approving of what he was doing. "That's Moose. He needs you to come back to him now. The movie's over and you need to go home."

He felt her stir, and as he watched, she closed her eyes and inhaled deeply, then slowly let out the breath.

"Good," Dr. Melton praised. "Take another breath."

She did.

"I'm going to count backward from twenty, with every number, you'll feel more and more calm and safe. By the time I get to the number one, you'll feel refreshed, as if you just took a two-hour nap. Twenty, nineteen, eighteen, seventeen..."

Moose kept his eyes on Penelope as the doctor slowly counted backward. When she hit number one, Penelope's eyes popped open again and locked on him.

Without thinking, Moose leaned forward, wrapped his free hand around the back of her neck, and pulled her into him. His lips found hers, and he showed her without words how brave he thought she was. How amazing. How fucking much he loved her.

He pulled back way before he was ready, but was

bolstered by the fact she'd kissed him back, seeming almost as desperate as he'd been.

"Hey," she whispered.

"Hey," Moose returned and dropped his hand from her neck, caressing her skin before he did so. Neither had let go of the other's hand, and even as she scooted to the edge of the armchair, Penelope kept hold of him.

"How do you feel?" Ivy asked.

"Okay. Not tired at all, which is weird."

"Do you remember what we talked about?"

For a second he thought she might lie, but after a moment of hesitation, she nodded.

"So you know that you did absolutely nothing wrong? That nothing you did or said made any difference to that mob of men, right?"

Penelope nodded somberly.

"I had forgotten that Wilson fled," she said softly.

"And does that make you think less of him?" the doctor pushed.

"No," Penelope said sadly. "Honestly, I wanted to run too. But there was nowhere to go. There were too many men. We were outnumbered, and I didn't want to do anything rash that would provoke them."

"Like Wilson did."

Penelope shrugged. "It was a combination of bad decisions and bad luck."

"Do you truly believe that, or are you just saying that because you think it's what I want to hear?" Dr. Melton pressed.

Penelope thought about the question for a moment before saying, "I believe it. I have to admit, I'm relieved that I wasn't the reason why White and Black were killed."

Dr. Melton nodded. "Good. You've done amazing here today, Penelope. That wasn't easy, and you did extremely well for your first time being put under. Most veterans I help don't do so well."

She shrugged. "I probably wouldn't have if Moose wasn't here." She looked up at him and gave him a small smile. Then her gaze dropped—and she gasped. "Holy shit! Did I do that to you?"

Moose followed her gaze and saw the back of his hand, where her fingernails had bit into his skin and drawn blood.

"It's nothing."

"It's not *nothing*. I hurt you!" she exclaimed. She started to stand, but Moose stopped her by placing his free hand on her forearm. "I'm okay, Pen. Seriously. I'd take a hundred times worse if it helped you fight your demons."

"Fight like a girl, right?" she said quietly.

"Exactly."

"I'd like to see you again," Dr. Melton said quietly, interrupting the moment. "After you've had some time to come to terms with your memory returning and what happened."

"For more hypnosis?" Penelope asked, standing.

When she wobbled a bit on her feet, Moose wrapped his arm around her waist and pulled her against him.

"No, I think you're good there. Simply to talk through everything that happened and help you put it all in perspective."

"I think I might like that," Penelope said.

The doctor walked closer to them and shook Penelope's hand, then Moose's. "Thank you for trusting me with your memories," she said. "And I'm very glad you have such a good support system to help you work through this."

"She's got more than just me," Moose said. "She's got her brother, and the rest of the guys at the fire station, not to mention, all their women and our other friends in law enforcement. She's also friendly with a special forces team here at Fort Hood, and another out in Riverton, California. She's got support coming out her ears."

The doctor grinned. "That's good. A lot of veterans don't have that. You're very lucky, Penelope. I know it doesn't seem like it all the time, especially when your memories take hold, but you are. Try to remember that."

"I will. Thanks."

"You can make an appointment today if you want, otherwise just call whenever you're ready and I'll fit you in."

"Thanks again."

"You're very welcome. It was an honor to assist you.

It's not every day you get to be up close and personal with a princess."

Moose tensed for a second, but relaxed when Penelope laughed. "Oh, jeez, not you too," she said with a roll of her eyes.

"I couldn't resist. And don't worry, client/patient privilege is firmly in place, my lips are sealed."

Penelope nodded, and Moose walked her out of the room and into the warm afternoon air toward his truck.

"You hungry?"

"Yes. I think I could eat a horse right about now."

"Well, I don't think I can find one of those...but if you're up to it, the guys from that Delta Force team are having a get-together at one of their houses...and I kinda said you'd be happy to go hang out for a while."

Penelope stared at him so long, Moose got uncomfortable.

Finally, she said, "What if I was in no condition to go and be social?"

"Then we wouldn't go."

"Just like that? What about the trouble the Deltas went to in order to set it up?"

"Pen, they're hanging out and grilling and drinking beers. I'm guessing it wasn't all that hard to arrange. If they're anything like our friends at the station, they probably jump at any excuse to hang out together away from work."

"True. But I would've appreciated a head's up."

"Noted," Moose said. "I'll try not to do something like this again. But I have to warn you, I *do* have something else I'm working on that you might not be too happy with."

She stared at him for another long minute before asking, "Why am I not more concerned about what you might be up to?"

"Because you trust me." It wasn't a question.

But Penelope nodded anyway. "I do."

"We don't have to stay long. After hearing why you were up here, and what was going on, the guys were concerned about you. You made quite the impression on them when they rescued you, and even though your connection is supposed to be hush-hush, enough time has gone by since you came home that I think it's fine. Besides, it was their idea, not mine."

"Fine. But don't complain if I fall asleep on the way home."

"Never." Moose picked up her hand and kissed the back of it before turning the keys in the ignition.

"One more thing."

"Anything."

"You let me help you clean up your hand when we get there. I don't like knowing that I hurt you."

"You didn't hurt me, sweetheart. But if it'll make you feel better, I'll let you play doctor."

"If you think me running hydrogen peroxide over your cuts is playing doctor, you've obviously been playing the game wrong."

Moose gasped, and his head turned so fast to stare at her, he almost got whiplash.

Laughing hysterically, Penelope said, "You should see your face!" Then she laughed even harder.

Moose simply shook his head and backed out of the parking space, but inside, he was grinning like a fool. His Penelope was coming back into her own. The session had already done wonders toward making her relax, and the shroud of guilt she'd carried on her shoulders for months seemed to finally be lifting a bit. He could never repay Dr. Melton for that. There wasn't enough money in the world.

Moose knew he, himself, would also have to process what his woman had gone through. Later. He couldn't think right now about how scared she'd been and what those assholes had done to her.

He did his best to change the focus of his thoughts from Turkey, and Penelope being a POW, to how she might be willing to play doctor with him in the hopefully not-so-distant future.

"Now what are you thinking about?" Penelope asked suspiciously.

"Just about where you might want to stick a thermometer," he said with a grin.

That sent Pen into more gales of laughter.

Moose smiled all the way to their destination.

CHAPTER NINE

Penelope sat on the built-in bench on the deck of Cormac "Fletch" Fletcher's house and grinned in delight at the sight of his daughter ordering around seven big Delta Force men and one huge firefighter. She'd set up an elaborate "battleground" in her backyard, and she was apparently the general of her troops. She was ordering them about from her position in some sort of homemade tank, which she was driving around like a maniac.

It was hilarious and heartwarming at the same time.

"How old is she now?" she asked Emily, Fletch's wife.

"Eleven going on eighteen," Emily answered.

"She's beautiful."

"Don't tell *her* that," Emily said with a chuckle. "She's currently in a phase where she thinks women should be admired for their brains and not their looks."

"She's not wrong," Penelope said with a shrug.

"It's good to see you again," Rayne told her.

"And good to see that your handsome firefighter is still very watchful of you," Harley added.

"I can't help but notice you still seem to be fighting whatever's between the two of you," Mary said.

Surprised, Penelope looked up at the woman. She'd seen her at the ceremony when Emily had married Fletch, and she looked a lot healthier this time. Moose had told her earlier that Mary had beaten breast cancer —twice—and that she and Truck had finally made things official and had gotten married. She was happy for the other woman.

She shrugged. "Things are complicated."

Strangely, at her response, all of the Army wives around her burst out laughing.

When Kassie got her breath back, she croaked, "You sound exactly like *we* did before we finally gave in and admitted we were head over heels crazy in love with our men."

Penelope wasn't sure how to answer that. She didn't really know some of the women much at all. Of course she knew Rayne, Emily, Harley, and Mary, because they were at Emily and Fletch's wedding, but the others had gotten together with their men after that, and Penelope had only met them face-to-face today.

"What is it about men like ours that makes everything so complicated when in reality, it's just a matter of them loving us and that's that?" Casey asked.

"So, you have PTSD and you were here getting hypnotized?" Mary asked bluntly.

Rayne rolled her eyes and told Penelope, "You'll have to excuse her. She's getting better, but she still hasn't mastered the art of subtlety."

"No, it's fine. It's actually somewhat refreshing. I mean, I'm pretty fucked up from everything that happened, and it's kinda nice that someone isn't treating me with kid gloves," Penelope said with a smile for Mary.

"You can't tell me that Moose is doing that," Wendy asked with a raised eyebrow.

"Well, no, but most of the time, when I've met with different veteran groups and their spouses, I can tell they're all dying to ask me questions about what happened but they're too polite or scared to do so."

"So...what happened to you?" Mary asked with a grin on her face.

Penelope couldn't help but smile back. "I'm sure you all know the basics from the newspapers. I was taken prisoner for months, forced to read their fucked-up manifestos, and then the SEALs and your guys swooped in and rescued me."

"I meant today," Mary clarified, pinning Penelope with her gaze.

"Are you okay?" Casey asked.

Penelope was still feeling a little off kilter from everything she'd remembered that day, but something about these women made her feel comfortable talking about it. Moose had told her a little about each of their stories, and she knew they'd understand some of her issues. Especially since, like her friends at home, some of them had been held against their will.

She didn't break eye contact with Casey as she said, "Things haven't been good for me lately. I found that I couldn't really do my job anymore, so I quit and basically went on walkabout. Tex helped hook me up with some of his military contacts around the country. I thought I was leaving to try to figure out why I was so messed up, but I pretty much was just avoiding my problems. It wasn't until toward the end of my trip that I realized what I'd done and really started trying to get my shit together."

"And did you?" Kassie asked.

"Get my shit together?" Penelope asked.

Kassie nodded.

Penelope shrugged. "I'm getting there. I saw a new psychologist today, and she hypnotized me...and I remembered for the first time what actually happened out in Turkey, how my friends and I were captured."

Everyone gasped, but it was Rayne who came forward and kneeled in front of her and put her hand on her knee. "And you're *here*? Do you need to get out of here and decompress?"

Penelope smiled at her. "This *is* decompressing," she admitted. "I've been terrified that I did something to get my friends killed. That I messed up somehow and was suppressing it, but I found out that I didn't. None of us did, really. We were just in the wrong place at the wrong time."

Rayne nodded. "I'm glad that you figured that out in your own head, but I could've told you that a long time ago and saved you some angst."

Penelope frowned. "I don't really even know you that well."

Rayne shrugged. "Maybe so, but at Em's wedding, I saw all I needed to know. You're a woman who takes charge. You didn't even hesitate to attack that asshole who was hell bent on hurting Annie and the rest of us."

"Moose did most of the attacking," Penelope mumbled.

"Not hardly," Emily said with a shake of her head.

"Look, we've all seen our share of shit," Rayne said, "but at the end of the day, the only thing that matters is being with the ones you love. Humans can be extremely awful to one another. I don't get it, and I never will. But the thing that gets me through when I wake up from a nightmare about what happened to me in Egypt is looking over at Ghost, and knowing no matter how fucked up I think I am, he loves me. Just as Truck loves Mary. Just like Beatle loves Casey. Etcetera, etcetera, etcetera.

"We aren't perfect, neither are our men, but that doesn't mean we love each other any less. Our experiences are part of who we are. You'll never forget your friends, ever. But life goes on, and I have a feeling they'd be pissed at you for letting even a moment of guilt stop you from living yours."

Penelope swallowed hard, then nodded.

"Right, and if you ever need another pep talk, or simply a place to go where you can hang with a bunch of women who won't judge you, you come up here. We'll hang out, have some drinks, and simply chill."

Rayne's words meant a lot to Penelope. Even though she already had exactly that. With Beth, Adeline, Sophie, Mackenzie, and all the other women down in San Antonio. But that didn't mean she didn't appreciate Rayne's invitation. "Thank you."

"You're welcome," Rayne said matter-of-factly, then stood and looked out into the yard. "Um...Em?"

"Yeah?"

"You might want to rein in your daughter before she runs over our men."

Everyone's heads swiveled toward the yard, where the men were all lying side by side, grinning like fools, as Annie swung her homemade tank around, obviously preparing to ride right over the guys.

"Annie Elizabeth Fletcher!" Emily yelled.

As if choreographed, all eight of the men's heads rolled to the right to look over at her, and instead of being cowed by the tone of her mother's voice, Annie yelled back, "It's okay, Mom! They said I could run them over!"

* * *

An hour later, Penelope was still on the porch, but this time she was hanging out with the Delta team and Moose. The women had all gone inside to raid the wine cabinet...and to give her time with the men. Penelope wasn't embarrassed by the obvious gesture on the women's part. As much as she enjoyed chatting with all the wives, she kind of felt more comfortable hanging with the guys. She'd almost always been the only woman in a group of men, so this felt normal.

"Moose says you had a tough day," Truck said, not beating around the bush. In a lot of ways, he reminded Penelope of his wife. She liked that, and could see that the two were meant for each other.

She shrugged. "I've had worse."

Everyone chuckled. That was another thing she liked about these guys. They had a warped sense of humor, just like her.

Moose put his hand on the back of her neck and slowly caressed her skin with his thumb, sending goose bumps down her spine. She'd somehow ended up on his lap on one of the love seats on the deck. Fletch and Emily had an entire living room of furniture set up outdoors, and when she'd asked about it, he'd merely shrugged and said that since everyone hung out over there so much, they'd decided to make things as comfortable as possible. The rest of the guys were either sitting or standing around, drinking beer and taking in the early Texas evening.

"Here's the thing, Tiger," Ghost said after a moment.

"We've been in a lot of situations where we've had to swoop in and rescue people. Civilians and soldiers alike. But no one has made such a lasting impression like you did."

Penelope wasn't sure how to answer, so she stayed silent.

"It wasn't so much your actions. I mean, you were a trained soldier, so ignoring your own injuries and doing what you could for the good of the team was somewhat expected. But what we didn't expect was for you to be so...calm."

Penelope couldn't help it. She snorted. "Calm? God, I was anything but."

"Seriously, Tiger. You weren't freaking out. You weren't demanding food and water, or crying hysterically. You were funny, sarcastic, and downright charming," Fletch said.

"Yeah, and that's so normal for someone in my situation," she protested.

Moose's hand tightened on her neck, but his thumb quickly resumed its gentle back-and-forth caress.

"It's *not* normal," Coach said, "which made it all the more extraordinary."

"We're not surprised you went to see a doc today..." Blade said.

"But we *were* surprised it took you so long." Hollywood finished his teammate's thought.

"We aren't saying there's anything wrong with you, Tiger, far from it," Beatle explained. "You handled what happened to you so well…almost *too* well, if you know what I mean. It was bound to catch up with you sooner or later."

Penelope narrowed her eyes at the men around her. "You all sound like you know way more about what's been going on with me than you should."

Ghost chuckled and shrugged. "We may or may not have been getting updates from Tex, who was getting them from Beth."

"That traitor," Penelope whispered.

"Don't be mad at her," Moose ordered.

"Why not?"

"Because the alternative is that she didn't care. That *these* guys didn't care. That they'd simply done their job and didn't think twice about the extraordinary woman who managed to keep herself alive for months of captivity, and who was willing and able to continue to protect herself and everyone around her after she was rescued."

Penelope stared into Moose's eyes and wished they were alone. She wanted to thank him for being by her side today. For never giving up on her. For believing in her. Even for loving her. She wasn't sure she deserved his love, but damn did it feel good.

"Oh," she said lamely.

"But I do have to say, we're all a little pissed at you too," Truck said.

Penelope tore her gaze away from Moose's and looked up at the huge man in surprise. He said they were upset, but that's not what his tone conveyed. She waited for him to continue.

"We're mad that you didn't come to us when you were hurting. We were there, Tiger. We know what happened. We know what went down. We may not have rescued you from that camp, or know all the details, but we've been on enough missions to have a good idea. After what you did at Fletch's wedding, how you helped take down those assholes who decided it was a good idea to rob a wedding party, you became one of us. A team member. And when one of us is hurting, we're *all* hurting. You need someone to talk to, and you don't feel like you can talk to your man there, you come to *us*. We'll set you straight."

Penelope felt Moose's hand tighten again, subtly, but she couldn't take her eyes from Truck. He wasn't just saying that. He meant it. All of it. He was upset, they were all upset, that she hadn't turned to them for help.

Yet more proof that she'd held the very people who could help her most at arm's length for way too long. And while she trusted Moose with her life, there were things that he wouldn't understand simply because he wasn't a soldier.

She didn't want to hurt Moose's feelings though. So she simply nodded at Truck.

That was apparently all he needed. What they all had needed. The somber looks on their faces faded and the tension on the deck eased.

Breathing out a sigh of relief, Penelope jumped slightly when Moose nuzzled against her neck. His lips brushed her skin, and she shivered. "You can *always* talk to me," he practically growled into her ear.

Penelope nodded again.

But he wasn't done. "I might not be a bad-ass Delta Force soldier, and I wasn't over there in Turkey, but I've seen and done my share of fucked-up shit. You need me, Pen, I'm right here."

She turned her head and placed a hand on the side of Moose's face. His brows were drawn down and he looked extremely distressed.

"I know, Moose. Why do you think I let you take me to my appointment today and insisted that you stay in the room when I was hypnotized? I knew you were right there by my side every second. I felt your hand in mine, and it gave me the strength to continue. If you weren't there, I don't think I would've trusted Doctor Melton enough to let her hypnotize me."

Her words were enough to clear the angst in his expression. He didn't say anything more about it, but turned his head into her hand and kissed the sensitive skin of her palm.

"You guys about done out here?" Emily asked as she stuck her head through the sliding glass door that led onto the deck.

"Yeah, what's up?" Fletch asked, heading for his wife.

"The babies are cranky. Ford needs to be put down,

Kate is screaming her head off, and Kassie has a headache as a result. And Annie is hyper and needs some quiet time before she goes to bed."

Hollywood was on the move before Emily had finished speaking. He crossed over to Penelope, kissed her on the forehead, then straightened. "It was good to see you again, Tiger. Don't be a stranger. Come back and visit us soon."

The other guys followed suit, telling her how much they enjoyed seeing her, even if it was because she was in town for some not-so-great reasons, then disappearing into the house to take their wives home. Only her, Moose, and Ghost were left on the deck.

Penelope had stood, and Moose did as well. Ghost got into her personal space and pulled her in for a long, heartfelt hug. Then he pulled back and put his hands on her shoulders. Penelope felt Moose's hand on the small of her back. She felt surrounded, but not smothered. It was a good feeling.

"I'm sorry you're hurting, Tiger. But out of everyone I know who's struggled with their PTSD, you'll be the one to break through quickest to the other side. Want to know how I know?"

"How?"

"Because the first time I met you, you said, and I quote, 'I don't know what the hell your plan is, but can we please get on with it and get the fuck out of here?' Anyone who can ask to hurry their own rescue is a woman who will not let anything hold her down for long."

"Fight like a girl," Moose murmured.

Penelope took a step forward and rested her forehead in the middle of Ghost's chest. "I'm tired, Ghost. So damn tired."

"Then stop trying to do everything by your damn self," he retorted.

Penelope's head came up at that. She'd somehow thought he would continue to be all soft and gooey with her. But his words were almost impatient.

His eyes were still gentle, however, as he turned her to face Moose. Ghost leaned down and spoke into her ear as she stared up at the man who'd helped her more than she could ever tell him.

"You've got a man standing right in front of you who would gladly take on those demons of yours. Ever since I met him at Fletch's wedding, he's had eyes for no one but you. Let him carry you when you can't walk anymore. He's more than capable. You'll never make it if you don't lean on those around you."

That was the thing…she trusted Moose with her life, but she wasn't sure she could trust anyone *else* anymore. Still, as she looked up into his eyes, she felt more relaxed than she could remember being in a long time.

Dude's words came back to her then, about letting someone else take over for a while and how freeing it could be.

She leaned forward again, and this time her forehead came to rest against Moose's chest. Inhaling, she sighed in contentment. He smelled so good. Like soap and the detergent he used to wash his clothes. Penelope felt his arms go around her, and she went limp. She hadn't lied. She was tired.

Tired of trying to be strong.

Tired of being so keyed up all the time.

Tired of worrying.

For once, she didn't want to think about anything. Not about her therapy session and what she'd remembered. Not about White, Black, and Wilson. Not about anything that had happened to her in Turkey. Not about what she was going to do with her life, her job. Nothing.

"Come on, sweetheart. You've had a long day. Time to go home."

She nodded against him.

"Thanks again," Moose said to Ghost. Penelope felt his hand move from her back and figured he was shaking Ghost's hand.

"Anytime. And I mean that."

"Tell Fletch I want to be invited to his daughter's graduation party. She's a hell of a girl, and I can tell she's gonna be a hell of a woman."

"Very true. I'll walk you guys out."

Penelope let herself be shifted in Moose's embrace until she was tucked against his side, under his arm.

She felt safe and cared for, and never wanted to leave that spot.

The thought should've freaked her out, but instead it just made her snuggle into him closer.

She said goodbye to Emily, Fletch, and Annie, and the next thing she knew, Moose had gotten her all settled in the passenger side of his truck. Before he started it up, he asked, "You want to go back to San Antonio or grab a hotel room up here?"

"Home," she said without thought.

The gentle look in his eyes told her she'd made the right decision.

"Go ahead and sleep, Pen. I'll get you home safe and sound."

"I know you will."

It was the last thing she remembered until being gently shaken awake by Moose inside his garage. He helped her into the house and up the stairs.

"You gonna be all right to get ready for bed?"

She nodded absently. The truth was, she wasn't really sure, as her eyes felt so heavy she didn't know if she could keep them open. Moose eyed her for a long moment before nodding and leaving her alone in the master bedroom. Smokey was still over at Adeline and Crash's house. They'd go and get him in the morning. So she didn't have to worry about her donkey hogging all the room on the spacious bed. She dropped her jeans and blouse on the floor by the dresser and pulled out one of Moose's T-shirts. It was huge on her, hanging well below her ass and more than adequately covering her.

She did a perfunctory brushing of her teeth and crawled under the covers, half asleep before her head hit the pillow.

Penelope had no idea how much time had passed since she'd gone to bed, but she knew the second Moose joined her. He pulled her into his side and wrapped an arm around her shoulders. She cuddled into him, bringing up one leg and hooking it over his own. Her arm tightened around his belly, and she realized for the first time that he wasn't wearing a shirt.

Being wrapped around him, resting her head on the bare skin of his shoulder, was extremely intimate...and comforting. Feeling as if she were melting, Penelope completely relaxed into the man at her side. She didn't hold herself stiff from nerves. She didn't worry about what he was thinking. She simply did what she wanted...and needed.

And that was to give herself over to him completely.

Just as Dude and Ghost had suggested, she needed this.

"That's it, Pen. I've got you," Moose murmured softly. "I love you. Just relax and sleep."

"Moose?"

"Right here, sweetheart."

"Thank you."

"You don't ever have to thank me for taking care of you. That's a given."

The words were beautiful and seeped into her soul. Moose wouldn't let her down, *that* she knew without a doubt. She fell asleep and slept soundly throughout the night.

For the first time since she'd come back from her impromptu trip around the country, she slept without having a nightmare.

CHAPTER TEN

The next two weeks went by fairly quickly. Moose had thought things would be easier for Penelope, now that she knew she had nothing to be ashamed about as far as her actions in Turkey went, but instead of becoming more confident, she seemed to be folding in on herself with every day that passed.

At first she seemed to be doing great after her session with the hypnotist. She seemed happy and relieved to have finally remembered everything that had happened. But when she'd had a nightmare only two nights later, she'd been visibly frustrated the next morning. She'd refused to talk to him about it.

Then, when she'd had another the *next* night, it outright angered her.

Since then, as the nightmares continued, she'd ranted and raved about how she was supposed to be fine now. That being hypnotized was supposed to have cured her of her "issues."

Moose tried to explain that wasn't how things worked, but she tuned him out.

He'd also tried to talk to her about what Wilson had done, and how she felt about it, but she merely shrugged and said she understood, that he was scared. But obviously, deep down, his betrayal still hurt, was still causing her issues.

In short order, when it became obvious that being hypnotized wasn't the cure-all she'd expected, Penelope withdrew more and more. Moose reiterated over and over that she wasn't responsible for her friends' deaths, but she refused to talk about it.

He was extremely worried and desperate to help her. He was frustrated that she'd gone from seemingly trusting him implicitly after their trip to Killeen, to being jumpy and short with him at every turn.

Today, they were participating in another law enforcement versus firefighter softball game, and instead of looking forward to spending time with his friends, and having a hell of a lot of fun thinking of new ways to cheat to try to win the game, he was irritated and grumpy.

He'd also woken up, once again, by himself.

For the last week, Pen had been heading up to bed extremely early. Most of the time she was asleep before he got home from Station 7. He'd missed talking to her. Telling her about his day. But he wasn't about to wake her up. He knew she was using sleep, when she could find it, as an avoidance tactic, and the only thing that made him feel slightly better was the fact that she was still sleeping in his bed.

Every evening when he got into bed next to her, she rolled into him and threw an arm and leg around him, holding him as tightly as he did her. Subconsciously, she reached out for him, but he hated that when she was awake, she was getting more and more remote.

It was about time she pulled her head out of her ass and got back to her life. He wasn't being heartless, but the more time she spent wallowing in her own insecurities and pain, the harder and harder it was going to be to get back to truly living.

Moose rolled out of bed and headed for the bathroom to shower. Fifteen minutes later, he wandered down the stairs and saw Penelope in the kitchen, standing by the stove. Her gaze was fixed on the pan of eggs in front of her, and even though he knew she'd heard him enter, she didn't turn around.

Mentally shaking his head at the way she was trying to avoid him, Moose slowly began to seethe. He was fucking done with her pretending nothing was wrong, and like they were roommates instead of...

What were they?

He loved her. More than anything. But she'd been treating him as if he was a buddy or something. If she hadn't snuggled up to him in bed every night, he'd probably have lost his cool way before now.

Moose poured himself a cup of coffee and took a sip before settling his ass against the kitchen counter. He stared at the back of Penelope's head, willing her to turn around and talk to him.

Finally, after a few minutes, Pen turned, and when she quickly glanced at him, he raised a brow at her.

"What?" she asked somewhat belligerently.

It wasn't a good start, but Moose was done tiptoeing around.

"So you *are* going to talk to me this morning, huh?"

"What are you talking about?" she asked. "I talk to you every morning."

"No, Pen, you don't. Sometimes you grunt. Other times you pretend I don't exist. I have to say, it's getting old."

She reacted as if she'd been just waiting for him to throw the first volley. "You think you're the best room-mate either? Ha! That's a joke."

A little taken aback by her tone, even though he'd been wanting some sort of reaction from her, Moose slowly put down his mug and crossed his arms over his chest. This was the first time in a week he'd seen any emotion in Pen, and while he didn't like that she seemed to be pissed at him, he was glad to see something could rile her up. "Is that what we are? Roommates?"

"Apparently," she fired back. "You left lights on down here again last night. You're wasting energy and it's annoying."

"Seriously?" Moose asked, beyond frustrated that she was bitching about the fucking electricity.

"Yeah, Moose. Seriously. And once again, I had to do the dishes this morning because you left them in the sink—*without* putting water in them, so the food was all dried and gross on the plate and pan that you used last night."

Moose clenched his teeth. She was being ridiculous. She didn't give a shit about the dishes. She was frustrated at herself, that she wasn't magically cured of her PTSD and issues after remembering what had really happened in Turkey.

At his lack of immediate response, she went on listing his apparent flaws as a live-in partner. "The clothes in the dryer were damp, and I'll probably have to rewash them today because they smell funky. The least you could've done was restart them before you came upstairs last night. And the door to the garage was unlocked, anyone could've just walked right on in the house. And if you leave the TV on one more time, I'm gonna scream."

She was beautiful all riled up. Moose was almost too pissed to appreciate the flush in her cheeks, and the way her chin came up at just the right angle that, if he wanted to, he could lean over just slightly and catch her lips with his own. *Almost.*

"You're so full of bullshit you can't see what's right in front of you," he bit out.

She let out a bitter chuckle. "Yeah? And what's that?

An inconsiderate man who thinks his shit doesn't stink? News flash, Moose, turning the fan on when you go into the bathroom doesn't mask the sound of anything you're doing in there!"

He wanted to scream in frustration, but instead, he let fly with the words he'd been holding back all week. "You're not pissed about the lights, or the dishes, or the laundry."

"Yeah? What am I pissed about then? If you're so fucking clairvoyant, you tell me!"

"You thought that remembering what happened in that refugee camp would cure you. Make it so you could instantly go back to the person you were before. But that's not how shit works. If you maybe *talked* about what you're feeling, it would help you work through it. But you're all fired up and so determined to do things on your own, you've blocked out the people who care about you the most."

"I suppose you think I can talk to *you* about it?"

"Yeah, Pen, I do." Moose did his best to control the anger and frustration in his tone, but wasn't sure he was all that successful.

"Because you have so much experience with being a soldier," she said sarcastically.

"Just because I was never in the military doesn't mean I don't know what you're going through."

"Riiiiight. Moose, your life has been one big fucking ball of sunshine. You've never had to worry about whether or not the next person who walks in when you're sleeping is going to decide to rape you. You haven't had to worry about if today's the day your head will be chopped off or you'll be burned alive. You haven't wondered if the next time you open your mouth, you'll say something that will goad someone into deciding you aren't worth their time and effort to keep alive. You have *no* idea what I went through, and I'm sick of everyone thinking if I just talked, I'd be magically cured! Especially when *hypnotism* didn't even help!"

That was it. Moose was done. He'd been treating Penelope with kid gloves for the last few months, but he was fucking done. If she couldn't see what was right in front of her face because of the blinders she'd willingly donned, he'd force her to open her eyes once and for all.

"You know what your problem is, Pen?"

She snorted. "Yeah, Moose, I do. I was fucking held captive for months and spent every day wondering if it was my last. But I suppose you're going to try to enlighten me anyway."

"Damn straight. Your problem is that you're so focused on yourself, you can't see that you're not the only one struggling with the shit life has thrown at them."

She rolled her eyes—and Moose saw red.

His voice lowered, but it was controlled when he spoke, which made the impact of his words all the more profound. "While you were gone, gallivanting around the country, refusing to talk to anyone but me when you found a precious few minutes to call and tell me you weren't lying dead in a ditch somewhere, your friends and family have been going through their own shit here at home."

Penelope glared at him, but kept her lips pressed together tightly.

"Yeah, Pen, that's right, you aren't the only one dealing with some serious issues. Life here didn't just stop, waiting on your return. Beth had a major relapse. She freaked out one night when she and Sledge went out to eat. He had to call 9-1-1 because she'd crawled under the table in the restaurant and refused to come out, and she had to be forcibly sedated. But you wouldn't know about that—because you didn't call your brother while you were gone. Not *once*.

"And what about your parents? Did you know your dad was hospitalized because he was having chest pains? I can see by your expression that you didn't. Don't worry, he's okay for now. But the doctors are watching him carefully and trying out several different cocktails of drugs to make sure his heart doesn't give out on him."

The rage on Penelope's face had drained, but Moose was already on a roll.

"What else? Let's see...Hope and Calder's baby almost died. Carter had an infection caused by bacteria and the doctors at first gave him only a fifty-fifty chance of survival. Luckily, he pulled through, but it was touch and go for a while. Hayden was injured on the job one night when some asshole pulled out a gun and started shooting as she walked up to his car on a traffic stop. The bullet only grazed her, and the asshole drove off, but it could've been so much worse. Coco was hit by a car when he ran in front of Adeline, trying to protect her because she wasn't paying enough attention when she was crossing a street. He almost died, but the vet was able to save him.

"Quinn's second laser treatment on her port-wine stain was rough, extremely painful, and she wasn't sure she wanted to continue them. She and Driftwood are also still dealing with the courts and the trials of some of the assholes who kidnapped and tried to kill her. Oh, and you haven't gotten to know Koren all that well, but when her condo burned down, she had literally *nothing* to her name. No clothes, no pictures, none of her childhood memories. It all went up in smoke. Everyone pitched in to help replace it all. Everyone but *you*, because you weren't here. You'd already checked out mentally, and then physically when you left town without a word to anyone.

"Did you know Sledge actually went and put in a missing person's report right after you left? He was terrified that something had happened to you. Because you didn't think about anyone but *yourself*. It wasn't until Tex called a week later that we learned you'd taken your tracker with you, and that you were safe.

You didn't bother to call *me* until another week had gone by."

Moose could see tears in Penelope's eyes...but he wasn't quite done.

"And what about *me*, Pen? I've loved you for what seems like forever. You leaving, and knowing I wasn't reason enough for you to stay...that hurt. A lot. I lived for your phone calls while you were gone. I wanted to know that you were all right. Safe. I went through the motions at work, not sleeping well at night because I couldn't stop worrying about you. Until one night, when I got off shift, I came home and couldn't relax. Couldn't sleep at all. I couldn't do *anything* but stare at my phone and pray you'd call. Then I lay down and couldn't breathe. My chest hurt and it felt like I was dying. I called Chief, and he called an ambulance."

"Moose," Penelope whispered, the tears in her eyes finally spilling over.

He steeled himself against the anguish on her face. He was being relentless, but he couldn't stop himself. She had to understand. Someone had to get real with her, and he loved her enough to be that person. To be the bad guy. It had to be done if she was going to come back from everything that had happened to her. She might hate him after this, but if it helped Penelope pull her head out of her ass, it would have to be worth it in the long run.

"I thought I was having a heart attack. My vision was blurry, and I couldn't take a deep breath without shooting pains in my chest. I had a full workup, MRI, CAT scans...you name it, I got it. But it wasn't a heart attack. Turns out it was stress. The doctor said that stress, along with working too hard and not getting enough sleep, had made my body rebel on me. I'm not working half shifts because you're home...well, not entirely. I was put on half duty because of my health. All I could think about was you, and whether you'd ever come back to me. If I'd ever see you again."

Moose sighed. "I'm not telling you all this to get your sympathy. It sucks, but I'm dealing, and I haven't had any real bad chest pains in a while now."

"Then why *are* you telling me all this?" Penelope whispered.

"It's not to cause you grief. If you believe anything I say, believe *that*. It's because you need to know that you aren't the only one going through pain. Life isn't fair, Pen. It's not. Every day we wake up is a gift. Everyone's hurting in some way. It's not just you. You're right, I've never been in the military, and I've never had to worry about being raped, but that doesn't diminish the things I *have* worried about. Everyone's tiptoed around you because they're afraid of doing or saying anything that might make you bolt again. You're loved, Penelope. So damn much...but you've got your head buried in the sand so deep, it's not even funny."

"Maybe I shouldn't go to the game today," Penelope said hesitatingly.

"Oh, no," Moose threw back at her. "You're going.

Everyone is going to be there. You know why? Because of *you*. Because they want to see you with their own two eyes to make sure you're okay. You might have come back, but you haven't made the effort to reach out to all of your friends. It's as if you're still gone. So they're all coming. Mackenzie, Mickie, Corrie, Laine, Erin and baby Lily, Milena with both JT and Steven, Hope with her son Carter, Adeline and Coco, Sophie, Blythe and Harper, Quinn...and even Koren, who barely knows you. But she wants to *get* to know you, because she's heard such wonderful things.

"And you know who else is making the effort to come see you, even though you haven't bothered to reciprocate? Beth. That's right, the woman who has agoraphobia, who would've already married your brother if you'd been around to give them your blessing, is going to be there. She's leaving the safety of her home to see you, for the *second* time since you've been back. And of course all the guys too. Can't have a softball game without the participants. So you're going today, and you're going to smile and pretend that everything is all right so your *friends* can breathe a sigh of relief. Even if you don't feel like it, you *owe* it to the people who love you to at least show up."

"Okay, Moose. You're right."

He did his best to calm down. He wasn't sure if he'd gotten through to her, but he hoped he had. He wasn't the best at grand speeches, but this had been the most important talk he'd ever had with her before, and he hoped like hell something he'd said sunk in.

"Go get changed," Moose said in as calm a voice as he could manage. "I'll let Smokey out one more time and start a new batch of eggs since those are burnt." He nodded to the pan of eggs still on the stove behind her.

Penelope took a step toward him, and he pretended he didn't see her, moving to the side so she couldn't touch him and picking up the spatula she'd left on the counter. If she touched him right now, he didn't know what he'd do. Haul her to him? Push her away? Neither action was all that attractive right now.

He felt the familiar twinges in his chest but ignored them. It was just stress. They'd fade.

Without a word, Penelope turned and headed to the master bedroom.

Waiting until he knew she would be at least halfway up the stairs, Moose turned and watched her disappear from sight.

Sighing, he closed his eyes. He felt like shit. He hated being upset with Penelope, and hated even more that he'd made her cry. It was for her own good, but that didn't make it any easier.

Smokey nuzzled his hand, bringing Moose out of his self-imposed pity party. "Hey, Smokey. Think any of that sunk in?"

Smokey brayed quietly and nodded his head up and down a few times. Moose couldn't help but laugh. "I hope so, boy. I really hope so."

* * *

An hour later, Penelope sat next to a silent Moose in his truck as they headed to the softball fields. Her mind was spinning with the stuff he'd dumped on her. She hated that she'd been kept in the dark about everything that had been going on, but at the same time, she understood. She really hadn't been that good at keeping in touch with people. Yes, she'd called to talk to Moose, but when she thought about their conversations, she realized that he'd done most of the listening and she'd done the talking.

She hadn't asked about their friends. She'd told Moose about where she was and who she was with and what fun things she'd been doing...but not once had she asked how *he* was doing. She hadn't called her brother or parents, had just assumed Moose would pass on word that she was okay.

She'd been a terrible friend, sister, daughter, girlfriend.

She'd been selfish...was *still* being selfish.

Thinking about what Adeline must've felt when Coco had been hit by a car. Or about Beth relapsing. Or the idea that Carter might not be here today if the doctors hadn't been able to help him fight his infection after he'd been born.

But the thing that really struck home the hardest was Moose and his health issues.

He was the strongest man she knew. Both physically and mentally. He'd been there for her with no questions asked. To know that he'd been in physical pain, was likely *still* in pain, and she had probably been *responsible* for that pain, was almost too much for her to handle. Not once had he let on that anything was wrong. And also, no one else had told her.

She *did* have her head up her ass.

Some people might think Moose had been too harsh, but he'd done exactly what she needed. What had happened to her had sucked. Big time. But was her sucky any worse than anyone else's? Maybe, maybe not, but she'd done her friends a huge disservice by not being there for them. For putting her pain above their own.

Glancing over at Moose while he drove, Penelope bit her lip. She had no idea how to make things right with him. She'd been distancing herself from him since her session with Dr. Melton because she'd been so frustrated that she wasn't instantly cured.

She'd also begun to second-guess herself...and their relationship.

What they were doing was weird. Sleeping together every night but not really being intimate. She knew Moose loved her, but she was afraid to love him back. What if he really only pitied her, and was confusing that with love? What if he loved the old Penelope, and was too stubborn or kind to admit he didn't like the person she'd become?

The bottom line was that she was scared.

White and Black would be ashamed of her. White would look down at her with his big brown eyes and shake his head, asking, "What happened to fighting like a girl?"

Because Black hadn't ever really had a serious relationship, she knew he'd tell her to grab hold of her man and never let go because life is short.

And life *was* short. Her experiences had proven that.

Penelope had no idea what to do to bridge the gap that had begun to form between her and Moose because of her selfishness. She wanted to. She knew now that some of her trust issues stemmed from Wilson's actions, from him trying to convince the terrorists to beat up on *her* instead of him. But Moose would never betray her like that. He wouldn't; she knew that down to the marrow of her bones. She knew his tough love this morning wasn't because he thought she shouldn't worry about healing herself; it was more because she'd been blind to everyone around her. Because he thought she should embrace her friends while working on her mental health...and she wasn't.

And that was exactly what *everyone* had said. Wolf, Dude, Caroline, Ghost...they'd all tried to make her understand that she could be broken, and still be okay at the end of the day. That her tribe would help her heal. She'd been trying to do everything on her own, and the bottom line was that she needed her friends. Needed Moose.

Had she completely screwed things up between them? Could he ever forgive her?

She hadn't thought of anything to say to break the tension between them by the time they arrived at the softball field. There were a few different games going on today on the other fields, so the parking lot was full and they had to park a ways away from their destination.

Without a word, Moose got out, lifted Smokey down from the back seat, and grabbed their bags. He waited for her to get out of the truck and come around to the front before heading for the field. Penelope fell into step beside him, leading Smokey, and tried desperately to think of something to say before they were no longer alone and she lost her chance.

"Moose?"

"Yeah, Pen?"

"I've been a selfish cow, and I'm going to try to stop wallowing."

She saw a corner of his lips quirk up, and even that little smile made her feel a hundred times better.

"Good," he said, not even trying to refute her words.

"Moose?"

"Right here, Pen."

"I'm sorry you've been stressed. I never meant for anything I did to cause anyone any pain. Certainly not you."

"I know you didn't. But now you know."

"Now I know," Penelope agreed.

Before he could respond, if he even wanted to, Penelope heard her name being called.

"Penelope!"

Looking toward the bleachers, she saw most of the women had already arrived and Mackenzie was waving her hand in the air like a complete dork as she called out her name. Chuckling, Penelope started toward her friends, then she turned back to Moose. "Um…can we talk more later?"

Moose nodded. "Of course. See you on our bench." Then he turned and strode toward the field, giving a chin lift to the police officers on the opposite benches as he headed for the guys from the station.

Penelope knew she didn't have a lot of time, since she was playing and needed to warm up, but after what Moose had told her that morning, she *needed* to say hello. To make sure her friends all knew how much they meant to her, and that she hadn't meant to be so remote.

"Hey, everyone," she said as she neared.

Various forms of greeting were called out.

"Penelope!"

"Pen!"

"Great to see you!"

The first person Penelope wanted to talk to was Beth, though. The other woman was sitting on the bottom row of the bleachers looking like she wanted to be anywhere but there. Penelope crouched in front of her and looked at her friend. "Hey, Beth."

"Hey."

Penelope tried to think of a good way to start this conversation, and couldn't. So she just blurted out, "I'm sorry I've been a shitty friend. Are you okay?"

Looking surprised, Beth nodded. "I will be."

Once more, Penelope was so impressed with her strength. Moose was right, shitty things happened to everyone. "Of course you will. And, just so you know, my brother hates getting dressed up."

"Um...okay?" Beth said, her brows drawn down in confusion.

"Which includes wearing a tuxedo or any kind of suit. So, not that I'm trying to tell you what to do or anything, but I'm thinking a small ceremony at your house, in your backyard, would probably be the best thing."

"Ceremony?" Beth asked, still not understanding.

"Yeah, ceremony," Penelope told her. "I can't believe my brother hasn't already married you. I can't wait until we're actually related, and I can call you my sister for reals."

Beth's eyes widened comically.

"I know I've been a shitty sister and sister-in-law-to-be, but you guys should just do it already. Everyone knows how crazy you are for each other and nobody cares that you don't want a huge shindig. Hell, we all know you'd hate it, and you and Cade would probably skip out early anyway, and why should you pay all that money for a reception you won't even attend? So just do a laid-back thing in your yard and be done with it already."

Without a word, Beth launched herself at Penelope, throwing her arms around her and physically tackling her to the ground. Smokey thought it was a fun game, and he nuzzled both Beth and Penelope, braying in excitement.

Mickie and Koren leapt to their aid, then stared down at the women in confusion when both Beth and Penelope started laughing hysterically.

"We didn't want to do anything without you here," Beth told her from her perch on top of her.

"I'm sorry. Start planning, Beth. Make an honest man out of my brother."

"What in the world is going on?" Corrie asked from her seat on the bleachers. "Laine, tell me what you see!" she ordered.

Penelope chuckled, and both she and Beth picked themselves up from the dirt.

"If it's okay with you," Beth told Penelope, "I'm out of here."

Not surprised, just feeling extremely honored the other woman had even made the effort to come to the game because of her, Penelope nodded and hugged her tightly. "Love you, Beth."

"Same. It's good to have you back," Beth returned. Then she waved at the other women before gesturing toward the field, letting Sledge know she was leaving, and jogging toward the parking lot.

Then Penelope did what she should've done way before now. She went from one woman to the next, saying hello, asking them how they were doing, and promising to be around a lot more. She handed Smokey's lead to Adeline and leaned down to pet Coco. She noticed where the shaved hair was still growing back on his side. "He's really okay?" she asked quietly.

Adeline nodded. "Yeah. It was touch and go for a while, but he's a trooper."

"He is. And so are you."

They stared at each other for a long moment before Adeline smiled. "Takes one to know one," she retorted.

Penelope hugged her, then said to the group, "Looks like everyone's getting impatient. Gotta go kick some police butt."

"As if," Mackenzie snorted.

And thus commenced the trash talking between the wives and girlfriends of the police and the firefighters. Smiling, Penelope made her way over to the firefighter's bench.

"'Bout time you got over here, shrimp," her brother mock complained. He put her in a headlock and gave her a noogie.

Penelope shrieked and did her best to get out of Cade's hold, but he was just as stubborn as her and wouldn't let go.

"Guess you don't want to know what I said to Beth about your wedding then," Penelope said between giggles.

And just like that, Cade released her. "What'd you say?" he asked.

Penelope smiled up at the man she'd loved and respected her whole life. According to what she'd seen and been told after she'd returned from Turkey, he'd single-handedly kept her case in the limelight, and she'd always know it was *his* doggedness that had convinced the President to send the SEALs after her. The thought that she'd done anything to hurt him and Beth cut deep. "I told her that you hated to dress up and that you'd be much more comfortable with a wedding ceremony in your backyard than having to put on a tuxedo or something."

The relief and love in Cade's eyes almost did Penelope in.

"Thank you," he whispered. "We didn't want to do anything without you here."

Penelope nodded. "Well, I'm here now, and I expect you to hurry the hell up and marry her already."

"I'd do it tomorrow if I could swing it," Cade said.

"I know. But you probably want to make sure Mom and Dad can be here. I'm not sure they'd get over missing it."

"You're right. I'll call them tonight and see when's the fastest they can get here," Cade said.

"Don't let this derail your concentration on the game," Crash grumbled.

"Fuck off, you're already married, asshole," Sledge grumbled.

"Yes, I am," he agreed, smiling and puffing out his chest.

Sledge punched him in the arm and everyone laughed.

"Before we go out there and wipe the cops' badges in the dust, can I say something?" Penelope asked.

"Make it fast, Pen," Squirrel said. "We've got a game to play."

"Right. I just want to apologize for up and leaving without a word to any of you. That was rude and wrong, and I regret it. You're all the best friends I've ever had, and you've always been there for me. I...I'm still not sure about coming back to work at the station, but you didn't deserve me leaving like that. I'm sorry."

She held her breath as seven pairs of eyes focused on her.

"Apology accepted. Now can we play this game already?" Driftwood muttered.

Everyone nodded and headed for the field. Penelope should've known the guys would let her off the hook. They weren't into drama, and they were obviously just pleased she'd come today.

Taco held back from the others and put a hand on her arm before she could head out onto the field. Penelope panicked for a second, wondering if he was going to lambast her for not being there for him when he'd needed her most.

But instead of telling her what an awful person she

was, that he didn't want anything to do with her, he wrapped his arms around her and pulled her close.

Penelope didn't breathe for a second, then she relaxed into him.

He didn't say anything, but then again, he didn't have to. He pulled back, looked into her eyes, then nodded before jogging out onto the field.

Penelope took a deep breath and started to follow him, when she noticed Moose standing nearby, watching.

He hadn't simply left her to face whatever Taco might say. No, he'd been there, ready to intervene if necessary.

Without a word, he turned and headed to the outfield.

She didn't deserve Moose. He'd shown her in a million different ways over and over again that he was there for her. That he loved her. She didn't give a shit about him leaving the lights on in his house or stupid dirty dishes in the sink. That was all just petty shit she'd dredged up that morning because she'd been feeling so off kilter and confused about where a relationship between them could go.

But it all disappeared the second she found out that he'd been in the hospital, and she hadn't known. Every time she called, she'd tried to convince him she was having the time of her life, even though she'd missed Texas, missed *him*, every minute of every day.

Knowing it would take time to come to terms with

what she'd missed out on, and to make it up to everyone, Penelope took a deep breath and headed out to the
field. She was on first base to start out with, just like
she always was. She preferred that to the outfield
because she wasn't the greatest at catching the ball, and
she loved doing what she could to cheat and make the
law enforcement guys get tagged out because she hid
the base, or moved it when they weren't looking, or
something equally nefarious.

The game started, and Penelope lost herself in the
joy of laughing and joking around with her friends.
She'd forgotten how fun this was. How a simple game
—okay, not so simple when every single person was
doing their best to cheat...and not hide it—could make
her forget her worries for a while.

Penelope leaned over, resting her hands on her
thighs and blocking Hayden's path to second base.

"Hey, move it, shorty," the other woman complained
as Penelope refused to get out of her way.

"You're only a few inches taller than me, I'm not
sure you can call me shorty," Penelope told her.

"A few inches might as well be a mile, *shorty*,"
Hayden shot back.

Penelope was smiling, thinking about how she
could best prevent Hayden from getting to second
base, when a few things happened all at the same time.

A fight broke out in the spectator area near another
field. The sounds of men yelling and fists hitting flesh
sounded across the field.

A siren in the distance wailed.

A car in the lot backfired.

And suddenly, Penelope was back in Turkey.

One second she was at the softball game, watching as Dax got ready to hit the ball, and the next, she was back in the refugee camp. She looked around and saw White and Black next to her, but then she blinked and they disappeared, and she was all alone.

Reaching for her rifle, she was horrified to find she'd lost it somewhere.

She was alone in the refugee camp and surrounded by armed terrorists. She knew when they got their hands on her, they'd hurt her.

Whimpering, she backed up, step after step, her hands in front of her, as if that could keep the men away. She heard her name being yelled, and she thought it was Black.

"Black?" she called out. "Where are you?"

He didn't answer.

Her back hit something and halted her retreat. The men slowly began to close in around her. They were talking, she could see their lips moving, but she couldn't hear anything they were saying. She was all alone and there was absolutely nothing she could do.

* * *

"Moose!" Hayden yelled. "Get over here!"

Moose looked to where Hayden was standing near

first base, and at first he thought she was just messing with him, trying to distract him so one of her teammates could steal home base—but the second he saw Penelope, he knew this wasn't a joke.

He sprinted over to where Penelope was staring into space. She was backing away from Hayden.

"Penelope?" he asked gently, but she didn't acknowledge him in any way. She looked much like she had when she'd been hypnotized. Her eyes were glassy, and she wasn't focusing on anything.

When her head swiveled and she called out for her murdered friend, Moose knew he had to do something.

By now, all the other guys on both teams had run over to see what they could do to help. They were gathered around Penelope in a semi-circle. She backed herself up until she hit the chain-link fence surrounding the field, her arms outstretched and her hands up, as if to stop the people in her head from coming any closer. Her mouth opened and shut several times, but no words came out.

"Don't get in front of her," Moose ordered. He had no idea what he was doing, but if Penelope was seeing anything, the last thing he wanted was for her to feel penned in, surrounded. That's what happened that day in the camps, before the terrorists had attacked.

"Black? White? Where are you? Come back! Help me!" Penelope wailed.

Moose cautiously approached Penelope from the

side. He didn't grab her, but very gently put his hand on her shoulder. "I'm here," he said softly.

"Thank God!" Penelope breathed. "Where's everyone else?"

Moose gestured to Sledge with his head and put his finger over his lips. Penelope's brother came up to her other side and put his hand on her shoulder as well.

"White? Is that you?"

"We're here," Moose said.

The other guys separated and slowly approached Penelope. One by one, they all put a hand on her. Quint crouched by her and put a hand on her calf. Chief approached from the other side and touched her hand. Conor crouched as well and touched her wrist.

With each touch, the muscles in Penelope's body got looser and looser.

"Thank God you came…" Penelope said brokenly.

Moose realized with a start that while the men had been approaching Penelope and him from the field side, their women had gathered around the other side of the fence. From the outside, it probably looked like a mob had gathered; a mob of people all squished together like they were wasn't exactly normal, but Moose didn't give a shit.

Penelope was still pressed up against the fence, and Mackenzie reached out and touched her back through the chain-link. Blythe did the same. Then Milena. Not all of them could get close enough to touch her, but they were all there. Supporting their friend, doing what they could to let her know she wasn't alone.

Adeline had walked around the fence onto the field, and was now coming toward the group with Smokey and Coco in tow. When she got close, she dropped Smokey's lead and the miniature donkey ran straight toward his mistress. He nudged her leg with his nose.

"Smokey?" Penelope asked, her voice wavering with confusion. "What...how?"

Then she was on her knees, and Smokey was in her arms. Moose had dropped to the ground with Penelope, and he carefully and slowly wrapped his arms around her from the side. The others took a few steps back and watched with bated breath.

Moose felt Penelope take a deep inhale. Then another. She blinked, then turned her head to stare at him.

"Pen?" he asked cautiously.

"Shit," she swore, then closed her eyes.

Everything in Moose sagged in relief. She was back. Fuck, she'd taken ten years off his life. "It's okay," he told their friends. "Give us a second?"

The women slowly backed away and went back to the bleachers, and the guys who minutes ago had been laughing, joking, and obnoxiously cheating walked about twenty feet away, but hovered there. Not willing to go back to the game until they knew Penelope was all right.

"I don't know what to do or say," Penelope uttered quietly.

"You don't have to do or say anything," Moose told her.

"I thought I was back there," she said. "I was in the camp, surrounded by the men who I knew were going to beat the shit out of me again, and I couldn't find White or Black. They disappeared. They left me alone."

"I know," Moose said, because he'd figured that out from watching her go through the flashback.

"I know they didn't really abandon me...but maybe a part of me still blames them. How fucked up is that?"

"I think it's to be expected. They were your backup. They were supposed to have your back, just as you'd have theirs."

"Exactly," Penelope breathed.

Moose took a chance and lifted her chin so she was looking at him. "That's why you couldn't go in to get Taco, isn't it?"

She frowned, and he could see her breaths coming too fast. She shook her head. "No, that's not—" Her voice stopped abruptly, and she stared up at him in shock. "I was scared that I'd get in there and get in trouble, and I'd be on my own again."

"I know this is going to take a while to sink in, but this isn't Turkey, Pen. We've got your back. Always. No matter what."

"You can't promise that," she whispered.

"The hell I can't," Moose countered.

They stared at each other for a beat before Moose asked, "What's the last thing White said to you?"

"Fight like a girl."

"Right. And why'd he say that?"

"I don't know."

"Okay, fair enough. Why do you *think* he said it? Come on, Pen, you knew him really well. What was he thinking?"

"He wanted me to be strong. To not give up. To let me know he'd do the same."

"Yes. He had to hate not being able to be at your back. He probably knew what was going to happen to him and Black. He wasn't stupid, Pen. He did what he could to let you know he loved you and admired you, and to give you words that he hoped would give you strength no matter what happened next."

Penelope's eyes filled with tears, and Moose hated it. Hated to see her so vulnerable and sad. "I miss him," she whispered. "I wish he could've met you and all the other guys. You would've loved him."

"I might not have met him, but I love him all the same," Moose replied. "He did his best to protect you. To give you what you needed to make it through all those months of captivity. I love him because he respected you and because he was your friend."

And with that, Penelope deflated as if she were a balloon that had been pricked with a needle. Moose caught her and Smokey nuzzled her leg in concern.

Moose stood up with Penelope in his arms and

carried her over to their benches. He could've left, but he thought Penelope needed to stay. She'd fought alone for far too long. He'd let her cry for now, but then she'd dry her eyes, watch the game for a while, and if he could convince her, she'd go back out onto the field and smile and laugh with her friends. They needed to see her do that, as much as she needed to do it.

He didn't like that she'd had a flashback, but she'd woken up and seen the love and support each and every one of her friends had for her. Things would be different from here on out. They had to be.

CHAPTER ELEVEN

In the truck on the way home from the game, Penelope felt surprisingly good for having a flashback in front of literally all of her friends and coming back to herself with them staring at her. But with Moose's help, she came to the realization that her friends didn't see her any differently now than they had before she'd flaked out on them.

She let Moose convince her to go back into the game, and while she'd planned on using her cop friends' sympathy against them, she'd underestimated them. Not once did any of them treat her like some delicate flower. They still talked smack. They still had no problem hauling her over their shoulders to physically prevent her from getting to the ball, and she loved them for it even more.

That's what she needed. To be treated normally.

She'd sat with the women for a bit toward the end of the game. She and Hayden had bowed out when the score was seventy-four to fifty-three in favor of the police officers. The guys had gotten a little rougher, and she and Hayden were more than willing to call it quits.

Penelope had felt her friends' hands on her. Not once did she think they were the terrorists. Somehow she'd simply known they were there. That they would stand by her no matter what happened.

It sounded crazy, but having that flashback when and where she did had done her a world of good.

Looking over at Moose, she realized that she felt different. More settled inside. She wasn't exactly ready to tell the chief that she wanted to come back to work, but for the first time, she was entertaining the thought.

"I like that," Moose said out of the blue.

"What?" she asked.

"The smile on your face. I haven't seen it a whole heck of a lot since you've been back, and I like it."

"Me too," Penelope admitted. "I need to thank you."

"No, you don't," he said immediately.

"You don't even know what I need to thank you for," she protested a little huffily.

"Doesn't matter, but you're still wrong. You don't ever have to thank me for anything. I'd do anything for you, Pen, gladly."

His words made her feel all gooey inside, but she was done being a taker and not giving in return. She kept quiet until Moose had parked the truck inside his garage and they'd entered the house. Moose went and let Smokey out into the backyard so he could roll around and eat some grass for a while.

When Moose closed the door and turned back to her, Penelope said, "You agreed we could talk later. It's later."

Sighing, Moose nodded. He walked over to the couch and sat on one end. Glad he didn't pick the armchair, Penelope sat on the other end of the couch and turned so one leg was hitched up on the cushion and she was facing him.

"You were right," she said without beating around the bush. "I've been wallowing in my own head and not paying attention to what's going on around me. I've been a shitty friend and an even worse housemate. I'm going to try to do better. But...I still don't think I can talk to you about what's going on in my head."

Moose frowned. "Why not?" he asked. "You know I won't judge you. The last thing I'd ever do was something to make you feel bad."

"I *do* know that," Penelope said. "But I need to separate what I feel for you from what happened to me. I don't want you to be my therapist. I need you to be my supporter. My rock. And if you're constantly worried about what I'm thinking and whether I'm relapsing or what the best thing to say to me is, I'm not sure you can be the man I need you to be."

She hadn't thought much about her words before

she'd said them, but seeing the look of gratitude and love on Moose's face confirmed she'd said the right thing.

"I'll never stop worrying about you, sweetheart. Nothing you can say or do will change that. But I understand what you're saying. A professional therapist can help you better than I could in that sense anyway. But you have to know I'll always be here for you. You don't have to say a word, I'll just hold you if that's what you need. I won't hold back to tell you when you're being unreasonable though, I hope you can handle that."

"I can," Penelope reassured him. "It wasn't easy hearing what you had to say this morning, but I needed that. You're right, I've had my head up my ass, and I feel terrible about it."

Moose scooted closer to her then reached out and palmed her cheek. His hand was calloused and felt amazingly good against her face. She leaned into it, and he took the weight of her head. "It's done. We're moving on."

Relief swept through her. If she was being honest, she was sick of her own angst. This wasn't like her. She'd much prefer to be the happy-go-lucky woman she'd been once upon a time. Before ISIS had tried to take it from her. Well, fuck them.

"What was that thought?" Moose asked, his brown eyes piercing in their intensity.

"If you must know, I was cursing ISIS and telling them to go to hell."

He smiled. "Good."

"Moose?"

"Yeah, Pen?"

"Are you really okay? I don't like the thought of you being in pain or that you had to go to the hospital."

"I'm okay. Promise. And you being here, safe, where I can simply turn my head to prove to myself that you're alive and well, has done wonders for my health." He dropped his hand, but didn't move away from her. He reached out and took one of her hands in his and held it.

"Good. And for the record, I wouldn't be staying with you, sleeping in your bed, if I didn't like you."

"I know."

"I feel bad though, for not...you know...putting out."

Moose immediately shook his head. "Don't. Contrary to what Pornhub might want women to think, men don't need to have sex every minute of the day. I'm perfectly happy holding you in my arms every night. In fact, I want you to promise right here and now that you won't let me make love with you until you think you can love me back. You know I love you, but I don't think you realize how much.

"When you were missing in Turkey, I was as concerned as everyone else, but that was kinda my big moment of clarity. The thought of those bastards hurting you, of terrorizing you, made me realize how much I loved you. Not as a sister, friend, or fellow firefighter. But as a man loves a woman. I wanted to tell you right when you got back, but you didn't need that. You were trying to acclimate back to your life. It killed me to see you struggling so hard. Then when you took off, the same feeling of terror hit me again, but this time because I thought you might *never* come back. Or that you'd fall prey to some asshole right here in our own country. When you came home, and said you'd stay here with me in my house, I felt like I could finally take a deep breath again.

"Things won't be easy. As you so nicely pointed out this morning, I'm not exactly the easiest person to live with. I'm almost forty and have been a bachelor for my entire adult life. I've never lived with a woman. I'll try to clean up my act and turn off lights and remember to make sure the clothes in the dryer are all the way dry, but I'm gonna fuck up, Pen. I'm never going to be a neat freak. That's just not who I am. As much as I might want to be that person for you, it's not going to happen."

Penelope wanted to laugh at the way Moose was blurting out every little thought in his head, but she felt bad that she'd made him so self-conscious about shit that just didn't matter.

"It's fine, Moose. I didn't mean all that stuff this morning. I mean, it's true that they're annoyances, but if that's the worst thing that happens between us, that I get pissed because you left a light on, I think we're doing pretty good. I'm not exactly perfect myself."

He resisted the opportunity she'd given him to list all of her faults, and instead he leaned forward and got into her personal space. Neither of them smelled all that great after being out in the sun and running around all day, but she didn't care. This was Moose.

"I'm serious, Pen. I'll hold you tight every night, for as long as you let me. I'm not saying I don't want more, because I want it all with you, but what I *don't* want is you giving me a pity fuck or some such bullshit. If you can't love me, I won't lie, it'll hurt. A lot. But what would hurt more is you letting me between your legs if you aren't intending to make this thing between us permanent. Don't give me a slice of heaven then take it away. That would be cruel, and one thing you aren't, is cruel."

Penelope shook her head. "I wouldn't do that to you, Moose."

"That's all I'm asking. But in the meantime, I'm gonna do my best to convince you that I'm the man for you."

"I'm not sure it'll take much convincing," Penelope admitted. She couldn't imagine her life without Moose in it. She loved how she felt lying in his arms at night. Safe. Cared for. But was that a result of what happened to her, and just being comfortable with Moose, or was it more? She wasn't sure, and that was why she couldn't tell him she loved him yet. She wanted to be sure.

"What if you decide that you were wrong?" she asked softly. "This isn't all one-sided. I'm not exactly a peach to be around all the time. I'm too quick to judge, apparently selfish, and I obviously have a lot of baggage. It's a lot, Moose, and the last thing I'd want is for you to settle. You might decide that you can't deal, or don't want to deal, with someone as fucked up as me."

Moose let go of her hand and cupped her face. He leaned in and kissed her forehead, then the tip of her nose. He pulled back far enough to look deeply into her eyes. She brought her hands up to curl around his wrists. "That's not going to happen."

"You don't know that," she persisted. "If you make me love you, then decide I'm not what you want anymore, I'm not sure how I'll deal with that."

"If you fall in love with me, I'm not *ever* going to let you go," Moose said, and it sounded like a vow. Penelope's stomach churned, and she felt all tingly. "I'm not an idiot. As I said before, I'm almost forty, Pen. Old enough to know exactly what I want. And that's you. So if you ever tell me you love me, that's it. We're getting married and you'll be mine, just as I'll be yours. Period."

"I don't want to let you down," she admitted.

"Impossible," he declared.

Penelope chuckled and rolled her eyes. "I wish I could be as sure about myself as you always seem to be about *yourself*," she said.

"Sure of myself?" he asked. "Sweetheart, I'm anything but. I'm shaking in my boots here. You scare the shit out of me because you're the one thing that can bring me to my knees. You're holding all the cards. You know I love you and that I want to marry you. While I could manipulate and seduce you to try to get you to love me back, that's not what I want. Your free will was taken away from you for months over in Turkey, and the last thing I'd ever do is coerce you into something you really don't want. I'm not sure of *anything* when it comes to you, or a relationship between the two of us. All I'm sure of is that I don't want to fuck this up."

"You aren't fucking anything up," she told him. Then added, "So far."

That broke the tension, and they both chuckled.

Moose kissed her once more on the forehead and pulled back. "Hungry?"

"Yeah."

"We can make something or order from one of those apps that delivers from any restaurant you want."

"Can we order from that popular steakhouse you like so much?"

Moose's eyes lit up. "Hell yeah, we can. Your app or mine?" he asked.

And that was one more thing Penelope liked about Moose. He didn't insist on paying for everything simply because he was the man. She had a feeling if things worked out between them, that might change, but for now, it felt good to be able to buy him dinner every now and then.

"Mine," she told him.

"Then get ordering, woman," he said. "I'm hungry."

She ordered their food, they both showered, and then they ate their dinner when it arrived while watching a documentary on TV. Instead of heading up to bed at eight-thirty, as she'd been doing, Penelope stayed downstairs and she and Moose continued to talk.

About his health and what the doctors said, about her parents and how they were doing, about *his* parents, about Smokey and how everyone had loved him on her road trip. They even touched on Taco and Koren, and what had happened that fateful night.

By the time they headed up to Moose's bedroom together around eleven, Penelope was feeling mellow and not at all anxious about what was to come. She used the bathroom first and changed while it was Moose's turn. She was waiting in bed when he came out. She watched as he stripped off his T-shirt and jeans. Wearing only his boxers, he crawled into bed next to her, and Penelope didn't hesitate to scoot closer to rest her cheek on his shoulder.

His arm came around her, and Penelope sighed in contentment. She still wasn't sure this was fair to him, wasn't sure what exactly she was doing, but she couldn't deny that the only time she truly relaxed was at night, when she was snuggled up to Moose just like this.

"Moose?"

"Yeah?"

"I like this."

"Me too, sweetheart. Me too."

Nothing more was said, and for once, he fell asleep before she did.

As she lay next to him, listening to his deep inhalations, Penelope couldn't help but think about how much she loved Moose. It scared her, but it also felt right. She wasn't ready to do more than what she was doing right now, sleeping in his arms, but the thought of Moose making love to her, of declaring her his and hauling her down to the courthouse to make it official, was far from unappealing.

Smiling at the thought, Penelope closed her eyes. And instead of dreaming about White's and Black's heads being chopped from their bodies as she did nothing but stand and watch, she dreamed she was standing in the middle of that refugee camp. As she stood there, legs trembling and waiting for the mob of men around her to close in and beat the shit out of her, as they'd done in real life and in past dreams…one by one, they began to disappear.

She caught one of the terrorists looking behind her in panic before evaporating in a puff of smoke.

Taking a chance, Penelope glanced over her shoulder—and was amazed at what she saw.

Her friends were all there. Standing with their arms crossed over their chests, frowning and looking as fierce as could be. They weren't holding any weapons, except for Hayden, who had a baseball bat over her shoulder. Hell, even the women who'd recently given birth were there, holding their children, and *they* looked as if they would scream bloody murder on cue if that would make the bad guys back off.

And of course, Moose was standing closest. When he saw her looking at him, he stepped forward and put a hand on her shoulder. No one said a word, but they didn't have to. Their presence spoke volumes.

By the time Penelope turned back around to face the mob of terrorists who wanted to use her for their own nefarious reasons, they were gone, and instead of being in the refugee camp, she was standing in the middle of her brother's backyard. Cade and Beth were standing in front of a judge, and now it was her standing behind *them*, supporting them and having their backs as they pledged their lives to each other.

But she still felt a hand on her shoulder. Moose was still there. Still being a silent supporter.

He leaned forward, kissed her shoulder and whispered, "I love you."

When Penelope opened her eyes, she saw it was morning. Moose was bending over her on the bed, and she knew without a doubt that he'd just kissed her like he had in her dream, and had once more told her how much he loved her.

"I'm headed to the station," he whispered. "Stay and sleep some more. I'll call later, okay?"

"M'kay," she mumbled sleepily, still lost in the feelings of peace and comfort she'd experienced from her dream. She felt Moose's lips once more brush against her forehead, and then she knew no more until she woke up hours later, feeling refreshed and revitalized.

CHAPTER TWELVE

It was time.

Moose had made all the arrangements, and it was now or never. Four days had passed since the softball game where Penelope had had her flashback. Two days after the game, she'd called the therapist from Killeen and had talked to her for an hour over the phone, and when she'd come out of his home office, she'd seemed better. Lighter.

In fact, every day, she'd seemed a little bit more like her old self. She hadn't talked about coming back to work at the station, though Moose hoped that would come in time.

But today was the day he'd been planning for, and he hoped what he'd done wouldn't make Pen revert back to the broken woman she'd been for months.

"What are your plans today?" she asked over breakfast.

Smokey lay at her feet, hoping for some scraps, which Moose knew without a doubt he'd get because Penelope was a pushover when it came to her donkey. He knew she fed the little bugger from her plate, and that she thought she was being sneaky, but the slurps and chewing from the animal gave them both away every time. But he pretended he didn't see or hear anything, just as she pretended she wasn't feeding her pet from the table.

"I thought we'd take a road trip," Moose said as nonchalantly as he could.

"Where to?" Penelope asked.

"Mississippi."

The woman he loved and wanted to heal more than anything stared at him in shock.

"Mississippi? What's in Mississippi?"

"Not what. Who. Makayla White."

Penelope put down her fork and stared at him without saying a word.

Feeling nervous, Moose started babbling. "I know, I know, this is a surprise, but she really wants to meet you, sweetheart. I've talked to her a few times on the phone. I got Beth to help me track her down and get her number. I guess White wrote to her about you, and she followed your story on the news. She told me she prayed every night that you'd be saved, and that she cried the day she heard you'd been rescued. I thought maybe you could get some closure if you went and talked to her. I think it'll be good. I wouldn't have arranged it if I didn't. And... You're staring at me. Say something, Pen."

"I... What if she hates me? If she blames me for her son's death?"

Moose got out of his chair and went over to kneel next to Penelope. "She doesn't hate you. She flat-out told me that on the phone. She doesn't blame you for White's death, she blames the terrorists who killed him. Besides, there's no way I would take you to see her if I thought for one second that she'd say something to hurt you more than you're already hurting."

"I don't know, Moose," Penelope said, the worry easy to see in her eyes and on her face.

"If shit goes south, I'm gonna get you out of there. Trust me, Pen. I'd never do *anything* to hurt you. To jeopardize the progress you've made. I even talked to your therapist, and she said she thought this could be a good thing for you."

"I do trust you," she said shakily.

"So you'll do it?"

"How long are we going to be gone?"

"Well, she lives in Biloxi, and it takes about nine hours to drive there. That's kind of a long way to go in one day, so I thought we'd take our time and stop in Beaumont the first night. So two days to get there, two to get back, one day to meet Makayla, and another day to spend at the beach or the casinos, whatever you want to do. So around a week, give or take."

"The chief gave you a week off?"

Moose smiled. "His exact words were, 'If giving you a week off to help get Turner's head on straight gets her ass back to the station sooner rather than later, you've got it.'"

"I still can't believe he didn't file my resignation," Penelope said, obviously stalling, processing what he wanted her to do.

Moose didn't try to convince her anymore. He simply kneeled by her chair and waited for her decision.

"What about Smokey?" she asked.

"What about him?"

"What will we do with him?"

"He'll go with us, of course," Moose told her with a slight frown. "I'm not sure either of you would be too happy if I left him behind for a whole week. Besides, Makayla is excited to meet him. The motel in Beaumont said he was allowed to stay as long as he was housebroken. And I rented us a yurt thing on the beach in Biloxi, so it's okay for him to be there too."

Penelope closed her eyes and reached for him. Moose grabbed her hand and squeezed as he held his breath to see what her decision would be.

"Okay, let's do this," she said in a rush, her eyes popping open to stare down into his. "I mean, why not? The worst she can do is yell at me and tell me I killed her only son, right? That's nothing that I haven't already thought myself."

Moose frowned. "Penelope—"

"I know, I know. I don't really think that anymore, especially after remembering what happened. But deep down, I think a part of me will always wonder what else I could've done. If something would've changed the ultimate outcome."

"She's not going to blame you for anything, and I'm hoping you'll feel a bit of relief after seeing her." Moose stood. "You done? You need to pack and we need to hit the road."

Penelope pushed back her chair and turned to him, wrapping her arms around his waist and tilting her head back so she could look at him. "You were so sure I'd say yes, you already made the reservations for where we're going to stay?" she asked.

Moose immediately nodded. "Yup."

She shook her head in exasperation. "That's kinda annoying, just so you know."

He chuckled. "I know. Now, get a move on. My bag is already packed and sitting in the closet. I'll wash the dishes and let Smokey out one more time while you pack your stuff. This is gonna be fun!" He hoped his enthusiasm leaked into her. The last thing he wanted was for Penelope to dread the trip. Yeah, it was natural for her to have some misgivings, but he'd talked to Makayla several times, and he knew beyond a shadow of a doubt that Penelope had nothing to worry about.

Before too long, they were on the road.

The drive the first day was fun. Penelope told him more stories about traveling with Smokey, and they stopped often to give him plenty of potty breaks. Every time they stopped, children would approach, wide-eyed and curious about the donkey.

Penelope had been great with them. She patiently explained how Smokey came to live with her and somehow managed to get across a "fire is no joke" message in a way that was *real*. With Smokey as a live example of how fire could be destructive, there was no doubt.

Watching Penelope and Smokey with the children gave him an idea as to what she might be able to do while she was debating being a firefighter again. Maybe she could travel around to schools on behalf of Station 7 and give fire safety talks. She was a natural with the kids, and of course Smokey would be a huge draw. Moose decided to talk to her about it later, after their visit with White's mother was out of the way.

But the next day, things weren't as easygoing. The closer they got to Biloxi, the more tense Penelope became. Moose knew she was worried, and he'd told her a thousand times she had nothing to be nervous about, but it didn't seem to reassure her.

By the time he pulled into Makayla's driveway a day after they'd left San Antonio, Penelope was a mess.

"Do you want to back out?" he asked after turning off the truck.

She looked over at him. "But we've come all this way."

"Don't care," he said with a shake of his head. He

reached over and took her hand in his and intertwined their fingers. "If you really don't want to do this, or can't right now, we'll go."

"I'm sure she's expecting us," Penelope said, glancing at the small but well maintained house. All the houses in the neighborhood looked similar. Brick construction, boxy, tiny.

"I'll call and explain when we get to the yurt," Moose reassured her. "This visit is supposed to make you feel *better*, not worse. But if you really can't do it, then we won't. We'll just spend some time on the beach instead."

Moose had always thought Penelope was one of the bravest people he'd met, and his opinion wouldn't change if she decided she couldn't meet White's mother.

She took a deep breath. "No. We're here. It's the least I can do. White always said such great things about his mom. Said she was funny, and that he gave her hell growing up and he always regretted it. They had a deep bond that was easy to see. Did you know they wrote actual letters back and forth?"

Moose nodded his head and let Penelope talk. He knew it was her way of trying to psyche herself up to step out of the vehicle and actually meet Makayla.

"Late at night, White would sit with his legs crossed, hunched over a notebook, and he'd write long letters to her. I'm not sure how often they got mailed, because most people used email to communicate with their loved ones, and not many mail runs were being done. Many times, he'd get two or three letters from her at a time because they'd get caught up in the postal system somewhere. He loved getting those letters. He always pretended his mom was a pain in his ass for insisting they actually write to each other instead of emailing, but I know deep down, he loved seeing her handwriting and reading her words the old fashioned way."

"Did Sledge ever write you a letter?"

Penelope snorted. "As if. No. But then again, I was too impatient for that. I wanted to know everything that was going on back home and what I was missing at the fire station. I bitched at him that he didn't message me enough. He accused me of being a nag."

Moose chuckled. "That sounds about right. What did you miss most?"

She thought about her answer for a while, then said, "I'm probably supposed to say something like, Whataburger hamburgers or puffy tacos from Henry's, but honestly, I missed sitting around Station 7 and shooting the shit with you guys."

Moose's heart almost broke for her.

"When I got emails from Cade, I could so easily imagine all of you kicking ass at a fire. Or working together to extract a vic from a car. I missed bitching about whose turn it was to wash dishes and complaining about the food, even though there nothing to complain about. I loved being a soldier and serving my country, but late at night, when I thought about the hatred we were seeing, both aimed toward us and toward the refugees who just wanted a crust of bread to eat and a place to sleep without having to worry about being murdered in their beds, I missed you guys terribly. White and Black did a lot to alleviate that. They reminded me of my friends back home."

"We missed you too," Moose said softly. "Things didn't feel the same after you left." He wasn't sure if he was talking about when she went overseas to do her tour with the National Guard, or her most recent disappearance. They missed her either way. It was almost harder the second time...knowing that she might never recover enough to come back.

Penelope took a deep breath. "Okay, let's do this," she said firmly.

Feeling proud of her, Moose lifted her hand to his mouth, kissed the palm, then nodded. "We'll leave Smokey here for now. Makayla seemed excited to meet him, but showing up on her doorstep with a donkey might not be the best thing right off the bat."

"Agreed," Penelope said.

After rolling down the windows to make sure there was enough air circulating in the truck and the donkey wouldn't get overheated, Moose climbed out his side of the vehicle and Penelope met him around the front.

He immediately grabbed her hand again and they headed for the front door. As they were walking up the short set of stairs to the porch, the door opened and a dark-skinned black woman stood there. "I thought you two were never gonna get out of that truck!"

Penelope swallowed hard. She almost turned around and bolted, but Moose's firm grip on her hand prevented her from doing just that. So she mentally pulled up her bootstraps and did her best to smile at White's mom.

"Hi. I'm Penelope."

"I know you are, girl. I saw all the news shows about you."

Penelope couldn't read her tone, and for just a second, she panicked. God, the woman hated her. She was going to lambast her for allowing her son to die. She just knew it.

But instead, Makayla White took a step forward and engulfed Penelope in a hug. She was taller than Penelope by several inches and outweighed her by at least a hundred pounds.

Penelope stood there in shock for a second, but then she slowly returned the embrace.

The second Makayla felt Penelope's arms go around her, she lost it.

Feeling and hearing White's mom crying made Penelope's own eyes tear up. The next thing she knew, they were both bawling together. Neither said a word, but they didn't need to.

Penelope had no idea why she'd dreaded this meeting. She was so glad Moose had come straight to the house when they got into town, rather than dragging things out and coming the next morning. She'd been kind of upset with him about surprising her with this trip, but standing in Makayla White's arms made all her fears and concerns disappear in a puff of smoke.

After several moments, Makayla pulled back and stared down at Penelope. Her eyes were rimmed with red and the streaks from her tears underscored her sadness. The older woman made a half-hearted attempt at wiping her cheeks and gave Penelope a small smile.

After wiping her own face, Penelope returned the grin. "Hi," she said.

Makayla chuckled. "Hey. Thanks for comin'. I never thought I'd get this chance. When your man here called me, at first I thought it was some kind of joke. Why would the American Princess come see *me*? You got more important things to do with your life than saunter down here to Biloxi to chat with an old woman."

"First of all, please call me Penelope. I swear if I hear that stupid moniker 'American Princess' once more time, I'm gonna scream. Second, I'm sorry I haven't come sooner. Your son was amazing. I'm just s-sorry he didn't make it home." Penelope was proud of herself for only stuttering once.

"Come on," Makayla said, and Penelope saw tears had once more filled her eyes. She had a feeling they'd both be crying on and off all afternoon. "I made all Henry's favorite foods for your visit. I figured it was only fittin'."

"Let me guess," Penelope said, "blue crab, fried chicken, collard greens, corn bread, po'boys dipped in comeback sauce, and Mississippi mud pie."

Makayla threw her head back and laughed. "My boy always loved his food."

"And he loved to *talk* about food. Day and night. He'd never shut up about it, which especially sucked when we were eating MREs," Penelope reminisced with a chuckle.

They entered the small house, and Penelope looked back at Moose. She almost laughed at the way he ducked when he came through the front door. He caught her staring and gave her a small, tender smile of encouragement.

Penelope had no idea what she'd do without him.

The thought stopped her in her tracks. From the time she got back from overseas, he'd been there for her. At first he was like an annoying big brother who browbeat her and nagged her to death. He made her eat lots of vegetables and protein to get her strength and muscles back. He was always by her side at calls, encouraging and watching over her, but not being overbearing or obnoxious about it. When she'd stopped thinking about him as a brother, and started having romantic feelings for him, she wasn't exactly sure.

They'd kinda snuck up on her. But she'd fought them because she didn't think she deserved someone as amazing as him. And she was still dealing with all the shit in her head.

And when she'd stood in the doorway of Koren's burning condo, she knew that if she fucked up, she could get *Moose* killed.

She hadn't trusted herself, and she hadn't trusted the men who'd always had her back. She'd been paralyzed with fear. For herself and for Moose. And she'd bolted.

But who had she called when she was on the road? Her parents? Her brother?

No. Moose.

"Pen?" Moose asked. She'd obviously been standing there staring at him for too long.

"Sorry, I'm good," she told him.

Makayla patted her arm. "I do that all the time, child. All the time. You just take your time and come on in when you're ready." Then she turned and headed for the kitchen.

Penelope was touched by how understanding the woman was. It wasn't exactly a surprise, as White had been almost as observant.

"You sure you're okay?" Moose asked.

"I'm sure. Have I told you thank you yet?"

He raised a brow. "For what?"

"For everything. For making me all those grilled chicken meals when I got back from Turkey. For forcing me to try harder in training when all I wanted to do was sit on my ass. For being there for me and Smokey. For letting him use your barn. For rebuilding your barn for him. For letting me talk to you while I was gallivanting around the country. For taking me to see the hypnotist. For letting me stay at your house. For arranging this visit. For always being there for me... There's so much I should've thanked you for, Moose, and I haven't. I've been so selfish and stuck in my own head, and I'm so sorry—"

"Shhhh," he said, putting his finger over her lips. "You don't have to thank me for any of that. I did it because I wanted to. So I guess you could say *I* was the selfish one."

Penelope reached up to grab his wrist. She turned his hand upside down and it was *her* kissing *his* palm this time. She saw his pupils dilate, but he didn't say or do anything. He just stood there patiently, letting her set the pace.

How in the world she'd somehow managed to catch this man's eye, she had no idea. But she clearly saw the love in his entire expression.

"I don't deserve you," she said quietly. "All I've done is take take take."

"You've given me more than you'll ever know," Moose told her.

She wanted to tell him right then and there that she loved him, but something held her back. A little part of her that said it couldn't last. That he'd figure out sooner or later she was the reason why so many people had died, even if indirectly. That she'd let him down and he'd leave.

As if he could read her mind, Moose said, "Stop thinking so hard, sweetheart. White's mom is waiting for you, and she apparently wants to fatten us up, if all the delicious smells are any indication."

She chuckled. "Thanks again for being here with me."

"Nowhere else I'd rather be," he said, then he put his hands on her shoulders and physically turned her toward where Makayla had disappeared. "Let's go eat."

Two hours later, after an amazing lunch and lots of laughter, Penelope sat on a love seat with Moose at her side. Smokey lay at her feet, snoring obnoxiously. They'd brought him in after lunch and Makayla had insisted on feeding him after making a fuss over how adorable he was. Makayla was currently sitting in a well-worn and comfortable-looking chair to their right.

They'd been talking about what White was like as a little boy, and how he'd decided to join the National Guard.

"He was a punk," Makayla said. "His friends were all little punks too. He'd managed to graduate from high school, but didn't have no job and wasn't even looking for one. He hung out with them all day and half the night. I know he was smokin' pot, and I also knew if things continued the way they were, I was gonna lose him. Pot could turn to some other, harder drug, and their petty little crimes and harassment of women walkin' by the house would turn into somethin' more. Somethin' I knew my Henry wouldn't be able to live with, no matter how tough he tried to appear."

"What'd you do?" Penelope asked, settling back more comfortably against the cushions...and Moose. The love seat wasn't huge, and Moose wasn't a small man. So her thigh was pressed up against his, and it felt only natural for him to put his arm around her shoulders and pull her into him.

"I left for a week and didn't tell him where I was going or when I'd be back."

Penelope stared at her in confusion. "I'm not sure I understand why or how that would straighten him out?"

"See, my Henry was a mama's boy. No," she said, when Penelope opened her mouth to defend her son. "He was. And that's okay. I'd done everythin' for him since he was a baby. His father didn't stick around when he heard that he'd knocked me up. So it was always me and Henry. I cooked for him. I did his laundry. I cleaned up after him. I helped him with his homework. He loved me and I loved him. But I couldn't deal with the man he was becomin'. So I left him completely on his own. And it did what I wanted it to. When I came home, he was pissed at me because he'd been worried, because I hadn't told him where I was goin'. He'd had to make his own meals. His favorite clothes were dirty, and he didn't have anythin' he wanted to wear." Makayla laughed. "It sounds stupid, he was a grown man at nineteen, but I hadn't done what I should've done—teach him what he needed to know to get by on his own in this world.

"Somethin' changed in him that day. He wanted to learn how to cook. He wanted me to show him how to get stains out of his clothes. I think me disappearin' like that made him understand for the first time how precious life can be. How we can be here one day, gone the next. We talked more after that. About stuff that mattered. About how whistlin' at a pretty girl walkin' by can be hurtful and demeanin'. How smokin' pot wasn't gonna get him anywhere in this world but into trouble. He wanted to change, but wasn't sure how. I took him down to the recruitment center and he joined the National Guard that very day."

"Why didn't he go into the regular Army?" Moose asked.

Makayla closed her eyes for a brief moment, and when she opened them, the tears were back. "He said that doin' the part-time thing would keep him closer to home and would be safer in the long run. He knew there was a chance he could be deployed, but that it was lower than if he joined up for the full-time gig.

And he loved his mama, and couldn't bear to be away from me for years at a time."

Penelope sat forward and reached over to put her hand on Makayla's knee. "He loved you *so* much. And you're right that he was a mama's boy, and there's nothing wrong with that. He talked about you all the time. About how much he admired you and how you taught him what it meant to be a man."

Makayla smiled and Penelope sat back. She felt Moose's hand curl around the back of her neck and his thumb caressed her skin. It felt nice. Soothing.

"My Henry wasn't a man to hold back his thoughts. He said what he meant, it's one of the many things I loved and admired about him." Makayla leaned over to the cluttered table sitting next to her chair and lifted a rectangular box. She put it in her lap and opened it, pulling out a stack of letters.

Penelope sucked in a deep breath. She recognized those letters and the handwriting on the front. How could she not? White was constantly writing his mother.

"I see you know what these are," Makayla said.

Penelope could only nod.

"They're one of my most prized possessions. I swear sometimes I can almost smell him on the paper."

Penelope couldn't help but laugh at that. Personal hygiene was tough over in Turkey in the camps. Too little running water and not enough time to thoroughly clean yourself when you were allowed to shower. They made do by using washcloths and a bucket of water most of the time.

Makayla's lips twitched as if she knew what Penelope was thinking, but she went on. "Seein' his handwritin', knowin' how long we worked on his cursive to make it legible, knowin' he took the time out of his day to write these for me is somethin' I'll treasure forever. If all I had was words on a computer screen, it wouldn't mean nearly as much."

Penelope agreed with her one hundred percent. She regretted not writing her own parents real letters. If she hadn't made it out of the desert, all they'd have is the short emails she'd sent them every now and then.

She mentally vowed to sit down that evening and handwrite a letter to her parents, letting them know how much she loved them and how thankful she was for them.

"I'm glad you have them," Penelope told Makayla.

She nodded. "There's one letter in particular I wanted to share with you."

Penelope shook her head. She wasn't sure she could handle hearing White's voice as if from the grave. She'd teased him about the letter writing, but he'd never shared what he'd written to his mom, and she hadn't asked. His thoughts were personal, and it felt almost sacrilegious for his mom to be sharing them with her.

"I don't think—"

"You need to see this," Makayla said firmly, interrupting her protest.

Penelope nodded woodenly. If White's mom needed to share it, she'd listen, but she wasn't necessarily happy about it.

Moose's hand tightened around her nape, as if reminding her she wasn't alone. That he was right there next to her. She needed that reminder. Her left hand slowly slid over and wrapped around the side of Moose's leg, right above his knee. It was an intimate touch, but she needed to ground herself. His free hand covered her own on his leg.

Makayla's gaze didn't miss anything, and she waited until Penelope was somewhat settled before ever so carefully opening one of the envelopes and unfolding the piece of paper inside.

Even seeing the white-lined paper made Penelope's heart hurt. She could clearly picture White's hand moving over the paper as he faithfully and precisely wrote to his mother.

Makayla leaned over and held out the precious piece of paper to Penelope.

She reluctantly took it, afraid to even breathe on it for fear of somehow messing it up. She'd never forgive herself if she ruined this beautiful piece of memorabilia.

Seeing White's handwriting made Penelope's heart hurt anew, but she pushed back her pain and began to read, aware that Moose was reading over her shoulder.

. . .

Mama,

Today's another day in the desert. Much like the ones that came before it. Except not. Tensions are rising in the camp and instead of smiles and waves when we patrol, people scurry out of our way and disappear into tents or into the blowing sand that's all around us. Rumor has it that there have been threats against us, "us" meaning all the international troops that are here to keep peace and to try to help with the food and water supply. Of course, no one knows where the threats are coming from, or from who specifically, so all we can do is keep patrolling and hope things stay calm.

But that's not what I wanted to talk to you about today. I've told you about the food situation here and how horrible it is, and about the weather, but I haven't told you about the people I work with. When I first got here, I wasn't happy that our National Guard company would be intermeshed with other companies and platoons from across the country. We were all thrown in together with soldiers we'd never worked with before, and it pissed me off.

But I lucked out. Big time. I was assigned to a four-person patrolling squad. There's me, a guy from Maine named Black, another guy named Wilson, and a chick from Texas named Turner.

At first, I was so annoyed. Black is as white as they come. As black as my skin is, that's how white his skin is. He has red hair and freckles from his head to his toes, and his skin is so pale it glows. He looks like that Opie character from that old show you like so much. He gets sunburned when he's out in the sun for five minutes.

But it was the woman I was most worried about. I know, I know, I can hear your lecture now, Mama. I should respect women. But out here, things are different. I have to be able to rely on these people to have my back if the worst should happen. And how can I rely on a short little runt of a woman who weighs less than the rifle and gear we have to carry?

You know what, though? That little runt of a woman surprised me. Not only that, but she has no problem carrying her gear. Or holding her own. She's proven time and time again that she's a great soldier...and a good woman. This isn't a combat situation, but I have no doubt that if the shit ever hits the fan, she'll be right there at my side, fighting like hell.

Back home in Texas, she's a firefighter. I know, I was shocked too. But, Mama, I bet she's the best firefighter in her station. She's smart as all get out and pays attention. She knows what's going on around her before I even have an inkling that something might be wrong. She's earned my respect a hundred times over, and I hope at some point, when we all get to go home, that you might be able to meet her someday.

I don't like her like that, so stop thinking about grandbabies. She's just impressed the hell out of me. When we go out and patrol the camp, I have no doubts about her abilities. She's in charge of our little squad, and I'm happy to let her do it. Once, when we got a day off from patrolling, the captain of our company arranged for us to do some hand-to-hand sparring. The same kind of thing we did in basic training. Well, there was this cocky older first sergeant who was sparring in the bout right before Turner's. After he won his match, he looked over at her, gave her a mocking chin lift, then said to the guy he'd just beaten, loud enough for everyone to hear, "You fight like a girl." He was trying to embarrass them both.

Well, Turner lifted her own chin and marched into the circle like she didn't have a care in the world. Mama, I wish you could've seen it. She took down this guy, who was six inches taller than her and at least eighty pounds heavier, in two minutes flat! When the sergeant was on the ground, she stood over him and said calmly, "That's how you fight like a girl." Then she turned her back on him and walked away.

Ever since then, we've used that mantra, "Fight like a girl," to mean fight like a mother-fuckin' badass (sorry about the language, but in this case it's totally warranted), because that's exactly what Turner is.

If something happens to me over here, you have to know it was something that went bad in all the ways something could go bad. Because I have no doubt, if there's a way to get out of it alive, Turner will find it. I know she'll do whatever it takes, including giving up her own life, to make sure me, Black, and Wilson make it out in one piece. I have that much respect and trust in her abilities as our squad leader.

I hope the weather there has cooled off a little bit. If the air conditioner continues to go out, let me know and I'll wire you some money to get a new window unit. It's not good for you to be in that little house sweltering in the heat. In fact,

I'm gonna do it anyway, whether you think you need it or not. I know you, Mama, you'll sit there and not complain until you're just a pile of sweat with eyes.

I love you, Mama. It seems as if the letters are getting here slower and slower, but don't stop writing. The highlights of my time here are mail call and when I get to hear from you.

Love, Henry.

Penelope could barely read by the time she got to the end of the letter because of the tears in her eyes. She held the paper away from her so she wouldn't cry on it and had no idea what in the world to say.

She'd known White respected her, he'd told her, but she'd had no idea exactly how much. She figured it was because she was a sergeant and he wasn't, but it had obviously been more than that. She'd respected the hell out of Henry White right back. He'd done what had to be done, without complaint, and there was a lot to complain about in the middle of that godforsaken desert. The heat, KP duty, patrol, cleaning up their tent...whatever it was, he did it. She respected him and knew she'd taken his support for granted.

Makayla leaned over and took the letter. She lovingly folded it back up, put it in the envelope, put it back in the stack in the box, and placed the box on the table next to her. "So now you see why I was so happy to meet you. My boy talked so highly about you. And believe you me, he didn't talk like that about many people. I don't know what happened that day, and I don't *want* to know. All the Army folks would tell me was that he was on patrol when he was overpowered and taken."

Her voice faltered then, and Penelope wished there was something she could tell her that would make her feel better, but unfortunately, knowing the details would only distress her more, so she kept quiet.

"But I know without a doubt, because of the respect my son had for you, that it wasn't your fault."

Penelope closed her eyes and tried not to burst into tears. She felt Makayla's hand on her knee and still didn't open them.

"Henry had his flaws. He didn't always see trouble when it was right there in front of him. But the sincerity in his words in that letter come through loud and clear. I watched every interview I could find of you, Penelope Turner, and it's obvious to me that you're strugglin'. I don't blame you after what happened to you, but if you're strugglin' over my Henry and what happened out there in that hellhole, you need to stop right now. He believed in you, and you need to honor his memory by believin' in yourself. War is hell, as many people have said in the past and will continue to say in the future."

"Thank you," Penelope whispered.

"You're welcome. Now, it's gettin' late, and I'm sure

you two have better things to do than sit around and chat with an old woman."

"You kicking us out?" Penelope joked as she opened her eyes and tried to get her equilibrium back.

"Yup," Makayla said without remorse. "But you're welcome to come back anytime. I mean that."

"Thanks. I'm going to take you up on that," Penelope warned.

"I hope you do. Henry was my only child, and things are a little quiet around here without him."

Penelope vowed to do what she could to bring some joy back to Makayla White's life. She'd ask for Tex or Beth's help in tracking down some veterans who lived in the Biloxi area, who might need a bit of Mama White's kind of support. The more she thought about it, the more she liked the idea.

Penelope stood and felt Moose right at her side. He hadn't said a word, but his silent support meant more to her than she could say. Smokey's head came up, and he stood and stretched, then nudged Penelope's hand as if to say, "Let's get going."

The foursome walked back to the door, and Penelope couldn't help but see some of the things in the house that needed a little TLC. A crack in the wall there, a smoke detector that was obviously not working because the batteries had been taken out. Things that White would've surely taken care of for his mother by now...if he'd been around to do them.

She was *definitely* going to talk to Tex, and see if he

could find someone or several someones to visit with Makayla and help her with the little things that needed doing around the house. It would be good for her *and* the vets.

Makayla opened the door and Penelope, Moose, and Smokey walked out onto the porch. Penelope handed Smokey's lead to Moose and gave White's mom a long, heartfelt hug. "Thank you," she whispered as they embraced.

Makayla shook her head. "No, thank *you*. Thank you for lookin' after my boy. For comin' to visit me when you had no obligation to do so."

After Penelope pulled away, it was Moose's turn to hand off Smokey's lead and hug the woman. She saw him whisper something in her ear, but couldn't hear what.

Whatever it was made Makayla smile huge and nod. She patted Moose on the cheek as a mother would do to a son. Then she said, "I hope y'all don't mind if I don't stand out here and see you go. Hurts my heart a little, to be honest."

"Would it be okay if I wrote you a letter now and then?" Penelope asked before she closed her front door.

"I'd like that," Makayla said with one last smile before she shut and locked the door.

Moose took hold of her hand and led her down the stairs back to the truck. He opened the door for her and put Smokey into the back seat, as she climbed up into the front. He then got in and started the truck, reversing out of the driveway and heading for the yurt he'd reserved for them.

Neither said a word for a long time, until Penelope broke the easy silence. "Thank you, Moose."

"You're welcome, sweetheart."

The Penelope who walked toward the fancy tent-but-not-a-tent that Moose had so thoughtfully rented so Smokey could come with them on their trip felt lighter than she had in months. She'd felt better after the visit with the hypnotist, but nothing felt as good as knowing White's mother didn't blame her for her son's death. And knowing how much White himself respected and trusted her went a long way toward making the guilt she'd carried around for so long dissipate. She knew it would never completely disappear. She'd always feel some sort of guilt for living when the others had died, but at that moment, she thought it just might be manageable.

Now all she had to do was figure out how to trust herself in a life-or-death situation again, and trust those around her to have her back, and she'd be golden. That, of course, seemed like a hell of a mountain to climb, but for now, she was going to do her best to enjoy spending a day or two at the beach with her pet donkey and Moose. The man she had a feeling she wouldn't be able to hold at arm's length for much longer.

CHAPTER THIRTEEN

"How'd it go?" Moose asked the second Penelope walked into the house. A few days had passed since they'd gotten back from Biloxi.

She'd seemed a lot better after talking with White's mom. She still had a lot to go through in her head, but he hoped and prayed that she'd be able to come to terms with the new Penelope.

"Good!" she said with excitement. "Really great. The kids loved Smokey, and he was *so* good. I told them the story of how he came to find me—leaving out the part that we were fighting that forest fire because Erin was being hunted by a crazy serial killer—and they ate it up. I loved it!"

Moose grinned and pulled her close when she tried to pass him. She immediately rested her cheek on his chest, and he couldn't help but sigh in relief. *Every* time he put his hands on her, he felt relief. He'd come so close to losing her, twice.

"Have I thanked you for helping me figure shit out?" Penelope asked, looking up as she kept her arms around him.

He smiled and did his best to not think about how good she felt in his arms, and how he could lift her up and plunk her ass on the counter behind him and she'd be at the perfect height to kiss. He wouldn't even have to lean over.

"Only a million times. I might've led you to the water, Pen, but that's all I did. You were the one who did all the hard work."

She shook her head. "I think we both know that without you, I might still be wallowing. I loved doing the fire safety thing with the kids today. I felt the same kind of enthusiasm that I used to about going to work. I'm not saying I'm ready to jump back into the swing of things, not that the chief would let me without some retraining, but the spark is there."

"I'm glad, sweetheart."

Her eyelids dropped for a second before she looked up at him once more—and Moose couldn't stop his body's reaction if he tried. He felt his dick get hard, and he tried to discreetly shift his lower body away from hers, but she wasn't having it.

Penelope looked up at him with longing in her eyes. She pushed him backward until he hit the counter, effectively trapping him. Yeah, he was bigger and stronger than she was, but at the moment, it felt as if she could control him without even lifting her pinky finger.

"Pen?"

"You're one of my best friends, Moose. I literally have no idea where I'd be if it hadn't been for you these last few months. I've been so selfish, and you've still always been there for me."

"You need to cut yourself some slack, Pen. It's not like you got a little singed while we were at a fire or something."

She chuckled. "I know, but still, you've never—not once—*not* been there for me. You've pushed and prodded and even pissed me off a time or two. Your own health has suffered as a result, and I hate that. Out of everything that's happened, I hate that you've had to cut back on work as a result of me."

"Pen, it's—" he started, but she interrupted him.

"No. Whatever you're going to say, it's bullshit. Also…I heard what you said the other day, and while I'm not quite ready to go all the way…I'm tired of just being your roommate."

"What do you mean?" he asked quietly, doing his best not to let the hope rising up inside him overtake his good sense. The last thing he ever wanted to do was pressure Penelope into something she wasn't ready for. Something that would obviously change their relationship for good.

"I mean that I've never met a man like you. Noble,

honest, so good. You've been my best friend for longer than I can remember, and you're so unselfish. When I started sleeping in your bed, I just needed someone there beside me, someone who I knew I could count on, no matter what. But over the last few weeks... something's changed."

"What's that?" Moose asked, holding his breath.

She pushed up against him so tightly, there was no way she could miss his hard-on against her belly. "When we were in Biloxi on the beach, and that woman walked by and oh so obviously tripped right in front of you, and you immediately went over, helped her up and smiled at her?"

She paused, and Moose frowned. "Yeah?"

"I was jealous as hell."

Butterflies took flight in Moose's belly. "There was no need. I only wanted to make sure she hadn't hurt herself."

"She was tall. Built. Her tits were practically falling out of that bikini top she was wearing."

"So? I wasn't attracted to her. Not in the least."

"But that's what changed," Penelope said earnestly. "Me. *I've* changed. I woke up and saw what's right in front of my face. I was so jealous...but I'm still scared to death you're going to get sick of always having to prop me up when I fall flat on my face. When I have a flashback or nightmare. That it's all going to get old and you can't handle it anymore."

"Not gonna happen," Moose said firmly.

"I don't want to be your roommate anymore," Penelope said, looking him straight in the eye. "I have no idea how this is supposed to work, since I'm already living with you, and since you already know all my faults. But I want...more."

Moose closed his eyes in gratitude for a brief moment, and when he opened them again, he knew his life would never be the same. He'd prayed for this moment for so long, he'd begun to think it might never happen. That Penelope would never be able to see him as anything more than an annoying older-brother type. Someone she worked with.

A friend only.

"I want more too," he told her, not that she didn't already know that. "I'm going to do everything in my power to make sure you don't regret this."

"I'm not going to regret it, and you don't have to do anything, Moose. You've already done it all. Don't you get it? You've literally pulled me up from the depths of hell back into the light."

"Don't agree to be with me because you're grateful," Moose said a little more harshly than he'd intended.

"I'm not," she said immediately. "I want to be your girlfriend because being in your arms at night makes me feel safe. It also turns me on. And lately, I haven't been able to think about anything other than climbing on top and straddling you and taking what I want."

Moose's dick got even harder, if that was possible.

And the little minx knew it, if her sly smile was any indication.

"I want to be with you because you make me want to be a better person. You force me to look outside myself and not be so self-involved. You were right, shit happens to everyone, and it's how we deal with that shit that dictates the kind of person we are. I've been a selfish bitch, not paying any attention to anyone around me, but I want to stop that…and I need your help. I've been thinking about you being in the hospital, and the fact that I had no idea, and it tears me up inside."

"Shhh, I'm fine," Moose reassured her.

"Damn straight you are," Penelope joked. But then she got serious. "I'm not cured, Moose. I'm probably going to have relapses. Times when I just want to stay in bed with the covers over my head and wallow in my own pain."

"Then I'll make sure I'm here to bring you food until you're done wallowing, then we'll do something together that takes your mind off your pain."

She smiled again.

Moose couldn't help himself. He leaned down slowly, giving her a chance to pull away or tell him she wasn't ready, but she did neither of those things. Instead, she stood up on her tiptoes and brought her hands up to curl around his neck.

When their lips touched, everything within Moose felt as if it settled into place. Like he'd been a jumbled mess, but now he was calm and everything was as it should be.

She opened under him, and Moose didn't hesitate to claim what he'd known was his for months. Maybe even years. She moaned under his onslaught, and her hands buried themselves into his hair. Moose wrapped his arms around her and picked her up, turning to put her on the counter, just like he'd fantasized. Their lips never parted, and once she was settled, she tilted her head and kissed him just as aggressively as he was kissing her.

Moose had never kissed anyone like this before. Like if he didn't imprint himself on her, he'd die.

For just a second, she fought for control of the kiss, then she melted into him, letting him take the reins.

When they were both out of breath, he pulled back and simply stared at Penelope in awe. Her lips were a bit swollen and, as he watched, she licked them, making his dick jump in his pants once more. She had a dreamy look on her face, and he didn't dare glance down at her chest. If he saw that her nipples were hard, he wouldn't be able to stop himself from grabbing her, thundering up the stairs, and throwing her down on their bed.

Instead, he gently brushed her hair away from her face and took a deep breath.

"Wow," she whispered.

"I knew it would be like that," he told her with one hundred percent certainty.

"Like what?"

"Beautiful. Life changing. Fucking amazing," Moose told her.

A blush bloomed on her cheeks, and he found it fascinating. The Penelope he knew from the past would never have let a simple compliment fluster her, but he hoped that meant she wanted more.

"Can we..." Her voice trailed off.

"What, sweetheart?" he asked. Her hands were still around his neck, as if she never wanted to let him go. And he was more than all right with that.

"Can we take things slow? I'm not ready to...make love yet. You asked me to be completely sure before we did, and while I'm very sure that I want to see where things between us can go, I'm not sure I'm ready to say the words yet."

Moose's respect for her increased tenfold at her request. "Of course. And I meant that. I don't want you to say something you don't mean with all your heart and soul. I love you enough to wait."

"I feel bad."

"About what?"

"That I'm not ready to say it back yet."

"Don't be," Moose told her immediately. "But you should know, while I'm perfectly happy taking things slow and not pressuring you for sex or to say that you love me, I'm not sure I can go back to the way things were. I want to be able to touch you, Pen. Kiss you. Make out on the couch and get embarrassed when Smokey sees us being inappropriate in front of him."

She chuckled like he hoped she would.

"I want to see you. All of you. I want to make you feel good, Pen. Show you what it could be like with me."

"I want that too," she whispered. One of her hands moved from around his neck down his body until she reached the hem of his shirt. She pulled it up slowly until her fingers touched the bare skin of his side. Moose inhaled sharply, but she didn't stop.

Her hand continued inching up his body until he couldn't stand it anymore. Moose grabbed her wayward hand and pulled it out from under his shirt and held it behind her back in an iron grip. "That's enough of that."

Penelope pouted. "But you said—"

"I know what I said, but if we're going to keep things light and easy, I need to be in control."

She shivered, and he saw the flare of lust in her eyes.

"You like that, Pen? Me taking charge of when and how we get physical?"

She nodded. "Someone once told me that giving up control would help heal me. Make me feel better than I have before."

God, she was killing him. "Think of it as a new form of therapy," Moose told her. "We'll practice on your trust issues."

"I trust *you*," she said huskily, leaning forward and nuzzling the side of his neck before kissing him there.

"Damn straight you do," Moose said before gathering her blonde hair in a fist and gently pulling her head back so she had to look him in the eye. "You're *mine*, Penelope. You have nothing to worry about when it comes to other women. The only one I want is you. You don't have to be jealous. Because the only lips I want on mine are yours. The only leg I want thrown across my own in bed is yours. The only pussy I want to sink my cock into is *yours*."

She blushed, but smiled and said, "Crude...but for some reason, I like it."

Knowing he needed to do something right this second other than throw the woman he'd wanted forever over his shoulder like a caveman and bring her up to his lair and have his wicked way with her, Moose took a deep breath and stood back. Penelope's gaze dropped from his face and went down his body, before her eyes widened.

He knew his cock was making it very obvious how turned on he was, and for the first time, he worried about their difference in size. He wasn't a small man, anywhere, and Penelope wasn't exactly built to take on someone like him.

He must've frowned, or in some way indicated what he was thinking, because Penelope hopped off the counter and put her hands on his chest as she looked up at him.

"Stop worrying," she ordered. "I'm not a fragile flower, even though I've kinda pretended to be one for the last few months."

He chuckled. "The last thing I think about when I look at you is 'fragile flower.' How about helping me with dinner?"

"Of course. Let me put Smokey outside then I'll be right back."

Moose watched with a much lightened heart as Penelope removed Smokey's halter and lead and went to the back door and opened it. Her donkey pranced out the door, nudging her hip as he went.

Knowing that Penelope might actually return his love made him happier than he could remember being in a very long time. It hadn't been an easy road, and he had a feeling they'd still have their speedbumps to get over, but for the very first time, he had real hope that they'd make it.

Two weeks later, Penelope lay under Moose on the couch in his living room and moaned in frustration. Ever since she'd given him the green light to be more than a friendly roommate, he'd taken it upon himself to drive her absolutely crazy.

He'd started with kisses that first night. And they'd clung to each other in bed, as usual, but it felt different. More intimate.

Then he'd moved on to kisses with lots of touching and fondling...on top of her clothes. That progressed to her whipping off her shirt one night, and Moose playing with her boobs for hours. He'd gotten her so worked up, she couldn't resist touching herself—but he'd grabbed her hand and told her she wasn't allowed to get herself off. That was *his* job.

Except he hadn't touched her that night.

Or the next.

By the time he *did* ease his big hand under her pants, she'd come apart embarrassingly quickly. When she'd apologized, he'd simply laughed at her and told her not to worry about it. That making her come so fast was a huge turn-on.

And so it went.

She'd gotten to touch him a few times, but he'd always stopped her before she could get him off. She knew he was masturbating in the shower in the mornings, as he'd flat-out told her. When she'd said she was worried that she somehow wasn't doing something right if he preferred his own hand to hers, he'd told her in no uncertain terms that she was wrong. That he was doing what he could to make her feel good with no pressure to reciprocate because he didn't want to rush her.

Penelope was done taking things slow. The more time she spent with Moose, the more she wanted him. She'd always liked and admired him, but now that she'd admitted she needed more, she'd begun to take notice of every little thing he did.

She'd been going to Station 7 with him for every shift, hanging out with the guys and doing small stuff around the station. When they got a call, Penelope stayed behind and either cooked or read a book. She was beginning to get the itch to return, and the chief was allowing the others to put her through her paces.

They weren't going easy on her. The drills they were making her do made her bitch and moan and curse their names. But throughout it all, Moose was an unwavering support system. Telling her where she could improve and praising her when she did something right. He also didn't seem to give a shit when the other guys made fun of him for being whipped.

In fact, he'd begun kissing her on the lips and pulling her onto his lap when they were just sitting around shooting the shit in the living area of the station. One night, after announcing he was going to bed in one of the back rooms, he'd stood and dragged her along with him, Penelope blushing the entire way. Their friends catcalled and whistled, but for some reason it didn't bother her, even though she blushed harder.

Moose was generous and sensitive, and any little things that may have annoyed her in the past, she no longer noticed. How could she give a shit about the dishes when he didn't get them done because he was giving her a backrub? Or care about the lights being left on when he'd finally admitted he did it because Smokey didn't seem to like the dark?

And while Penelope had always known Moose was an extremely patient man, his current level of fortitude was reaching epic proportions. When he wanted something, he set out a course of action to achieve it—and he followed that course to the letter.

But right now, lying under him on the couch, his lips around a nipple, his hard-on pressing against her thigh, Penelope wanted to kill him. She knew he'd make her feel good, she had no doubt about that. He'd more than proven that he was capable of giving her orgasm after orgasm, all without even removing most of her clothes. He was being very careful to not push her to make love with him before she was ready.

But damn it, she *was* ready.

More than ready.

She loved him.

Had loved him for months.

She was head over heels, completely in love with the man—and now she had no idea how to convince him she wasn't just saying it so he'd fuck her.

She knew if she said it now, he'd smile at her, make her come, then carry her upstairs and cuddle her until she fell asleep.

But she wanted to make him feel good.

Wanted to feel him under her.

Wanted to know that she could satisfy him as well as he satisfied her.

"Moose," she gasped.

"Mmmm?" he responded, as he sucked her nipple into his mouth, making her arch her back even higher, pressing against him, trying to get some relief from the amazing feelings coursing through her.

She tried to push him so he was on his back, but he didn't budge. Not even a little.

"Moose, I need to talk to you."

"I must not be doing this right if you can still think about having a conversation," he murmured before nipping at her bud once more.

It felt amazing, but Penelope was determined to get through to him. Knowing she was fighting dirty, she said, "I want to talk about *us*."

That got him. His head came up and he stared at her with worried eyes. "Us?" he asked.

"Yes. Can you please turn over?"

He'd been happy to control their making out over the last couple of weeks, and Penelope had been happy to let him. It *had* been freeing to not have to make any decisions about how far they'd go and what she'd allow Moose to do to her. She knew he wouldn't go further than she wanted because, one, he was as in tune with her body as he was his own. And two, because he'd promised to let her make the decision about going all the way with him.

Before she knew it, Penelope was straddling Moose's stomach and his hands were holding her tightly against him. She could feel his fingers digging into her sides, as if he was nervous about what she had to say. The cool air of the room made her nipples tighten, and she knew she was blushing. She wasn't used to being topless around him, or anyone, and knowing he was staring up at her was a little unnerving.

Deciding to just say what was on her mind, Penelope blurted, "I want you."

His fingers lost some of their death grip on her hips.

"If you hadn't interrupted me, I'd've made you come already," he said a little cockily.

Rolling her eyes, Penelope shook her head. "No, Moose. I *want* you. I want to touch you. See you. All of you. Feel you against me. Inside me."

He stilled, and his fingers tightened again. She saw his chest rising and falling rapidly as he took in what she was saying.

"You know what I need to hear, Pen," he said softly.

When she opened her mouth to say the words, his finger covered her lips and cut her off.

"But if you say them, you're mine. I told you that before, and nothing's changed. I'm not letting you go. I'm not asking Sledge for permission to marry you. I'm not going to wait months and months for you to pick out a dress and make plans for a big party. I've waited what seems like my whole life for you, and if you agree to let me make love to you tonight, there's no going back. Understand?"

He was so intense, Penelope almost had second thoughts. How could he be so sure? She was still a mess. She hadn't been able to stomach the thought of actually going into a fire again. She wasn't sure she ever would. She could probably get a job as an EMT and handle car wrecks, heart attacks, and hospital transfers, but walking into a burning building again was a whole other thing.

When she looked down at him, he hadn't moved even an inch, except to take his finger off her lips. He was staring into her eyes, not leering at her naked chest. She could feel his erection against her ass, but he wasn't pushing it into her, or trying to influence her one way or another.

But he didn't have to. The thought of a life without Moose by her side was abhorrent. She couldn't walk away from him. Not again.

"I love you. I love how you hate when I put my cold feet against you when we're in bed, but you let me anyway. I love how your face scrunches up in disgust when you pick up Smokey's poop. I love that you'll actually still go out and *pick up* Smokey's poop. I love how you've always been there for me, even when I'm being a bitch. I love how big you are to my small, but you won't let anyone pick on me about it. I love the way your eyes seem to follow me when we're at the station, even if it annoys me that you feel like you have to keep watch over me. I love that you let me be independent, but that you make sure I know you're there if I need you.

"I think I've loved you for ages, but I haven't had the guts or the strength to admit it until now. It scares me to death because if I lose you, I'm not sure I'll be able to deal. I'd probably fall right back into the pit of despair I was in when I got back from Turkey, and there wouldn't be anyone to pull me out like you did. *I love you*, Moose. Now...will you please fuck me?"

"No," he said immediately, and Penelope stiffened.

Oh, God, had she just massively embarrassed herself?

"I'm not going to fuck you. Not now. At some point in the future, absolutely. Hell, it might be later tonight, even...but first, I'm going to make love to you the way I've fantasized and dreamed about. I have no idea if we'll even fit, but I'm going to do whatever it takes to make sure you enjoy it. I love you, Pen. So damn much."

She sagged over him in relief. The second she went limp, his arms banded around her, pulled her in tight as he swung his legs over the side of the couch.

Penelope screeched a little and grabbed ahold of Moose for dear life. But he wasn't going to let her fall. No way. One arm went under her ass, and the other tightened around her back, holding her to him. He strode toward the stairs and took them two at a time.

He entered the master bedroom and instead of

dropping her on the mattress, he stopped beside it. "Let go," he said in a low, gruff voice.

Penelope dropped her legs and stood in front of him, feeling a little awkward but a lot excited.

"Strip," he ordered in a forceful tone she hadn't heard from him before.

CHAPTER FOURTEEN

Penelope stared up at Moose and bit her lip. She'd thought he'd get on the bed with her and they'd maybe undress each other before he used his hands and lips to make her lose her mind once more.

But he took a step back, leaving her to stand by herself at the side of the bed.

"Strip, Penelope," he said again. "I want to see you completely naked for me."

Since all she had on were her pants and underwear, it didn't take long for her to do as he asked. She kicked away the denim and did her best to not feel self-conscious. She'd long since gained back the weight she'd lost while captive in Turkey, and she was in good shape. But being naked wasn't a state she was used to.

Just when she was about ready to turn and grab up the comforter and hold it in front of her body, Moose said, "So fucking beautiful. Go ahead and climb on the bed."

Penelope felt a tingle go through her. Moose had always been a bit bossy, but he usually smiled when he asked her to do something, or he bossed her when they were working, and she did what he said without a second thought.

But this was different.

Scary.

Exciting.

Knowing the last thing she wanted to do was turn her back on him and let him see her butt up close and personal, she sat on the mattress then slowly scooted backward, never taking her gaze from his.

She thought he would start taking off his own clothes before joining her on the bed, but instead, he simply stood there, watching her.

"Moose?" she asked tentatively.

"Yeah?"

"Um...aren't you gonna join me?"

"Of course. But I'm savoring this moment."

"You've seen me in this bed before," she reminded him, unsure what exactly he was savoring.

"I have," he agreed. "But not like this. Not after you told me you loved me, that you were mine...and you've never been naked in it before. And if I'm being honest, I'm doing my best not to fall on you like a starving jackal. I'm trying to calm myself down so I can make this good for you, so I don't hurt you."

His words turned her on even more and settled her nerves at the same time. "You would never hurt me," she said with conviction.

"Damn straight," he told her. Then without fanfare, he stripped his T-shirt off over his head and unzipped his jeans. Within seconds, he was standing in front of her in nothing but a pair of boxer briefs, which clung to him like a second skin.

Penelope sighed. God, he was beautiful. She knew he was muscular; she hugged that body every night. She'd also seen him work out and knew he took care of himself. But seeing him like this practically made her mouth water. His chest was so broad and lightly sprinkled with hair, and even as she watched, his pecs tightened and relaxed. His fingers curled into fists at his sides, as if he was doing everything in his power to keep from reaching for her. He was aroused, that was obvious, and she wanted nothing more than to pull the cotton down over his cock and finally see him in all his naked glory.

She didn't worry about being able to take him. The female body was designed to stretch, and she knew he'd make sure she was damn good and ready before entering her.

Shifting on the bed, she felt herself get wet, her body preparing itself.

By the time her gaze made it back up to his face, he was grinning at her.

"Like what you see, Pen?"

"You know I do," she replied.

Leaning over to the drawer in the nightstand next to the bed, Moose pulled out a box of condoms. He opened it and placed one at the edge of the table.

Penelope knew she was blushing, but she appreciated his foresight. She didn't even think about being upset that he'd apparently been planning this. If he hadn't thought about birth control then making love might not be in the cards for them tonight, because she wasn't on the pill, and the last thing she wanted was to chance getting pregnant. Not this early in their relationship, anyway.

Moose sat on the mattress and reached out with his hand to gently caress her cheek. "Relax, Pen."

"I can't," she admitted. "I want this to be good for you, and I'm afraid I'm going to screw it up."

"You won't," he said immediately. "That's impossible."

"Seriously, Moose—" she began, but he cut her off by shaking his head.

"No. There's no way you can screw this up. I've thought about this so much and for so long, and you've already exceeded all my expectations. And...I'd like you to consider something."

She stared up at him, more than ready to get on with things.

"What?"

"I want to be in charge this first time. You mentioned something about it previously, and I can't get the idea out of my head. I don't want you to think about anything other than what I'm doing to you. Not what you think you *should* be doing. I want you to completely relax and let me take care of you."

Penelope bit her lip, remembering Dude's talk with her in California. "You want me to submit to you," she clarified.

Moose shrugged. "Not in the technical sense, no. I love the kick-ass woman you are, Penelope. I'd never try to change that, ever. But I know you have a tendency to think too hard sometimes. Try too hard. For our first time, I just want you to relax. You don't have to worry about where to put your hands or what to say or not say, I'll tell you exactly what to do. All you have to worry about is feeling good."

"Will I get to touch you too?" she asked. That was the one thing she wanted more than anything. Now that she'd admitted she loved Moose, she wanted to put her hands all over him.

"Eventually, yes," he told her.

Taking a deep breath, and hoping she wasn't going to regret this, Penelope nodded and said, "Yes."

The grin that formed on Moose's face was worth just about any uncertainty she felt.

"Do I need a safe word?" she asked.

The grin widened. "Just what do you think I'm going to order you to do?" Moose asked, even as he was shaking his head. "No, don't answer that. No safe words. This isn't a BDSM thing. I'm not going to get out chains, whips, and crops. If there's something I'm doing that you hate, all you have to do is tell me. But I'm not going to attempt anything that will hurt, and I can almost guarantee that you'll love everything I do. I just want you to relax and put yourself in my hands."

"I'll try." But she already knew she wasn't going to have any problem trusting him. This wasn't a life-or-death situation. She didn't have to worry about anything she did resulting in his demise.

"So beautiful," Moose said reverently, turning his hand over and running his knuckles down her cheek, then over her collarbone, then over one of her nipples. It immediately hardened, and Penelope moaned.

"Stay still," Moose told her, and Penelope swallowed hard and nodded.

He continued to tease her with his knuckles. Running them over her belly, then her sides, then skimming the trimmed hair between her legs.

Penelope started to move her legs apart, but he narrowed his eyes at her and shook his head.

"Sorry," Penelope whispered. "I'm trying."

"I know you are," Moose said. "Close your eyes and concentrate only on my touch and how it's making you feel. Stay very still and quiet until I tell you otherwise, okay?"

She nodded and closed her eyes. The second she did, all her focus seemed to narrow in on the hand touching her. When he moved his hand again, goose bumps broke out in the wake of the path his skin made on hers. She was hyperaware of how he smelled and every time he shifted next to her. She could feel the heat from his thigh so close to her own.

But a funny thing happened as she lay there and did her best to let Moose explore...

She relaxed. Completely and utterly.

She didn't worry about what she looked like, if she was too skinny, if the moans she was making sounded funny or if she should be touching him back. She was completely focused on where he was touching her... where he might touch her next.

"That's it, Pen. You gave yourself to me tonight, and I'm going to do everything possible to make sure you never regret it."

Penelope pressed her lips together, loving that she didn't have to respond. He'd told her to stay quiet, so that's what she was going to do.

How long he sat next to her, lightly brushing his fingers against her body, she had no idea. All she knew was that she was more turned on than she'd ever been in her life. She wanted him to push her legs apart and take her, hard. But she had no control over this. He'd only do *what* he wanted, *when* he wanted. And it was hotter than any other sexual experience she'd ever had.

She knew the second he moved, but he never lost contact with her as he did so. His hand rested on her thigh, his fingers almost wrapped all the way around it. She'd never been so intensely aware of their size difference. Knowing that he could physically move her in any position he wanted with ease made her squirm on the bed.

She felt the mattress dip as he gently pushed her legs open and settled between them. Penelope might have gotten embarrassed over how wet she was, but he didn't give her time.

One of his large palms rested on her lower belly, his fingers nearly spanning from hip bone to hip bone. He used his other hand to lift her left leg. She felt it rest over his shoulder, his short hair tickling her inner thigh.

Then his shoulder nudged her other leg to the side, and she heard him inhale deeply.

Penelope licked her lips and held her breath. She'd never been able to enjoy oral sex too much in the past. The guys she'd been with had obviously done it just to get what they wanted faster...to fuck.

But Penelope knew without a doubt that Moose wasn't like those other men. She felt his nose nuzzle against her inner thigh. He took his time, building her anticipation until she thought she was going to go crazy.

She wasn't sure what to do with her hands, and her fingers moved restlessly against the sheet at her sides.

"Feel free to touch me, Pen," Moose said, his warm breath wafting over her lower lips, making her shift once more under him.

The second the words were out of his mouth, Penelope reached for him. The only place she could really touch him was his head and shoulders. She ran one hand over his head, and then felt his sigh of contentment against her wet folds.

"Don't worry about holding still," he told her. "I'm gonna be here a while; I'm not moving until I've had my fill. Nothing you do or say will deter me either. So feel free to hang on to me if you need to."

That was all the warning she got before Moose lowered his head.

For some reason, she thought he'd ease into eating her out. With all his soft and patient touches that had led up to this point, she figured he'd tease her with his tongue, then gradually increase the pressure of his touch.

But she'd been wrong.

So damn wrong.

The first thing Moose did was cover her clit with his mouth and suck—hard.

Her stomach muscles clenched and her back arched at the exquisite sensation. She'd masturbated plenty, but it had *never* felt like this.

Moose was ravenous. He attacked her clit with his tongue, stroking hard and fast, then sucking on the small bundle of nerves until she wanted to scream.

When she thought she was about to go careening over the edge, he moved to her folds, licking and sucking on her so enthusiastically, she knew she'd never be the same. There was nothing polite about what he was doing to her. He slurped and licked and nipped, using his chin and his five o'clock shadow to abrade her sensitive skin, then his tongue to soothe the slight pain. He used his nose to nudge her clit as he licked her from bottom to top.

He shifted, and Penelope held her breath, wondering what he was going to do next. When one finger eased inside her soaking-wet sheath, she lifted her ass off the bed. But she didn't get far; his hand on her belly kept her right where he wanted her.

She felt his hand turn, and he eased another finger inside her at the same time he leaned down and began to lash her clit once more.

Oh, God. She'd never had a G-spot orgasm before, but everything inside her was coiling higher and higher. She panted as if she'd just run a mile in her bunker gear. Penelope's head swung back and forth on the pillow, and her fingers curled into his shoulders as she held on for dear life.

She could hear slick noises as his fingers began to move faster, in and out of her body. She was soaking wet, and she might've been embarrassed at how turned on she was, but Moose didn't give her time to think about anything other than how he was making her feel, just as he'd promised.

"So fucking beautiful," Moose murmured, but Penelope could barely hear him. There was a rushing sound in her ears and every muscle in her body was taut, waiting for the pinnacle of pleasure that was hovering just out of reach.

She opened her legs as far as she could get them and whimpered.

Moose leaned down once more and sucked hard on her distended clit at the same time he curled his finger inside her, pressing on that special place.

That was all it took.

Penelope shuddered, and every muscle in her body went tight as she flew over the edge. She didn't worry about what she looked or sounded like, all she could do was tremble and shake in Moose's bed.

Just when she was coming down from the most intense orgasm she'd ever had in her life, Moose's fingers, which had stilled inside her as she came, began moving once more.

"Moose, I can't…" Penelope moaned.

"You can and you will," he countered, right before he moved his other hand down to her clit and began to stroke it firmly.

"Oh, God!" Penelope cried as she felt herself fly right over the edge again. There was no buildup this time; one second she was coming down from the first orgasm, and the next second, she was once more quivering in blissful excitement.

How *long* she quivered in bliss, she had no idea. But when she finally came back to herself, Penelope could feel Moose leisurely licking between her folds. Slow and easy. He wasn't trying to turn her on, but he was anyway.

Forcing her fingers and muscles to relax, she took a

deep breath and let her hands fall back to the sheet at her sides.

"Holy crap," she muttered.

She felt Moose chuckle, but he didn't stop licking her.

"Moose?"

"Yeah?"

"Um…are you gonna…" Her voice trailed off.

"Oh, yeah, sweetheart. I'm gonna," he reassured her. "In my own time and in my own way though, remember?"

She'd forgotten. He was in charge, and it was obvious he was perfectly happy where he was. And who was she to argue? His tongue felt good against her. Between his scratchy beard and the force of his fingers moving inside her, she was a bit sore. She knew it was nothing compared to how she'd feel after he actually made love to her, but she wanted that burning ache more than anything. If he could make her feel that good with just his mouth and fingers, what could he do with his cock?

Penelope lay boneless under Moose as he worshiped her. Eventually, his hands roamed up her belly to cup her breasts. He started out gentle and easy, but after a while, his fingers found her nipples and began to play. He pinched one hard, and when she squeaked, he immediately loosened the pressure, only to pinch the opposite one just as hard.

Penelope never knew when his light touches would

turn to something harder. But every time he pinched her, she felt it all the way to her clit. Soon, she was shifting restlessly under him once more, trying to push up against his mouth, needing and wanting another orgasm.

"Open your eyes, Pen," Moose ordered.

She did so immediately and winced at the bright light from the lamp next to the bed. He climbed from between her legs and shoved his boxer briefs off. Penelope was lying spread-eagle on the mattress, her sex bare to his gaze, but she couldn't focus on anything but Moose.

He was impressive fully clothed...but naked, with his erect cock almost touching his belly button, he was fucking phenomenal.

One of her hands moved from her side to touch him, but Moose took a step backward.

"Ah-ah," he reprimanded. "Hands at your sides, Pen. I'll tell you when you can touch."

She pouted, but secretly loved his bossiness.

"You'll get your chance. But if I let you touch me right now, with the taste and smell of you in my mouth and nose, I'll explode. And the first time I come, I want to be inside you. Your pussy is so fucking tight. You gripped my fingers so hard, I know you're going to strangle my dick."

Penelope couldn't have stopped her quick breaths if her life depended on it. She'd had no idea Moose was such a dirty talker. He'd been so polite and nice, always.

She supposed he'd been trying not to scare her away. But she liked this side of him. A lot.

He reached for the condom on the nightstand and quickly rolled it down his cock. Penelope licked her lips, wanting to taste it. Give him as much pleasure as he'd given her.

"Jesus, you're gonna be the death of me," he muttered, before climbing back between her legs. But this time he wasn't lying down, and she kept her eyes on his.

The brown irises were almost indistinguishable because his pupils were so dilated with lust. His nipples were hard on his chest, and as badly as Penelope wanted to reach up and touch him, he hadn't given her permission to do so yet. She was determined to do exactly as he instructed.

His hard erection brushed against her inner thighs and she lifted her knees, putting her feet flat on the mattress. She spread herself open for him, wanting him inside her more than she could ever say.

Moose leaned over her, staring with an intensity that was almost scary. His face was still damp with her juices and when she inhaled, she could smell herself on him. It was messy and carnal, and she loved every second of it. This was how sex was supposed to be. She wanted him with a desperation she'd never felt before. Feeling as if he didn't get inside her in the next three seconds, she was gonna die.

How in the world he was able to hold himself back,

Penelope had no idea. If it had been up to her, she would've grabbed his ass and pulled him inside already. But it wasn't up to her. Moose was in charge. And everything he'd done to her so far had been amazing. She trusted him to make their first time coming together unforgettable. She trusted him with everything that was in her.

At that thought, Penelope stilled.

She trusted Moose to always have her back. He'd never leave her. Never put her in a position where she could get hurt. If she was trapped, he'd move heaven and earth to get her out.

It was an inappropriate time for an epiphany...but then again, not really. She trusted Moose with her body and her heart. Completely and totally.

While she'd been thinking, Moose hadn't moved a muscle. She could feel him throbbing against her, but he hadn't inched forward to put himself inside her. It was as if he was waiting for her to give him some sort of sign that she was ready.

Apparently what she'd been thinking showed in her eyes, because he nodded and scooted up farther on the bed, widening her legs even more. The tip of his cock brushed against her folds, and Penelope whimpered.

"Can I touch you?" she whispered.

The muscles in Moose's jaw ticked as he hovered over her, and he nodded again.

Penelope immediately grabbed hold of his biceps, feeling them flex as he shifted his weight. One hand

283

held him aloft, while the other moved down between them to grab hold of his cock. He brushed it along her folds, lubricating himself with the evidence of her earlier orgasms.

He looked her in the eyes and said, "Say it."

For a second, Penelope was confused. Then she smiled. "I love you."

"Again," he ordered.

"I love you."

He notched the tip of his cock to her opening and pushed in slightly.

Moaning, Penelope gripped his biceps harder.

"*Again.*"

"I love you!" She would say the words as many times as he needed to hear them.

"You're mine," Moose growled as he pushed inside her body.

Penelope winced at his size, but he didn't stop.

"I told you once that if you let me inside your body, you'd never get rid of me. I wasn't kidding."

Penelope sucked in air through her nose but didn't otherwise respond. It had been a long time since she'd taken anyone inside her, and he wasn't exactly small.

"We'll go to the courthouse and get married the day before Sledge and Beth tie the knot. That way your parents can be there. All our friends will be together for their reception, and we can celebrate our marriage with everyone at the same time," he informed her.

Penelope wasn't exactly surprised. He *had* warned

her that if she said she loved him, he was going to marry her as soon as possible. She really didn't mind. But she made a mental note to make sure *Beth* didn't mind them kinda honing in on her wedding celebrations.

Thoughts of her soon-to-be sister-in-law faded when Moose pressed the rest of the way inside her.

Her thighs rubbed against his, and she could feel his pubic hair brushing against her own. Looking down, she could barely tell where he ended and she began. He held completely still, giving her time to adjust. But she could see it was costing him. The muscle in his jaw ticked again, and his lips were pressed together hard.

Just to mess with him—because while she might be submitting to him sexually, she'd never been that good at following orders to the letter—she tightened her inner muscles, squeezing him as hard as she could.

"Fuck!" Moose swore before narrowing his eyes. "Careful, woman, or you might find you've got a starving jackal in your arms after all."

She giggled, and even that small movement made the nerve endings inside her stand up and take notice. "I know I'm not supposed to give any orders, and that you're in charge, but if you don't start moving in the next ten seconds, I don't know what I might do."

He grinned and slowly, ever so slowly, pulled most of the way out of her.

Penelope immediately felt empty inside. But then he was gliding back in, just as slowly. There was still a slight twinge of discomfort, but when he repeated the movement again, then again, the discomfort slowly gave way to pleasure.

On the next thrust, her hips came up to meet his.

Moose asked, "Okay now?"

Penelope wanted to cry. Of course he was aware that she might've been in some pain. He'd never hurt her. Ever. She nodded.

"I love you, Penelope Turner. I'm proud of you. Proud to call you my friend, lover, and teammate. I'll always have your back, never doubt that. I'll support anything you want to do, whether that's coming back to work at the station or hanging up your bunker gear forever. You're amazing, and I'm never letting you go."

"I love you too, Moose."

Then neither said another word as he began to make love to her. Moose's thrusts were slow and steady. He did his best to drive Penelope out of her ever-loving mind.

Penelope lost all track of time, and even where she was at one point. Moose's control was the stuff of legends. He fucked her missionary style, then rolled them and let her fuck *him* for a while. When she was almost out of control, he pulled out, flipped her over onto her hands and knees, and entered her from behind. Penelope loved how easily he could manipulate her body. There was certainly something to be said for having a lover who was a foot taller than she was, and way stronger.

Finally, he turned her onto her back again, pulling her ass into an elevated position on his lap. He couldn't thrust into her very well in this position, and Penelope wanted to complain, but he was in charge. And frankly, she was more than happy to let him do with her as he wished.

He was buried as deep inside her as he could get, and his eyes were glued to where they were joined. He used his thumb to caress her clit, and Penelope found herself climbing the peak once more. This time, when her body clenched, she could feel his hard length inside her, and it gave a whole different feel to her impending orgasm.

"That's it, sweetheart. I can feel you squeezing my cock... Fuck, I'm gonna come without having to move if you keep that up."

Penelope wasn't consciously doing anything, her body had taken over. As he thumbed her clit, using her own juices to lubricate his movements, she arched her back and pressed harder into him. Her legs were spread wide, and she threw her arms over her head.

"God, you're gorgeous," Moose said, his gaze going from where they were joined to her tits. "Come on me," he ordered. "That's it, Pen. I can feel you pulsing around my dick. Fuck, it feels so good. Just a little more. *Yesssssssss!*"

Penelope let out a loud moan as Moose forced her over the edge. Between feeling full of his cock, and his finger on her clit, she couldn't stop the orgasm. It rushed over her like a freight train, and as every muscle clenched in ecstasy, she felt Moose's body tighten under her...within her.

His groan as he came was enough to send a smaller orgasm shooting through her system. When she was done, she lay with her ass in his lap, boneless and unable to move.

Moose didn't move for several minutes either. He only shifted away from her when his cock softened enough to slip out of her body. He didn't go far, though. He used his thumbs to spread her folds open and watched as her juices slowly leaked from between her legs.

"Moose?" she asked after a minute, feeling uncomfortable.

"Yeah?"

"Don't you need to take care of that condom?"

"In a bit. I'm busy."

Penelope closed her eyes and did her best to relax. She had a feeling nothing was going to be out of bounds with Moose. She needed to get used to his scrutiny. When it seemed as if he'd finally had enough of studying her, he slipped the condom off, wrapped it in a tissue from the box next to the bed, and dropped it on the floor.

"Um...shouldn't you throw that away?" she asked as he shifted until he was lying next to her.

It took a second for him to get the covers straightened out, but as soon as she was curled into his side, he said, "Nope. Getting up to go to the bathroom to throw it away means I'd have to leave you. Not happening."

It was a good answer, but it wasn't as if he could spend the rest of his life glued to her side. She told him as much, and he came up on an elbow, pushing her onto her back. He brushed a lock of hair off her forehead and stared down at her.

"I know, Pen. I know you're an independent woman who doesn't need me at her side at all times. But I just had the most intense and beautiful experience of my life, making love to the woman I want to spend the rest of my days with, who told me she feels the same. We're getting married, and I just had all my fantasies fulfilled. The last thing I want to do is leave her side for one second. Okay?"

"Okay," Penelope said immediately.

Moose nodded and gathered her to him once more, spooning her from behind.

"Close your eyes and rest for a bit, Pen."

She nodded. She was feeling completely mellow after four orgasms. She could still feel Moose between her legs and inside her. She throbbed down there, but in a good way. She could definitely sleep.

"You should know I'm gonna be waking you up to fuck you in a couple hours," Moose said nonchalantly.

And with those words, Penelope was wide awake once more. Her mellow mood gone in a flash. All sorts of carnal images whipped through her brain like a movie reel. She *wanted* Moose to fuck her. She wanted to fuck *him*. She hadn't gotten nearly enough time on top of him. She wanted him at her mercy, wanted to suck him off and have him come in her mouth. When he'd had Penelope on her hands and knees, he'd taken her nice and easy, but she wanted to know how it felt to have him pound into her from behind. He could use his hands to manipulate her clit, or she could do it herself.

Her dirty thoughts made her shift restlessly against him.

One of his large hands dipped between her legs and cupped her. "You like that thought." It wasn't a question.

Penelope nodded anyway.

"Fuck it," Moose muttered. "Who needs sleep?" One finger slipped inside her, and Penelope moaned as she found herself on her back with him hovering over her once more.

"Say it," he ordered.

"I love you, Moose," she obliged.

"Damn straight you do," he said, before leaning down and taking one of her nipples into his mouth.

This time, Penelope immediately brought her hand up and tangled her fingers in his short hair, holding him to her. He hadn't told her to keep her hands to herself, and she'd submitted to him that first time. Now she wanted to be an active participant.

When she felt him grin against her flesh, Penelope smiled. This was going to be fun.

CHAPTER FIFTEEN

The next morning, when Moose's alarm went off, Penelope groaned. Moose agreed with the sentiment, but he had to go into work. The last thing he wanted to do was leave, but unfortunately, real life was intruding.

He'd never been so happy in all his life. Penelope was everything he wanted in a woman. Smart, tough, and she matched him move for move in bed. Remembering how they'd laughed throughout their second bout of lovemaking the night before immediately had his cock hardening.

Knowing Pen was way too sore for any kind of quickie before he headed off to the station, Moose pushed down his own discomfort and climbed out from under the covers. The chilly air of the room was a shock, but he quickly pulled the sheet over Penelope to keep her from getting cold.

"If you feel like it later, stop by the station," he whispered.

"Uh-huh..." she mumbled.

Moose smiled again. Then he walked over to his dresser naked as the day he was born and pulled open one of his drawers. He rummaged through it for a second before finding what he was looking for.

He walked back to the bed and lifted Penelope's left hand. He slipped the one-and-a-half carat emerald-cut diamond onto her ring finger, then smiled as she grumpily pulled her hand out of his and tucked it close to her chest.

He couldn't help but chuckle as he pulled the sheet and comforter up to her chin once more. He wished he could be there when she finally got up and noticed the ring on her finger. She said she loved him and hadn't protested his plans for a courthouse wedding the day before her brother got married. It would be perfect; her parents could be there, and there wouldn't be a chance of the press getting wind of it. While the newspapers and news shows hadn't been hovering around her anymore, Moose knew if they found out the American Princess was getting married, they'd make a nuisance of themselves again.

He didn't really blame them; Penelope's rescue was a miracle, and the American people loved a feel-good story. They liked knowing someone who went through something so horrific could live happily ever after.

And while Penelope wasn't exactly there yet—she

was still dealing with some demons, always would be—she'd certainly overcome a lot of shit that had been piled on her head.

"I'll call later to see how you're doing. Take a bath when you wake up, it'll take away some of your soreness."

"M'kay," she mumbled.

"Love you," Moose told her.

"Love you too," she replied.

Wishing he could forget work and crawl back under the covers, Moose forced himself to stand up and head for the bathroom. Luckily, they had the rest of their lives together and would have lots of lazy mornings to spend in bed.

Three hours later, Penelope woke up feeling sore, but refreshed. She felt better than she had in a very long time. Too many times to remember, she'd woken up depressed and dreading simply getting out of bed. Smokey had helped a little with that, but as time went on, she felt less and less like facing the day and what it might bring.

But this morning, she practically bounded out of bed. She knew Moose was working a twenty-four-hour shift. He'd been approved by his doctors to go back to the longer shifts. The chief still wasn't putting him back on the regular schedule of two days on, two days off, but they both knew it was only a matter of time.

Making mental plans to stop by the station and see Moose and the other guys, it wasn't until she was brushing her teeth that Penelope noticed the ring on her finger.

She stared at it in shock, foam coming out of her mouth and dripping onto the counter beneath her. She didn't remember Moose giving her the ring, but there was no denying what it was.

She spit out her toothpaste and lifted her hand to look at the ring closer. It was an emerald-cut solitaire. It was set low, so it didn't stick up on her finger, which Penelope appreciated. She could wear it all the time and not worry about it snagging on the gloves she had to wear when they went to medical emergencies, and it wouldn't get in the way of her bunker gear.

She figured she should probably be mad at Moose for presuming, but she couldn't be. She knew what she was getting into when she'd told him she loved him, and agreed to make love with him. It's why she put it off for so long. But he'd been sure enough for the both of them, because he'd already had a ring picked out, one that was perfect for her. And apparently he'd already thought about when and where they'd get married.

Penelope didn't need a big flashy wedding. She just needed Moose. She didn't care if they did a small ceremony at the courthouse, but she was touched that he'd known she would want her parents there. Really, it was a perfect solution, to get married the day before Cade and Beth. She didn't think Beth would care, she'd probably be thrilled to share her wedding weekend, simply because it would take some of the attention off of *her*.

Feeling happier than she had in ages, Penelope took a long bath to soothe her aches and pains, then quickly showered and washed her hair afterward. She put on a pair of cargo pants and a Station 7 T-shirt and went downstairs.

Smokey had been sleeping soundly on his special cushion Moose had bought for him when they'd first started staying the night. When he saw her, he perked up and came running over on his little legs. The enthusiasm and excitement he always exhibited when he saw her never failed to make Penelope smile.

She let him out, ate a quick breakfast of a bowl of cereal and a granola bar, then let Smokey back in and put on his halter. Her original plan had been to get up with Moose and go to the station with him, but obviously that hadn't panned out. She wanted to talk to the chief about expanding the fire safety education program. Smokey had been such a huge hit that she knew they could make more of an impact by going to as many schools as possible. It was a great chance to not only talk about fire safety, but about adopting animals as well.

But more than that, Penelope wanted to talk to the chief about going back to work.

She couldn't lie; she was nervous as hell about that. Even though he hadn't accepted her resignation, Penelope wasn't sure if he'd changed his mind after all this time. Not to mention, she'd fucked up pretty badly the last time she'd been working a fire, and she didn't know how she'd react the first time she was put back into a situation like that, but she knew without a doubt the guys would let her ease back into things. She didn't need to start out rushing into burning buildings. There was always enough to do behind the scenes. Things like water relay, rolling hoses, safety compliance, and even sticking to the medical side of things.

For the first time in a very long time, Penelope missed being a firefighter. It wasn't all about the fires though. A lot of their calls were medical. Often, the same people called time and time again for lift-assists, or because they were lonely and didn't have anyone to talk to. She missed seeing some of their regular patients and reassuring them. Holding their hands and telling them they'd be all right.

She also missed the camaraderie between her and the guys. Missed hanging out and shooting the shit. Spending time with her brother. Hearing how Adeline was doing, now that her life was nearly seizure-free. Talking to Chief about his culture and hearing about the trips he and Sophie took to the reservation. Teasing Squirrel, and bringing tacos in for lunch and watching Taco see how many he could eat before he exploded. Discussing the medical side of Quinn's port-wine birthmark and how her laser treatments were coming along. Cooking and laughing with Moose.

She'd gotten close to White, Black, and Wilson to some extent because of their circumstances. It was different with the guys at the station. They were truly family. They irritated and picked on her, but she admired the hell out of each and every one of them. She'd seen them in action. Had seen them put their own lives on the line more than once. They were her people. Her tribe. Part of the reason she'd felt so lost when she came back from Turkey was because she'd been holding them at arm's length. Not letting them in. But she was done with that.

The more she thought about it, the more she wanted back in the fold. She had a lot to prove. She had to show them that she wasn't the flakey person she'd been for way too long. And the great thing about her friends and teammates was that they'd give her the chance to prove it. They wouldn't hold a grudge.

After Penelope got Smokey settled into the passenger seat of her PT Cruiser, and she'd gotten into the driver's side, she couldn't help but sit and admire the ring on her finger for a second. The sunlight made it sparkle, and Penelope couldn't stop thinking about the night before.

"How'd I get so lucky?" she whispered…then pressed her lips together tightly.

Lucky? For so long, she'd thought she was the most unlucky person on the planet. After all, how many people were held prisoner by terrorists? But for the first time, her thinking had reversed.

She'd *survived* being held captive by terrorists. White hadn't. Neither had Wilson nor Black. Or those Army pilots. She had a loving family and a job. She had a man who loved her and would do anything, *had* done everything, to help her get past her mental issues. She had a support system of military men and her own friends to lean on when she needed them.

She had a home, a pet, and her health. So many veterans didn't have any of that. And yet she'd wallowed in her own head, feeling sorry for herself. She was suddenly ashamed of the person she'd allowed herself to become.

"No more," she vowed out loud. "I might not be perfect, but damn it, I'm pretty damn lucky, all things considered."

Smokey nudged her elbow as if he was agreeing. Or he was just telling her to hurry up and start the car. He loved sticking his head out the window and feeling the wind in his hair.

Chuckling at the donkey's antics, Penelope started up her car and backed out of the driveway. She rolled down the windows and simply enjoyed being alive.

Moose's house was about twenty minutes from Station 7, so Penelope turned up the radio and sang along to old eighties songs. She knew she looked goofy as hell, with a donkey sitting next to her and belting out songs at the top of her lungs, but she didn't care. Today was the first day of the rest of her life, and damn it, she wasn't going to wallow anymore.

She'd taken some back roads toward town just for something different, and because her friend TJ, a former Army sniper and a member of the Texas Highway Patrol, had impressed upon her how important it was to vary her routine, which meant not taking the same route to work every day.

Penelope was only about five miles away from the station when she first saw the smoke.

She didn't think anything about it at first, as someone was always burning leaves or trash in their yard. But when she got closer and pulled down a residential street, she saw that the smoke wasn't coming from a burn pile, but from a house.

It was a one-story bungalow with an attached garage. Penelope could see flames through the window of the garage on the side of the house.

Almost without thinking about what she was doing, she slammed on her brakes and pulled over. She took the time to roll up the windows partway so Smokey couldn't try to follow her, then she leaped out of her car and ran toward the house.

There didn't seem to be anyone around, but it was mid-morning, so most people were at work. Sending a prayer upward that the house on fire was unoccupied as well, Penelope ran to the front door.

Almost the same moment she reached it, a woman

burst out of the house looking completely panicked and freaked out.

Penelope grabbed her by the shoulders to keep from getting run over. The woman screamed and tried to fight for a moment.

"I'm a firefighter!" Penelope told her urgently. "Are you the only one in the house?"

The woman shook her head. "No! I've got four kids and they're all sleeping! There was so much smoke in the hall where their rooms are, I could barely breathe. I panicked and came outside. When I tried to go back inside to get them, the smoke was thicker, and it was really hot! Oh, God! Help them!"

Feeling her stomach clench in fear, Penelope fought it back. "How old are they and which direction are their rooms?"

"Eight, six, four, and seventeen months," the mother cried, then pointed back at the house, the same side where the fire churned in the garage. "We all had a hard day yesterday, it was the one-year anniversary of my husband's death, and I told them they could skip school and we'd have a fun family day today. We were all sleeping in. Oh my God, I can't lose them too!" the woman wailed.

Penelope grabbed her phone out of her pocket and shoved it at the terrified mother. "Take my phone. Call 9-1-1. Tell them about the fire. Make sure you tell the operator that you see flames in the garage. Also inform them that an off-duty firefighter is on scene and there are four children still in the house. Whatever you do, do *not* go back into the house. Hear me?"

The woman's eyes were huge in her white face. "My kids..." she moaned. "I shouldn't have left them! They're all I have left. Please save them!"

"I'm gonna get them out. I promise. But I need you to call for help."

Penelope waited for the woman to nod before she turned back toward the house. The smoke coming from the garage was dense, which wasn't a good sign. The thicker the smoke, the faster the fire would spread. It was also slowly beginning to change from a white smoke to a light gray. Also not a good thing for the children still inside the house. Almost all solid materials started out emitting white smoke, which was mostly moisture. As whatever was burning dried out and broke down, the smoke would change color. Wood materials changed to tan or brown smoke, and plastics and painted or stained materials would emit gray.

She'd learned in her fire classes that faster/darker smoke was closer to the fire, whereas slower/lighter smoke was farther away.

Penelope was at least relieved to see it hadn't turned into thick black smoke yet, as that meant an impending flashover and temperatures of more than a thousand degrees. Which wasn't something anyone could survive, not even a firefighter in turnout gear.

The bottom line was that she still had time to save the kids.

Not thinking about it another second, Penelope ran toward the front door, which was still standing open from when the woman had burst outside. Not pausing even a second, Penelope entered the house and turned left toward where smoke was rapidly filling the hallway. The doors to the rooms were all open, and Penelope mentally shook her head. Bedroom doors should always be shut at night; it could give whoever was inside an additional few minutes to escape if a fire broke out, like it had in this case.

Deciding to go to the room at the end of the hallway first, as it was closest to the burning garage, Penelope made a beeline for the twin-size bed. She leaned over the child still oblivious to the danger she was in and didn't even bother to try to wake her up slowly. Time was ticking and with each breath of the smoke-laden air, Penelope knew she was going to be cutting things close.

"Time to get up," she said as she picked up the toddler.

The little girl seemed lethargic and confused, and Penelope was somewhat thankful. It meant she was less likely to fight her. She hurried out of the room, slamming the door behind her. Maybe by cutting off some of the fire's fuel, it would give her a bit more time.

She hurried across the hall to another room and was relieved to find two children. Kneeling by the bottom bunk, Penelope shook the boy sleeping there.

She had a hard time waking him up, which was yet another bad sign.

"Can you hear me? You need to get up," Penelope told him urgently. She stood and reached to jostle the older boy on the top bunk. "Wake up!"

"What's going on?" the first boy asked as he sat up. His eyes were huge in his face and he looked scared.

Shaking the older boy once more, she looked down at his brother. "We need to get outside. There's a fire," she said succinctly.

"Where's my mom?" the older boy asked, and Penelope was happy to see he was up and already moving to climb down off the top bunk.

"She's outside waiting for us," Penelope told him.

"Dad told us we shouldn't talk to strangers," the smaller boy said.

"And he's right," Penelope agreed. "But this is an emergency, and I'm a firefighter, so it's okay."

"Where's your uniform?" the older boy asked suspiciously.

Knowing they didn't have time for this, but that she literally couldn't drag both of these boys out while holding their little sister and still needing to get the baby, Penelope tried to explain. "I was on my way to the fire station when I saw the smoke coming from your house. I stopped to help. I need you both to be big brave boys while we go and get your brother or sister."

It was obvious the older boy was finally waking up. He saw the smoke filling their room and looked at

Penelope, his brother, then his sister, his face filled with fear.

"We need to go," she said when he began to frantically look around the room, as if he was going to try gathering up his precious toys to save them.

"I can't carry your sister and you guys too, so you're going to have to help me. Be junior firemen, do you think you can do that?"

Their eyes huge in their faces, both boys nodded.

Penelope mentally sighed in relief. The smoke was getting thicker and time was running out. "Good. I knew you could. I need you to hold each other's hands, and then grab on to my waistband with the other. Under no circumstances should you let go. Not of me and not of each other. Understand?"

Both boys nodded, and the younger boy had begun to cry. "Okay, grab hold," she said. Wanting to give them something else to concentrate on, she added, "And when we start walking, I need you to count our steps. It's important to know exactly how many steps it is from your room to the front door." It wasn't exactly a lie, but it was a bit late for that piece of advice now.

She started shuffling toward the boys' door and she felt their little fingers holding on to her pants for dear life. When they got into the hall, she could feel the difference in the fire. The smoke was changing to a darker color and was rolling a little faster across the ceiling. *Shit.*

Not bothering with shutting the door to the room

they'd just left, she hurried to the last bedroom. There was a crib inside, and Penelope didn't hesitate to pick up the baby with her one remaining free hand. The children were heavy, but at that second, she didn't feel their weight at all. Her only concern was getting them out of the house and safe.

The four-year-old in her arms started to cry, which woke up the baby, who also started to wail. Not bothering to try to shush either child, Penelope turned her head to the boys. Thank God they were still holding on to both her and each other like she'd instructed them to. If one or both had panicked, and run back into their room or farther into the house, she wouldn't have been able to follow them right away. She would've had to get the girls out, then come back for the boys.

"Ready, junior firemen?" she asked, even as she turned to head back toward the hallway.

"Yeah."

"Yes."

The boys answered in unison even as they began to cough.

Penelope's eyes were burning, and she too was finding it hard to breathe. She'd never missed her bunker gear as much as she did in that moment. Flames weren't what killed most people in structure fires, it was the smoke that would do them in long before the fire even reached them.

"Keep counting!" she told the boys as she shuffled out of the room and down the hall, away from the flames that were threatening to break through the wall between the garage and the rest of the house. If she'd been even five minutes later, she wouldn't have been able to get to the kids.

She didn't rush, but kept walking in a slow and steady pace that the boys could keep up with. The last thing she wanted to do was yank herself out of their grasp, even if that's what her brain was telling her to do.

The front door was still standing wide open, and Penelope had never seen a more welcome sight. She shuffled out the door into the bright morning light and the children's mother came running toward them.

"Oh my God, thank you so much! Joel and Robert, are you guys all right?" she asked as she took the little girl out of Penelope's arms and cradled her. "I'm so sorry I couldn't get you out!"

Penelope kept hold of the baby as she urged the family to back away from the house.

"We're okay. Where's Buster?" the oldest boy asked his mom.

Penelope's stomach clenched at the question.

The woman pressed her lips together then shook her head. "I'm sorry, Joel. She's still inside."

The boy, who'd been so brave and had followed her directions to the letter, started to cry. "B-but she's probably scared. Dad got her for us! We can't leave her in there to die!" he exclaimed. "I promised Dad I'd take care of her!"

Making a split-second decision she hoped she wouldn't regret, Penelope handed the baby off to the mother, who automatically reached out a hand for her, even though she was already holding her other daughter.

She kneeled down in front of Joel and put her hands on his shoulders. "Is Buster a dog or cat?" she asked.

"Dog," Joel said immediately.

"How big? What's she look like?"

"Medium. She looks like Benji. You know, the dog from the cartoons?"

Penelope nodded. "I'm going to do my best to find her, but you have to promise to stay out here with your mom and brother and sisters. Okay?"

He nodded, leaning into his mother's side heavily.

Penelope stood up and asked the woman, "Do you have any idea where she might be?"

"You can't go back in there," the young mother yelped, instead of answering Penelope's question.

"Did you call 9-1-1?" Penelope asked.

She nodded.

Penelope quickly estimated how many minutes had passed and knew she had time for one last quick search. If the woman cooperated and helped point her in the right direction. "Where would the dog go?"

"She woke me up," the mother said. "I was sleeping, and Buster came in and jumped up onto my bed. She knows she's not allowed up there, but she pawed at me until she got my attention. I…I don't know where she went after that! I was too worried about getting us out of the house."

Penelope nodded. "Where's your room?"

Sighing in relief when the woman pointed toward the opposite side of the house from the garage—and the fire—she nodded. Then without a word, she turned and ran back toward the house.

The smoke was heavier now, and dark gray. Taking a deep breath at the front door, Penelope reentered the burning house.

Thankful that the house was one story, Penelope knew she could always go out a window if necessary. She ran through a room off the kitchen and made a mental note of the fact that this was an older house. It wasn't an open concept, which would work in her favor. It meant more walls that could burn, but that also meant it would slow down the fire some.

She went through a formal dining room and entered a hallway. Visibility was lessening, but she could still walk upright, which was good. She opened one door and flicked on the light. Bathroom. She opened another door…laundry room. Penelope made a beeline for the door at the end of the hallway, but stopped and backtracked when something on the wall caught her eye.

It was a picture. There were about a dozen framed pictures set up like a mini gallery in the hallway. The kids were smiling in each one, posing perfectly for the photographer. But it was the last one that had caught her eye and made her stop.

It was of the young mother and a man wearing his dress blue Army uniform. His arm was around the woman, her front against his side. Her hand was resting on his chest and she was looking up at him as if he was the most important person in her life. But more than that, the man was looking down at her the same way.

Penelope had seen that same look on Moose's face only a few hours ago. They'd just made love for the umpteenth time, and he'd been propped over her on an elbow, playing with the hair at her temples. She'd almost melted at the look of love in his eyes.

Without thought, Penelope reached for the picture. She closed her eyes and smashed it against the wall. The glass shattered, and Penelope felt a burning in her hand. Ignoring the small cuts from the flying glass, she grabbed the picture out of the ruined frame and quickly rolled it up, then stuck it in one of the deep pockets of her cargo pants.

Knowing she'd been stupid for taking the extra thirty seconds that could literally be life or death for her and Buster, Penelope continued down the hall. By the time she reached the door to what she hoped was the master bedroom, she could no longer stand straight up. The smoke was too thick and the temperature in the house had begun to climb too high.

Penelope entered the room and slammed the door

shut behind her. If the dog wasn't in this room, it was as good as dead.

Remembering something she and Moose had talked about once, she took the time to run to the attached bath and grab a towel. She went back to the door, opened it a crack, hung the towel on the knob on the outside of the door, then eased it shut once more.

Then she turned back to the room. "Buster?" she called out, and heard no response.

Penelope felt bile rise to the back of her throat. She couldn't bear to go back outside and tell those poor kids that she couldn't find the dog their deceased dad had given them, and that had probably saved all their lives.

She first looked again in the bathroom, and when she didn't find the dog, she shut the door. Then she checked the small closet. She threw shoes and random bags of shit out to make sure the dog wasn't hiding behind anything, and when she came up empty, she shut the closet door as well. The last thing she wanted was the poor thing going into the bathroom or closet and her not noticing.

Just like kids, and even adults, animals tended to try to hide when they were scared or trying to get away from smoke. Crawling on her hands and knees now, Penelope called out Buster's name over and over in as reassuring a tone as she could muster.

Just when she despaired of finding the dog and figured that she must've run out of the room and hidden elsewhere in the house, Penelope caught sight of two glowing eyes looking out at her from under the dresser.

Sighing in relief, Penelope crawled over to where she was hiding and lay down on her belly. She put her hands under the dresser and hoped like hell the dog didn't bite her.

"Hey, Buster. I know this is all pretty scary, isn't it? I know I'd be terrified if I were you. You probably smelled that smoke first thing and came in to wake up your owner, didn't you? What a good dog!"

The dog whimpered, and Penelope hoped that was a good sign.

"I've come to get you out of here. Your mom and the kids are waiting for you outside in the nice fresh air. Come 'ere, baby." She wiggled her fingers, silently pleading with the dog to trust her.

She could stand up and move the dresser, but there was no guarantee the dog wouldn't bolt under the bed or something and she'd be right back to where she'd started. The best thing in this kind of situation was to have patience, but time wasn't on their side.

"I promise there will be a huge bone and lots and lots of pets waiting for you outside. But you have to come to me first. We'll go out there together and you'll see that I wasn't lying. That your owners really are out there. Come on, Buster. I've got ya. Trust me."

Miraculously, the dog inched closer to her fingers and sniffed at her. The urge to lunge for her and grab her scruff was strong, but Penelope forced herself to stay still. She could hear Buster's tail thumping against the floor slowly and knew she had her.

"That's it, baby," Penelope murmured, trying to hold back the cough that was threatening. The last thing she wanted to do was startle the poor dog. Buster scooted forward a little more, until Penelope was awkwardly petting her head in the confined space.

Reacting instinctively, Penelope grabbed hold of Buster's scruff and pulled.

The dog immediately stiffened and did everything in its power to prevent being yanked out from under the safe space beneath the dresser, but it was no use.

The second Penelope had Buster free of the dresser, she scooted back and enfolded the dog in her arms. She estimated her to be around thirty pounds or so. She was adorable, but scared out of her mind.

Buster fought Penelope's tight hold and managed to clamp her teeth around Penelope's forearm.

Clenching her own teeth against the pain, Penelope refused to let go. She kept speaking in low tones to the frightened creature, and finally, after a minute or so, the dog let go of her and buried its head into Penelope's underarm.

Sighing in relief and ignoring the throbbing of her arm, Penelope tucked Buster closer into her and turned to face the room.

Shit.

She'd taken too long. Even with the closed door, the

smoke was rolling inside. And it was black now. A bad sign.

Crawling awkwardly on her knees over to the window she'd seen earlier, Penelope ripped down the blinds—and stared in disbelief at what she was seeing.

It was boarded up. There was literally a plywood board nailed over the window.

Why the fuck would a single mother have the only egress route from her room sealed off? The quick exit she'd hoped to make was no longer a possibility.

She was fucked. Her *and* Buster.

Coughing harder now, Penelope refused to give up.

"She called 9-1-1," she told the little dog, now shaking uncontrollably in her arms.

Penelope sat on her butt under the window and curled herself over the dog. "Moose and the others will be here any second. We just have to wait for them to get to us. And they *will* get to us," she promised Buster. "Hang on, girl. Just hang on."

CHAPTER SIXTEEN

Moose sat in the back of the fire truck, his eyes glued out the window as they raced toward the structure fire. He had his helmet in his hand and his face mask and regulator at the ready. The woman who'd called had said her children were trapped inside, so he and Taco were prepared to enter the building for a rescue.

As the large fire truck turned down the street, they could all see the gray and black smoke rising up into the morning sky. But while Taco and the others were studying the scene, Moose's eyes were fixed on something else.

A light blue PT Cruiser parked across from the burning house.

He knew that car as well as he knew the back of his hand.

It was Penelope's, and while he had no idea what in the hell she would be doing here, he immediately began to panic. He could see Smokey in the front seat of the car, looking at the flames, and even though he couldn't hear over the sirens and the headset he was wearing, he could see the donkey was throwing his head back and braying frantically.

By the time the truck had stopped, Moose was already halfway out the door. He paused just long enough to pull his mask and regulator over his head and put on his helmet. The oxygen tank was already on his back, and he quickly hooked up the hose to the air source. He grabbed something from under the seat he'd been sitting on and started for the house without looking right or left.

A woman was standing off to the side of the house with two small children in her arms and two more clinging to her sides. She started yelling the second the firefighters had emerged from the truck about a woman being inside. That she'd saved her kids, but had gone back inside for the dog.

Moose knew without a doubt that the woman inside was Penelope. If her car and frantic donkey weren't enough proof, the tingle at the back of his neck was.

"Wait up!" Taco yelled, running after him. But Moose wasn't waiting. Fuck protocol. His Penelope was inside, and he wasn't going to wait even one second to go in and get her.

He felt Taco's hand on his arm and he did his best to shake it off, but Taco wouldn't let go.

Moose opened his mouth to blast his friend, but before he could, Taco spoke.

"The woman says she went to the master bedroom to look for their dog. It's to the right after entering the house. On the far side, away from the garage."

Moose nodded, and he felt a flicker of hope flare deep within him. Penelope wasn't stupid. She wouldn't have gone back inside for the dog if she didn't think she had time to get to it and get out. With the way the fire was raging, however, her time had run out. She didn't have the gear or air to make it out of the house without help.

The second he entered the house, he had to get down on his knees. The smoke was pitch black and rolling along the ceiling. It was only a matter of time before a flashover happened and the entire house went up in flames.

He crawled as fast as he could to the right. He bumped into several things, but didn't even hesitate to push them out of his way when possible, or go around them when it wasn't. He felt Taco at his back, keeping in close proximity so they didn't get disoriented and lose track of each other.

Crawling as if he knew exactly where he was headed, Moose kept going. Later, he'd wonder how in the world he didn't get turned around. Or why he hadn't accidentally veered off into one of the many rooms in the old-fashioned house. But for now, he just followed his instincts down a hallway.

There were several doors, all of them shut. Any one of them could be the master bedroom, but when he looked up, the smoke seemed to magically clear—and he saw a towel hanging off the doorknob at the end of the hall.

He almost laughed.

He and Penelope had been joking one night a couple months ago about how much easier it would be to search and clear a house if people left some sort of sign to what room they were in. Much like the tried-and-true way people used in college to let a roommate know that they shouldn't come inside, by leaving a towel or sock hanging on a doorknob.

His Penelope, in the midst of this crisis, had the foresight to leave him that signal.

He crawled as fast as he could down the hallway to the door. Reaching up, he turned the knob and the door opened easily. He and Taco entered and, for just a second, he panicked when he didn't see Penelope anywhere. There was smoke in the room, but it hadn't totally obscured his vision yet. There were two other doors inside, and he crawled toward one.

But then he saw her. The bed had been blocking her from his view when he'd first entered. Penelope was sitting under a boarded-up window holding a scruffy fur ball.

Amazingly, when she saw him, she smiled and said, "It's about time." Then she began to cough. The dog in her arms was limp, but Moose was more concerned about the blood on her forearm and the smoke to think too much about the animal.

He quickly crawled over to her side and grabbed the extra face mask and ventilator he'd grabbed out of the truck and hooked to his side before he'd entered the house. Seeing it, Penelope's eyes widened and she leaned forward and let him settle the mask over her face. As he was doing that, Taco was attaching the tube from the regulator to Moose's air pack so they could buddy breathe.

The second the air was turned on, Penelope took a deep breath, and Moose knew he'd never forget the sight of her chest rising as she inhaled her first bit of clean air in who knew how long.

She motioned to the window and said unnecessarily, "It's blocked. I had planned to be outside waiting on you guys by the time you got here."

As proud as he was that she wasn't hysterical, Moose wasn't in the mood to joke just yet. Not until they were out and he'd had someone look her over to make sure she was all right.

Maybe not even then.

Moose reached for the dog in her arms and Penelope shook her head, hard. He didn't have time to fight with her, so he gestured for Taco to lead the way out of the room. They couldn't go back out the front door. Not with the way the smoke had filled the front room and how quickly the fire was spreading. Penelope couldn't crawl and still hold the dog, so they hunched over and walked as fast as they could to the first room in the hallway.

The heat was intense, and Moose was more than aware of Penelope's hand gripping his pants as they went. She was trusting him to get them out of there, and he wasn't going to let her down.

All three of them pushed into the laundry room, which had a small but functioning window. Taco quickly opened it and jumped out head first. Moose knew it would be a tight fit for him, especially since he was wearing an air pack, but it couldn't be helped. He was very thankful for all the training he'd had in getting through small spaces while wearing his bunker gear and air pack.

He looked out the window and was relieved to see Sledge, Crash, and Chief waiting for them. He also could see several police cars on the street now as well. He had a feeling word had gotten out, and their friends who were on duty were probably all racing to the scene.

Moose turned to Penelope and held out his hands for the dog once again. This time she didn't hesitate to put the poor pooch in his arms. It was still limp, and Moose hoped like hell Penelope hadn't risked her life only to have the mutt die. He turned and passed the dog out the window to Crash, who immediately ran toward one of the trucks. They carried some specialized equipment for dogs and cats, and he knew that Crash would do whatever he could to revive the dog.

Moose's attention went back to Penelope. He pulled her toward him until she was plastered against his front. Her eyes were huge behind the mask, but he could see the love she had for him shining out loud and clear. Incredibly, she lifted her left hand and pointed to her ring finger and the diamond resting there. She tilted her head and narrowed her eyes as if to ask, "What the hell, Moose?"

Shaking his head, Moose put his hands on her shoulders and forcibly turned her to the window. Sledge was right there, ready to help her out. Moose hated to do it, but he had to disconnect the oxygen before she crawled out. He tapped her on the shoulder then pointed to where the tube was connected to his tank. She took one last deep breath, then nodded.

Moose quickly unscrewed the tube and she pulled off her mask and regulator. Then she practically dove out the window, right into the arms of her brother, who immediately turned and carried her away from the burning building. Chief was there to help Moose get out the window, and after a little struggle and wiggle, he popped free. He ran side-by-side with Chief over to where Penelope was sitting on the bumper of an ambulance.

Ripping his face mask off, Moose kneeled down in front of her, practically pushing the poor EMT who was trying to assess her out of the way.

Penelope was coughing, but not in the scary desperate way he'd seen smoke inhalation victims do in the past. Her eyes were red-rimmed and she winced as if she had a raging headache, but she was alive. And smiling at him.

Standing, Moose pulled her into his arms, taking her off her seat on the bumper. He felt her legs curl around his hips as she held on to him for dear life. How long they stood like that, he had no idea, but eventually he felt Sledge shaking his shoulder.

"She needs to be looked at Moose. Put her down."

Reluctantly, he loosened his hold on her and Penelope's legs fell from around his hips until she was standing in front of him. Not ready to let go of her yet, Moose put his hands on either side of her face and forced her head up to look at him.

"Are you okay?" he asked in a tortured tone. He had no idea what to expect. Would she be freaked out? Right back where she'd been months ago before she'd taken off with Smokey? He wasn't sure he'd be able to deal with her backing away from him again, not now. Not after everything they'd been through and after last night.

"I'm good," she told him. "Great, actually."

"Really?" Moose asked skeptically, not sure if she was just saying what she thought he wanted to hear.

"Really," she confirmed. "I knew you'd come. All of you. This house is so close to Station 7, I knew you'd be first on scene, and I had no doubt you'd come and get me."

Moose studied her intently, trying to get a feel for

where her head was at. If she was telling the truth, this was big. Huge. "Do you understand what you're saying?" he asked.

Penelope nodded. "Yes. I trusted you to come get me out of there. When I found that window had been boarded up, I knew I was fucked. I couldn't go back into the hall, not with the smoke as thick as it was and without a mask or air pack. So I stayed put and waited for you to find me."

Everything within Moose wanted to fall into a puddle at her feet. He saw no doubt in her eyes. In fact, he saw a bit of the old Penelope staring back at him.

Somehow, by some miracle, she'd fought her biggest demon and learned to trust again.

Moose knew how important this moment was, and he wanted to cry at the sheer joy of it all. But of course, his Penelope was having none of that.

"I think we need to talk about your conceitedness," she said with a quirk of an eyebrow. She pointed to her left ring finger again.

"Is that what I think it is?" Sledge asked from next to them, but Moose ignored him.

"No, we don't," Moose countered. "You agreed last night and we're getting married."

"You aren't going to ask?" she asked.

"Don't need to. You agreed when you said you loved me."

Penelope smiled. "I guess I did."

"Seriously, you guys are getting married?" Sledge asked again.

Penelope reached up and grabbed one of Moose's hands, intertwining her fingers with his and pulling it away from her face. She looked at her brother. "Yup. The day before you and Beth have your ceremony. Figured Mom and Dad would be in town, and we could just get it done fast and easy at the courthouse."

Sledge smiled huge and tugged her out of Moose's grip. "It's about time," he said in her ear.

"Can I look at the patient now?" the EMT asked rather grumpily from next to them.

Knowing she was going to be okay, and she wasn't sinking back into her head because of what happened, Moose turned Penelope and helped her sit back down. He let go of her, but stayed close as the EMT began his assessment.

He hooked up some oxygen and made her put it over her face. "What happened to your arm?" he asked.

Penelope looked down at herself as if she'd forgotten her forearm was even injured. "The dog was scared," she said simply. Then her gaze sought out Crash and the dog she'd risked her life to save.

He was sitting on the ground with the dog and had just taken the cone of oxygen off her snout. Penelope inhaled sharply in fear...then sighed in relief when the dog picked up its head and whimpered.

The two boys she'd rescued kneeled down beside their pet and cried.

"Looks like she's going to be okay," Moose said.

Penelope nodded.

They watched as a group of men and women gathered around the woman and her children. Two took the toddler and baby out of her hands, and the woman approached them at the ambulance.

Penelope took off the oxygen mask and stood.

The EMT growled in frustration, but he didn't insist she sit back down or put the oxygen back on. Penelope held a wad of gauze against her arm and stared at the woman as she stopped in front of them.

"Thank you," the woman said with obvious emotion. "Seriously, I...I wasn't thinking when I left the house without my kids, and they're my whole world. I already lost my husband..." Her breath hitched, but she forced herself to keep going. "I don't know what I would've done if I'd lost my children too."

"You did the right thing," Penelope said, reaching out and putting her hand on the woman's upper arm. "If you weren't standing outside, able to tell me where your kids were, I probably wouldn't have risked going inside to see if there was anyone home."

The woman's eyes fell to Penelope's arm, still covered in the bandage. "Did Buster do that? I'm so sorry!"

"Nothing to be sorry about," Penelope said easily. "She was scared. I don't blame her for one second. It looks like she's going to be okay."

The woman nodded. "Yeah, I think so." She looked

into Penelope's eyes. "My husband got that dog from the pound right before he was deployed the last time. He told my sons that she'd help look out for us. And she did. She jumped on my bed and woke me up when smoke started to fill the house. I'm not sure I would've woken up in time to do much of anything without her."

Penelope didn't hesitate to reach out and hug the woman. They held each other for a long moment before the widow pulled back. "I just wanted to come over here and thank you again." She glanced at the house, which was now fully engulfed. Firefighters were doing their best to put out the flames, but it was obvious it was a total loss. "I know it's just stuff, and that the most important things in my life are safe, but..." She stared at the flames. "It feels weird to have absolutely nothing. No clothes, no toys, not even a toothbrush."

Her eyes filled with tears. "And even though I've got my husband here in my heart," she put a hand on her chest, "I've lost all the pictures of him. His parents will have some, I'm sure, but it hurts all the same."

Moose watched as Penelope reached down with her good arm, into one of the pockets along her thigh. She pulled out something rolled into a small tube and held it out to the grieving woman in front of her.

"I don't know what made me do it, I've been warned time and time again and trained not to stop for any kind of material possession when we're inside a burning structure, but I couldn't walk by this and not grab it."

Moose was as curious as the woman, and he leaned forward to see what it was that Penelope had rescued from the burning house. He was planning on reprimanding her later for stupidly taking the time to salvage *anything*—but when he saw the look on the woman's face, he changed his mind.

She held the picture as if it was the most precious thing she'd ever owned in her life. She stared down at the image of her and her late husband as if she was seeing a ghost. "I…you…I don't know what to say."

"You don't have to say anything," Penelope reassured her. "I lost some good friends while overseas myself. It hurts. But I can't imagine losing the man I love." She glanced up at Moose, then kept going. "I saw the picture and something about it called to me. It's obvious how much in love the two of you were, and I just didn't want this physical reminder of that love to be lost. You're going to make it through this. It's gonna suck and there will be some days when you just want to quit, but you've got four of the best reasons to keep going that you'll ever need."

The woman was crying, but she nodded. "Thank you," she whispered.

"You're welcome," Penelope told her.

One of the boys called out from across the lawn, "Mom! Buster just licked my face!"

The adults chuckled. Then the woman stepped

close, hugged Penelope once more, and turned and left without another word.

Moose knew it was because she was overwhelmed. He would be too. But it was obvious she had a ton of support from friends and neighbors. She'd be okay in the end. She had to be, for her kids.

"I don't think you're in imminent peril of collapsing," the EMT said dryly, "but I still suggest you go to the hospital to get checked out. At the very least, they can clean that arm and, if you need stitches, take care of that."

"I'm okay," Penelope responded. At the same time Moose said, "She's going."

She glared up at him, so much like the Penelope he knew years ago that it was almost startling.

Sledge spoke before he could.

"You're going, Pen."

"Cade, I'm fine. I can have Chief bandage me up and I'll go to see my doctor in the morning. Besides, I can't leave Smokey and my car. He's probably freaking out."

The donkey wasn't happy, that was for sure, but Moose had seen Hayden in the crowd of people and knew she'd moved Penelope's car away from the fire scene and was taking care of her pet. "Hayden's here, and she's got both your car and Smokey under control," Moose told her.

"She is? Where?" Penelope asked, her head whipping around as she looked for her.

"Please," Moose said softly. "Humor me and your

brother and go to the hospital and let them look you over. You know as well as I do how dangerous smoke inhalation can be. You were in that house for long enough to inhale too much of that shit."

Penelope stared up at him for a long moment before sighing. "Okay. But I'm definitely not spending the night there."

"Okay," Moose said immediately. He had no idea what the doctors would say, but if they wanted her to stay, she was staying. He wasn't going to mess around with her health.

Sledge hugged his sister tightly, and Moose heard him say, "You scared the shit out of me, sis. Don't do that again."

She smiled up at him. "No can do, big brother. You know you'd do the exact same thing if it had been you who had gotten here first."

The EMT helped Penelope up and into the back of the ambulance, and Sledge clapped Moose on the shoulder. "I'll catch up with you guys later. Take care of her, Moose."

"I will," he promised. "I love her."

"No shit," Sledge said with a smile. "That's not something I've missed in the last few months. I couldn't ask for a better man for her. She's different today. Whatever happened between you two recently has been for the good."

"It's not me." Moose shook his head. "It's all her."

"I think you're wrong, but whatever. I'm just glad to see my sister back."

"She's still gonna have things to work through," Moose warned.

"I know. But I think with the two of you being all official now, those things will become easier and easier to deal with. Give me your air pack and get her out of here and text me if something major's wrong. I'll bug out of here when I can and meet you at the hospital."

Moose shrugged out of the SCBA he was still wearing on his back and handed it to Sledge. "I will. But I think she's gonna be all right. If her attitude is anything to go by anyway," Moose said.

"Are you guys gonna stand out there shooting the shit all night or am I going to the hospital?" Penelope called out from inside the ambulance.

Moose and Sledge grinned at each other.

"Why you'd want to tie yourself to my ogre of a sister, I have no idea," Sledge said with a wink.

Moose simply shook his head and stepped up into the ambulance.

CHAPTER SEVENTEEN

Penelope shook her head in bemusement as she looked around the crowded courtroom. They actually had to change rooms because the usual room where weddings were conducted was too small.

It was a few weeks after the house fire that had changed her life. Well, there were lots of things that had happened that changed her life in the last couple of months, but when she'd been inside that bedroom, with no escape, she one hundred percent trusted that Moose and the others would find her and get to her in time. All she had to do was wait.

It was that innate sense of trust that made her realize she was finally back. And not only did she trust her friends completely, but she trusted *herself*.

She hadn't hesitated to enter the burning house and save those children. She hadn't even hesitated to go back in for Buster. She'd read the smoke conditions and knew she had enough time. It was instinctual; she hadn't analyzed it to death or doubted herself. The feeling of getting that confidence back and trusting her own decisions was such a relief.

The Miller family had lost everything in that fire. Everything but each other. Remi Miller brought her kids by the station all the time, and she'd been semi-adopted by the firefighters and their wives. Not only that, but the police officers got involved as well, doing a fundraiser so the family could buy the things they needed to get back on their feet.

Remi had reframed the picture of her and her late husband, and it now hung in a place of prominence in the apartment they were renting.

All in all, Penelope's decision to drive down that street had saved more than just the Millers, it had turned her life around as well.

And now it was finally time to marry the man she loved more than she ever could've thought possible. Smokey hadn't been allowed inside the courthouse, so they'd left him sleeping on his special pillow at home.

Their "small courthouse wedding" had gotten out of control. Not only were her parents there, but so were Moose's. Cade and Beth had also wanted to be there to see them get married. And of course, they couldn't leave out their fellow firefighters and their significant others. And when their law enforcement friends found out it was no longer Moose and Pene-lope getting married with just a courthouse witness, that everyone else was going, *they* all wanted to come too.

And to Penelope's shock, Tex had shown up that morning with his wife and two children in tow. He'd told her the Delta Force team, as well as the SEALs out in California, had all sent their regards, as well.

Not only that, Makayla White had also come. She was sitting next to Moose's parents, and she fit in with everyone as if she'd known them her entire life.

So now there were almost forty people in attendance to witness their ceremony.

"Are you pissed?" Moose leaned over and whispered into her ear when they were standing in front of all their family and friends.

Penelope couldn't stop smiling. "Of course not," she told him, looking up into his beautiful brown eyes. "How could I be mad that everyone wanted to celebrate with us?"

"Maybe because we're standing in the middle of an actual courtroom and not having the intimate ceremony we talked about a few weeks ago?"

Penelope looked around. It *was* a bit humorous that they were getting married in a place where criminals were tried for their crimes. Her parents and Cade and Beth were sitting in the first row of bench seats behind the railing that separated spectators from the criminals and the lawyers. Moose's parents were sitting across the aisle from them, and the rest of their friends filled in the seats behind.

It was almost as if she and Moose were on trial. If she was still in the headspace that she was a few months ago, she might've worried about having nightmares about being on trial for White's and Black's murders, with all her friends and family sitting in the courtroom staring at her. But thanks to Moose's determination to help her find her way back to herself, a new and improved Penelope, she would remember this day with nothing but love and fond memories.

The magistrate came into the courtroom and looked around in surprise at the number of people who were there. Then he smiled and proceeded up the aisle. He asked for their names and, after ascertaining they were the correct people who were there to get married, he started the ceremony.

Penelope stared up at Moose, wondering how in the world she'd gotten so lucky, so she didn't hear most of what the magistrate was saying. It didn't matter. All that mattered was that by the end of the day, they'd be man and wife.

"Would you like to exchange vows?" the magistrate asked.

Moose nodded.

Penelope's eyes widened. They'd talked about this. Had agreed to keep things simple, which meant no need to write sappy vows that they'd recite to each other. She narrowed her eyes at Moose. Of course he'd change things up on her.

She panicked for a second, wondering what in the

hell she was going to say to him, but then he squeezed her hands and started talking...and all her worries faded away.

"I know we agreed on no vows, but I can't let this opportunity, with all our friends and family here watching, slip through my fingers. I love you, Penelope Turner. Exactly how you are. I'll do whatever it takes to make sure you always feel safe and happy. At work, at home, and wherever life might take us. Thank you for trusting me. You'll never know how much I treasure that trust. I won't let you down. I might irritate you and piss you off sometimes, but you can always trust me to have your back no matter what."

Penelope refused to cry. One of the reasons why she wanted a nice quick ceremony was because she didn't want to get all emotional. But Moose was certainly ruining *that*.

She may not have planned any words to say, but they spilled out of her without thought. "I might've lost myself for a while, but you helped me find my way back," Penelope told him. "I trust you more than anyone I've ever trusted in my life. I'm proud to be your wife and will spend every day of the rest of my life trying to be a woman you can be proud of."

"You already are," Moose said softly, then leaned forward and kissed her. It wasn't exactly an appropriate kiss for the middle of a courtroom, but because it was their wedding, Penelope figured they'd be forgiven.

"I guess that's that," the magistrate said with a laugh. "I'd say you may kiss your bride, but I guess you already are. By the power invested in me by the state of Texas, I now pronounce you husband and wife."

Later, Penelope was told that people walking in the hall outside the courtroom were shocked and curious when a loud cheering sounded from within the room. They didn't know if a verdict had been reached in a case that was being tried, or what else might be happening.

After the ceremony, they were led into an office to sign the wedding license. Cade and Beth were their witnesses, and immediately after Beth signed, she left the room, and Crash, Chief, Squirrel, Driftwood, and Taco filed in.

Penelope wasn't sure what was happening. Once the magistrate had left to file their license and get copies for them, Moose spoke.

"I told everyone that we didn't want or need wedding presents. We've got everything we need already, and I told them to save their money. Of course, they didn't like that and insisted on doing something to prove how happy they were for us."

Penelope nodded, not sure where this was going.

"So...I told them about White, about the whole 'fight like a girl' thing, and this was all their idea, not mine."

Penelope felt the tears behind her lids threaten again. "What'd you guys do?" she asked.

One by one, the guys rolled or pushed up their sleeves to show her their brand-new tattoos.

She could only stare at them in disbelief.

Taco and Squirrel had gotten the new ink on their biceps, while the others all had it on their forearms. The tears that had been threatening spilled over, making all her friends blurry. She shut her eyes to try to control herself, but it was no use.

She felt Moose put his arm around her and tug her into his side, and she gave him her weight, not sure she could stand up.

"I'm gonna get one too, but knew I couldn't do it before the big reveal because there's no way I could've kept you from seeing it," Moose told her. "You like to see me naked a little too much."

At that, Penelope's eyes popped open and she smacked her new husband in the arm. "Shut up," she complained, but secretly she was glad he'd lightened the mood. She grabbed her brother's wrist and pulled him to her so she could see the tattoo up close.

It was the Maltese cross that was synonymous with fire service. In the center was a fire helmet with the number 7 on it, and a mask and regulator. Two axes crossed behind the helmet and the words "Fight Like a Girl" were across the top, with "Never Quit" along the bottom. It was bad-ass, while at the same time a heartfelt tribute to her strength and fortitude. Whoever had designed it was a genius and the tattooist was truly an artist.

She was beyond touched. "You guys…it's…I don't know what to say."

Cade pulled her into him and hugged her tightly. "You don't have to say anything. We're honored that you're one of us. You're a hell of a firefighter and a hell of a soldier too. If me and Beth ever have a daughter, we want her to be exactly like you."

"Cade," she whispered.

"Any girl you two have is gonna be a hellion," Taco teased Sledge. "She'll probably want to be a Special Forces operative who's a genius with electronics."

"Damn straight," Cade told his friend.

He held his sister in front of him and looked her in the eyes and said seriously, "You're responsible for entertaining everyone tomorrow night at the reception so I can escape upstairs with Beth."

Penelope laughed. "Whatever. It's *your* reception, not mine."

"Wrong. You know Beth will hate it. So it's my duty as her husband to take her inside and find something to do to keep her mind off her agoraphobia."

Now she rolled her eyes. "Yeah, right. We should've just had another softball game or something."

"Probably," Moose agreed, taking her from her brother's arms. "Now if you guys don't mind, I'd like to take *my* wife home. We'll see you all tomorrow."

Penelope ignored the taunts and innuendos from the guys as they filed out of the room. She turned to her husband and reached up to twine her arms around his neck. "That was rude," she chided.

"Don't care. Besides, we need to get home to check on Smokey. And later this afternoon, I have an appointment to get my tattoo."

"So soon?" she asked in surprise.

"Yup. Except mine is gonna have an addition."

"What kind of addition?" Penelope asked.

"Dog tags hanging from the cross, with the names Thomas Black and Henry White on them."

"Moose," Penelope whispered, more touched than she could put into words.

"Those guys were your friends. They would've done anything for you. They were important to you, so they're important to me too. I wanted to honor them."

"I love you," Penelope told him.

"And I love you."

"Do you think the tattooist would be able to sneak me in too?" she asked.

He smiled. "I may or may not have already put you on his schedule," Moose told her.

Penelope got up on her tiptoes and he leaned down to meet her halfway. She kissed him with all the love and respect she had in her heart.

When he pulled back, they were both breathing hard. "So where're you gonna put it?" Moose asked.

"Stamp tramp," Penelope said without hesitation.

"Good choice," Moose told her. "I can see it when I'm taking you from behind."

Penelope loved when he took her that way. "Maybe we should get home so we can practice, and you can make sure that's where you want it," she suggested.

"Maybe we should," Moose agreed, taking her by the hand and rushing her out of the room.

The next day, Moose stood in Sledge's backyard, watching as his friend married the love of his life, Beth. Moose had his arms around Penelope, and she was careful not to rub against his forearm, where his brand-new tattoo had been inked the evening before.

Moose had taken his wife home after their courthouse wedding, fucked her hard, then made love to her before they'd both gone to the tattoo parlor to get their new tattoos.

Smokey was walking around, eating up the attention everyone was lavishing on him, although he always kept Penelope in view. He'd been a bit traumatized by being stuck in her car while she went into a burning building, and didn't like to let her out of his sight. But with a lot of love and attention, he was mostly back to being his goofy self.

When the ceremony began to drag on a bit long, Moose looked around, studying all their friends, and he couldn't help but smile. Everyone was there.

Tex and his family had stayed for Sledge and Beth's wedding. Everyone knew how Tex had been the one to find Beth and Summer when they'd been taken hostage by a serial killer out in California, and how he'd helped get Beth involved in the work she did for the government. Moose had a long talk with the man before the ceremony, thrilled to be able to thank him for looking out for Penelope while she'd been wandering around the country.

Dax and Mackenzie had finally gotten engaged, and Moose knew that Dax wasn't going to wait long to make Mack legally his. He'd asked a lot of questions about their courthouse wedding, and Moose wouldn't be surprised if they got an invitation to return to the courthouse soon.

Mickie and Cruz were standing close together, much like he and Penelope, and Moose couldn't help but notice Cruz's hands frequently strayed to Mickie's belly, where he stroked her lovingly. He wasn't the most observant man in the world, but he'd bet everything he had that Mickie was pregnant. They'd wanted kids for a long time, and it looked like they were finally going to have them. The pair wasn't married yet, but obviously love didn't require a piece of paper from the government to flourish.

Quint sat next to Corrie, holding her hand. Every now and then, he'd lean over and speak into her ear, probably telling her what was going on around her. Corrie couldn't see the ceremony because she was blind, and Moose knew Quint would be describing it in detail.

Weston King and his wife, Laine, were also there, but Laine was too busy taking pictures of the ceremony to stand still next to her husband. That didn't keep Wes from keeping an eye on her.

Boone and Hayden were also in attendance—and Moose was somewhat shocked, because he very rarely saw Hayden in anything other than her sheriff's uniform or jeans and a T-shirt. Today she was wearing a light pink dress that went down to her ankles and suited her perfectly. Boone had on his normal cowboy hat and jeans, and somehow the two of them still looked absolutely perfect together.

Erin and Conor were there with their daughter Lily. For the moment, she was sleeping soundly against Conor's shoulder, but Moose wouldn't be surprised if she woke up and started screaming any second now. She was a handful, but it was obvious that her parents doted on her.

Milena and TJ Rockwell sat in the first row of chairs with their two kids. JT looked as cute as could be in his little tuxedo. He'd been the ring bearer, responsible for carrying the rings to Beth and Sledge on a little pillow. He'd dropped them twice, and it took forever for him to walk from the house to where the couple was standing, but no one cared because he was so darn adorable. Their other son, Steven, was awake and sitting in his father's arms. The infant looked around as if he was taking everything in.

In contrast, Hope and Calder's son, Carter, had

started screaming bloody murder the second the ceremony began, and no matter what the couple did to try to calm him down, it didn't work. So Hope had left Calder and her other son, Billy, outside and had gone inside the house with Carter. She was watching through the patio window so as not to disturb everyone.

Moose loved their law enforcement family more than he could put into words. They worked in different fields, but frequently saw each other at car crashes and other medical scenes they were called to. They'd all been through their own different kinds of hell and were all very aware of how lucky they were to be alive and healthy. They hung out together frequently outside of work, as well.

Moose could relate. He spent almost every day with his firefighter friends, but he never tired of being around them or their families.

Currently, Adeline was sitting next to Crash with one hand resting on his thigh. Coco lay at her feet, snoring so loudly everyone couldn't help but crack up every other time he inhaled. She pretty much didn't need her dog as a medical alert pet anymore because after her surgery, her epileptic seizures had just about stopped. Now, Coco was a beloved companion.

Sophie's pregnancy was progressing well, and both she and Chief looked extremely happy and content. Chief didn't let her out of his sight, and when she'd insisted she wanted to stand for the ceremony, the better to see, he'd done his best to convince her to sit anyway. When she refused, Chief leaned against the house and pulled her against him. His hands were resting on her belly, and she was practically glowing as they watched Beth and Sledge get married.

Squirrel was holding baby Harper while Blythe was inside, trying to help Hope calm her baby. She'd had a hell of a time dealing with her postpartum depression, but Squirrel had informed everyone that, after finding the right medication, they thought she was over the worst of it.

Quinn and Koren had become very close, and they'd been discussing their own wedding plans all afternoon. Driftwood and Taco had complained teasingly, but Moose knew without a doubt, whatever their women wanted, they'd bend over backward to make sure it happened.

The chief of Station 7 had even shown up. He was currently standing off to the side, looking a little lonely...but Moose couldn't help but notice him eyeballing one of the caterers as she bustled around, making sure everything was good to go with the food.

Yes, their little band of brothers and sisters was as strong as ever. They'd all been through their own kinds of hell, and had somehow managed to come out the other side better people as a result. Moose knew without a doubt if he ever needed anything, he could call on any one of the men and women in Sledge's backyard, and they'd be there for him in a heartbeat.

And seeing the babies who would soon be old enough to laugh and play with each other as if they were siblings, he couldn't wait to start a family with Penelope. They hadn't talked about children, but he knew she'd be an amazing mother. She'd teach their sons to be brave and to stand up for those weaker than them. And their daughters would take after their mom, strong, take-no-shit warriors. What more could he ask for?

"What're you thinking about so hard over here?" Penelope whispered, tilting her head upward so she could see his face.

Leaning down, Moose kissed her forehead and shook his head. "Nothing much. Just how happy I am."

Penelope squeezed his arm. "Me too."

As the officiant named Beth and Sledge husband and wife, and told him he could kiss his bride, Moose closed his eyes in contentment. This was what life was all about. Celebrating the little victories and enjoying the company of your friends. It had been a hell of a bumpy ride for him and Penelope, but they'd made it. Any other issues that cropped up would be child's play compared to what they'd already been through. What *she'd* already been through.

"Love you," Moose told her.

Penelope turned in his arms and looked up at him. "Love you too. Think Squirrel will let us steal Harper away for a bit?"

Moose looked over at his friend, then back down at

Penelope. "Not a chance in hell. But I wouldn't mind giving it a try."

She beamed at him. "Seeing you hold one of the babies is pretty hot, Moose."

"Yeah?" he asked, pleased as hell she thought so.

"Yeah."

"I was thinking maybe we could try for our own in a few years, but that look in your eye makes me think you might not want to wait that long," Moose said a little cautiously.

Penelope didn't take her gaze from his. "I'm not saying I want to get pregnant tonight, but I'm not averse to starting a family sooner rather than later. And look…I think Smokey would love a baby to hover over as well."

Moose turned to look at their miniature donkey and chuckled. JT had apparently gotten bored with the ceremony and had wandered over to play with Smokey. They were both sitting in the grass. Smokey had his head in JT's lap and the little boy was pulling up clumps of grass and feeding the animal. His little tux was covered in donkey slime, but neither seemed to care. Moose loved to see how gentle Smokey was being with the little boy, and a vision of the donkey sleeping next to and guarding his own child flashed through his mind.

He couldn't hold himself back anymore. Moose wrapped an arm around his wife's waist and hauled her off her feet. Then he kissed her as if it hadn't been only a few hours ago that he'd been balls deep inside her. After several moments, when he needed air, he lifted his head and stared down at the beautiful woman in his arms.

He was so thankful she was here. That she was his wife and loved him. Lord knew he wasn't perfect, but for her, he'd move heaven and earth to try to be so. "How long do we have to stay again?" he asked.

She chuckled as he put her back down so her feet were on the ground. "Longer than we have so far. Come on, let's go mess with Squirrel."

He loved teasing his friends, but he loved being with his wife more. He watched Penelope's ass as she walked in front of him toward Squirrel and his baby, and couldn't help his grin. He sent a silent prayer upward as she said hello to their friends as they passed.

Thank you, White, for looking after Pen when I wasn't there to do it myself. I swear I'll do everything in my power to treat her well, and I swear my children will know all about their mom's friend who helped keep her positive and strong when she needed it most. "Fight like a girl" will never be an insult in my house, not as long as I can help it. Rest easy, White.

Then Moose put his hand on the small of his wife's back as they stood in front of Squirrel, and he scowled at Penelope when she tried to take his little girl from him.

Yes, life was good.

EPILOGUE

One year later

Makayla–

I'm sorry it's been so long since I've written you back. Things here have been crazy, but that's no excuse. I got your last letter right before we left to go to Chicago for the special interview with Oprah.

It's still a little weird that I was sitting on Oprah's set being interviewed by her. I mean, I know that I'd been avoiding any kind of interviews after I got back from Turkey, but I never thought Oprah *would be interested in hearing my story.*

I hope I did your son proud. I really wanted the entire country to know that, while I might've been rescued, too many good soldiers have died fighting for the US. It was important to make sure that White, Black, and Wilson were recognized. Not only them, but Lieutenant Love and Sergeant Hess, the pilots who died when our helicopter was shot down.

Funny story, we were in the middle of the interview and I felt the familiar signs of impending pukedom. I didn't even say "excuse me" to poor Oprah, who must've thought I was crazy, I just bolted off the couch while she was in the middle of asking me a question and ran for the restroom. Luckily, Moose was right there and managed to get the door open for me, so I didn't barf all over the floor of Oprah's studio. Lol

And yes, that was why Oprah totally put me on the spot on camera, bringing up my marriage to Moose and slyly asking if we were planning on starting a family. So I apologize for not telling you privately first, but when Oprah asks if you're pregnant right after you almost puke all over her feet from afternoon sickness, you kinda have to fess up.

So, me and Moose are expecting our first child in about five months! If it's a boy, his name is going to be Henry. I couldn't think of a better name for a little boy. And stop crying, I can "hear" you all the way over here in Texas. :)

So anyway, because I'm pregnant, things with work have changed. I loved being able to fight fires with the guys again, and I think I was a better firefighter because of everything that happened and my newfound trust in my team. But that's obviously not a good situation for an unborn baby. So Smokey and I have been ramping up our fire safety classes. It's been a ton of fun, and the kids just love being able to pet Smokey after the talk. And I actually taught Smokey how to stop, drop, and roll. It's hilarious!

I'm glad that Liam is working out. I know you had some reservations about him, but Tex reassured me that he was a good guy and just needed a break to get back on his feet. I know it was hard to let someone help you, but letting Liam do some of the things that need doing around the house gave him the confidence he needed to branch out and start his handyman business.

Don't be surprised if Tex sends more veterans your way! There are always men and women who need some extra money, and it seems that Mama Makayla's becoming well known in the Biloxi area for being a hard taskmaster, but fair. (That, and they can't stay away from your home cooking either! Ha!)

I talked to Remi Miller the other day, and she and her children are doing great. They just moved into their new house. They even got a friend for Buster. Remi is as busy as ever, but she's doing really well.

The other thing I don't think I told you about was the good news for the Fight Like a Girl Foundation. You know I wanted to help people like Remi get back on their feet after losing everything to a fire, and that's how it started. We raised some money and were able to give her and her kids ten thousand dollars to buy clothes and other necessities. When I started giving speeches to groups about my ordeal, and how it's okay to need help in dealing with the stuff life throws at us sometimes, I made sure I mentioned the foundation, and that we were accepting donations.

Well, Oprah also happened to mention it—as you know, if you saw the show—and I cried when I saw that within a week of the show airing, we'd had over a million dollars in donations!

It was unbelievable. Now we can help so many more people. I think focusing on assisting those who are in the fire service, and those who have been touched by tragedy because of a devastating fire, is doing so much good for the community, filling an important niche.

I never thought Fight Like a Girl would get as big as it has, but I know, deep in my heart, I have your son to thank for it. He gave me the courage and fortitude to continue on when I thought I couldn't last another day in captivity. He believed in me and had no problem in letting everyone know it.

Anyway, now I'm crying, so I'm going to wrap this up. I have a meeting this afternoon with the family of a firefighter from Station 6, that's in our district. He just found out he has testicular cancer and the foundation is going to arrange to have someone come to his house and clean it once a week so his wife doesn't have to worry about that on top of everything else. We'll also get those ready-to-make meals delivered three times a week, and arrange for childcare in the afternoons so he can recover from the chemo in peace. His prognosis is very good, and being able to help a fellow firefighter because of White and the foundation is amazing.

It's been too long since I've seen you, and I've already told Moose he needs to take me to Biloxi before our child is born. We're also planning on heading up to Maine to meet Black's parents. I contacted them a few months ago, and they weren't ready, but I'd like to think seeing me talk so highly of their *son on TV—if they saw the show—might've helped convince them that I want nothing more than to thank them for raising such a wonderful human being.*

Take care of yourself. And it goes without saying, but I'm saying it anyway—if you need anything, all you have to do is ask. Don't be a stranger, and I can't wait for your next letter.

Love, Penelope

*

Thank you to everyone for reading the Badge of Honor series. As I stated in the very beginning, I have the upmost respect for our police officers and firefighters. They put their lives on the line when citizens need them the most.

While this might be the end of this series, I wouldn't be surprised if you continued to see the characters you know and love pop up in other books!

If you loved this series, you'll love ALL my other books! If you haven't already, be sure to check out the SEAL of Protection: Legacy series as well as book 1 in the new Delta Team Two series, *Shielding Gillian*.

Are you interested in reading the Station Chief's story? Of course you are! Ethan caught a glimpse of Viviana at the wedding, and now he can't stop thinking about her! Reina Torres has written this fabulous story in my fan fiction world! It's coming out in Nov, so SOON! Go pick it up now! Shelter for Viviana.

*

JOIN my Newsletter and find out about sales, free books, contests and new releases before anyone else!! Click HERE

Want to know when my books go on sale? Follow me on Bookbub HERE!

Also by Susan Stoker

Badge of Honor: Texas Heroes Series

Justice for Mackenzie

Justice for Mickie

Justice for Corrie

Justice for Laine (novella)

Shelter for Elizabeth

Justice for Boone

Shelter for Adeline

Shelter for Sophie

Justice for Erin

Justice for Milena

Shelter for Blythe

Justice for Hope

Shelter for Quinn

Shelter for Koren

Shelter for Penelope

Delta Team Two Series

Shielding Gillian

Shielding Kinley (Aug 2020)

Shielding Aspen (Oct 2020)

Shielding Riley (Jan 2021)

Shielding Devyn (TBA)

Shielding Ember (TBA)

Shielding Sierra (TBA)

Delta Force Heroes Series
Rescuing Rayne
Rescuing Aimee (novella)
Rescuing Emily
Rescuing Harley
Marrying Emily (novella)
Rescuing Kassie
Rescuing Bryn
Rescuing Casey
Rescuing Sadie (novella)
Rescuing Wendy
Rescuing Mary
Rescuing Macie (novella)

SEAL of Protection: Legacy Series
Securing Caite
Securing Brenae (novella)
Securing Sidney
Securing Piper
Securing Zoey
Securing Avery (May 2020)
Securing Kalee (Sept 2020)

Ace Security Series
Claiming Grace
Claiming Alexis
Claiming Bailey
Claiming Felicity
Claiming Sarah

Mountain Mercenaries Series

Defending Allye

Defending Chloe

Defending Morgan

Defending Harlow

Defending Everly

Defending Zara

Defending Raven (June 2020)

Silverstone Series

Trusting Skylar (Dec 2020)

Trusting Taylor (TBA)

Trusting Molly (TBA)

Trusting Cassidy (TBA)

SEAL of Protection Series

Protecting Caroline

Protecting Alabama

Protecting Fiona

Marrying Caroline (novella)

Protecting Summer

Protecting Cheyenne

Protecting Jessyka

Protecting Julie (novella)

Protecting Melody

Protecting the Future

Protecting Kiera (novella)

Protecting Alabama's Kids (novella)

Protecting Dakota

Stand Alone

The Guardian Mist

Nature's Rift

A Princess for Cale

A Moment in Time- A Collection of Short Stories

Lambert's Lady

Special Operations Fan Fiction

http://www.AcesPress.com

Beyond Reality Series

Outback Hearts

Flaming Hearts

Frozen Hearts

Writing as Annie George:

Stepbrother Virgin (erotic novella)

ABOUT THE AUTHOR

New York Times, USA Today and *Wall Street Journal* Bestselling Author Susan Stoker has a heart as big as the state of Tennessee where she lives, but this all American girl has also spent the last twenty years living in Missouri, California, Colorado, Indiana, and Texas. She's married to a retired Army man who now gets to follow *her* around the country.

She debuted her first series in 2014 and quickly followed that up with the SEAL of Protection Series, which solidified her love of writing and creating stories readers can get lost in.

If you enjoyed this book, or any book, please consider leaving a review. It's appreciated by authors more than you'll know.

www.stokeraces.com
susan@stokeraces.com